MATTHEW HENSON and the ICE TEMPLE of HARLEM

GARY PHILLIPS

Copyright © 2020 by Gary Phillips
Cover and jacket design by Chuck Regan

Hardcover ISBN 978-1-951709-35-8
eISBN: 978-1-951709-24-2
Library of Congress Control Number: 2020947864

First Hardcover edition Niovember 2020 by Agora Books
an imprint of Polis Books, LLC
44 Brookview Lane
Aberdeen, NJ
www.PolisBooks.com

LOSING YOUR WAY ON A JOURNEY IS UNFORTUNATE.
BUT, LOSING YOUR REASON FOR THE JOURNEY IS A FATE MORE CRUEL.

H.G. WELLS

CHAPTER ONE

Her tiny eyes blinked rapidly behind the heavy lenses of her glasses. She was on tiptoe looking through the peephole. "Yes?" she asked, frowning. Then, gasping in disbelief, "My goodness, you're... *him*?" she exclaimed.

"I am, ma'am," said the voice familiar to many Harlemites.

"Bless your heart," she replied. "Me and a few of my friends from our ladies' auxiliary enjoyed that talk and slide show about the ancient library at Timbuktu you gave at First Baptist last year."

"Thank you. Would you mind if I used your living room window?"

"Oh, yes, yes, come on in, Mr. Henson." She unlatched the door and opened it wide. The elderly light-skinned black woman wore a quilted housecoat and slippers.

Matthew Henson wasn't particularly tall. But at a shade under six feet and what with his sturdy build, he gave the impression of being larger as he regarded the older woman's modest apartment. The diaphanous curtains were ironed, and bright white doilies were scattered about. There was a built-in sideboard containing what he presumed were the dishes and silverware only brought out for her ladies' auxiliary meetings.

"You look loaded for bear," she said, eyes wide behind her glasses, noting his appearance. He filled the doorway in his workingman's clothes, a rope knotted at intervals connected to a grapple coiled around his substantial chest. There was also an ice axe, an ulu in the

Inuktitut language, a small utility knife, and other such items attached to a custom-made tool belt he had on. He came farther into the room and the older lady quietly closed the door.

"I'm sorry to intrude on your quietude, Mrs...?"

"Celow. The late mister was a railroad man. Oh, child, he traveled all over this country on them rails." She looked off toward a mantle with various framed photos on it as well as a good-sized Santa Fe railroad enameled shield.

"Yes, ma'am, where would we be without the railroads?" He eyed the window across the room but wasn't going to rush things and make her more nervous. No matter what might be transpiring just below them. He'd learned long ago in far harsher climes to pace himself.

"Lord yes," she went on, "'our peoples' means of freedom in many ways, isn't that right?"

He prayed they weren't about to have a revival. "That is so." He inched forward a notch.

"Would you like some tea?" she offered but instead of the kitchen, she glanced toward her sideboard and its lead glass cabinets. "Though I imagine an outdoorsman like yourself might want something a might more bracing."

"About that there window, Mrs. Celow."

"Oh, yes," she started as if waking from slumber, "you didn't come here to chitchat."

"Maybe some other time when the clock's not against me."

She beamed up at him. "Really? Would you come speak to the auxiliary as my special guest?"

"I would be delighted."

"The ladies would be beside themselves, Mr. Henson."

"Matt will do."

She clapped her hands together appreciatively. "Fine, fine."

He went on past her to the window. He undid the lock and slid it up easily. After moving her easy chair and lamp aside, he secured his pronged grapple hook on the frame and sill. The sharp ends dug into the wood and would leave gouge marks but there was no helping that. Mrs. Celow didn't raise a fuss, being too polite, he figured.

"Is this a government mission, Mr...Matt?" the widow asked as he put a leg outside the open window.

"No, this is a private engagement, Mrs. Celow."

"I see," she said, her dubiousness evident.

Henson was aware there was a persistent rumor that many believed he was an operative for an outfit called the International Detective Agency. There was no such organization, but he knew the source had been a serialized story in a magazine several years ago called the *Black Sleuth*. Elements of the popular story got transferred from the page, as these things do, into speculation in conversations in cafes and beauty salons throughout Harlem and elsewhere. From there, over time, fiction took on the trappings of gossip which always had its own reality.

"I'm thinking once you're gone, you're not coming back tonight."

He was half out the window. "Unlikely."

"How do I get in touch with you?" she asked.

"Just leave word for me at May-May's Diner."

"Over on Lenox?'

"Yes, near 132nd. Now if you would, once I'm outside, please don't go near the window," he added, figuring she might take a gander as he descended. He also hoped bullets wouldn't be coming through to ruin her nice flooring from the story below.

"Very well," she said resignedly. He was depriving her of some of the excitement of having Matt Henson in her apartment, but she'd still have more than enough to tell her church ladies.

His booted soles firm against the building's bricks, Henson, who'd slipped on supple seal skin gloves, held himself in place on the rope a few inches below the older lady's window. He'd lowered the sash, cognizant the warmth of the day was giving away to the early evening and not everyone liked the cold as he did. From where he was now, the window he wanted was below him to his left. He clambered down and cursed under his breath. The curtains were drawn—no way to tell what was going on inside, except a slight gap between the curtains showed the lights were on.

Henson worked the rope around his veined forearm, holding his body in place. His other hand free, he got his axe lose. He had one of his miniature smoke bombs with him as well as an incendiary type. The latter was based on a grenade developed by the Germans toward the close of World War I. He wasn't of a mind to start a fire in the room beyond—at least if he didn't have to, but better to be prepared.

Henson clenched the axe handle between his teeth and, unlimbering the rope, got both hands on it as he slipped down again. He came to rest just above the curtained window, not worried if those inside detected movement or not. What had that blowhard Peary always barked? "Find a way or make one, Henson."

"Well, shit," he smiled thinly as he pushed backward once, twice, and on the third time, muttering, "Whoop halloo," got enough arc as he swung back toward the building and let go of the rope. His boots and legs burst through the glass. Though it looked like he would land on his butt, the airborne Henson tucked his body into a ball and he landed neatly in a roll. One side of the curtains ripped from its pole as the material caught in the fold of his leg.

A hood who'd been sitting in a chair eating a sandwich gaped at the unexpected entrance. He spat roast beef and tomato from his mouth, his hand darting for a .45 in a shoulder holster draped on the back of a chair. He got the gun in his fist, but too late, Henson was upright and sprang on him.

"You goddamn jumping jigaboo," the white gunman blared.

"Jump on this," Henson said as he punched the man in the side of his head. He stumbled sideways, dazed. A pocket door to another room slammed home. A second gunman in a garish tie came out firing a drum-loaded Thompson machine gun. He raked the room in a sweep of bullets, hunks of wood, cloth and porcelain flying everywhere as the rounds blistered furniture and exploded the bric-a-brac.

"Watch where you're shooting, Eddie," the one Henson had struck yelled. He'd crawled behind a wingback chair.

"Aw, stop being a crybaby," Eddie groused. He looked around, not sure where their intruder had gone. There was a swinging door to the kitchen, and several bullet holes had penetrated the door.

"The darkie must be in there," said the first hood.

"He's as good as on the slab," Eddie vowed, sending another burst through the door, making it flap back and forth. His companion, gun in hand, joined in. The door now hung loose, the plaster and frame now nearly non-existent. From inside the kitchen, it got kicked all the way off and fell on the machine gunner.

"Goddammit," Eddie said knocking the door away from his body.

But Henson had already deployed his smoke grenade, and the thick stuff spread quickly through the compact quarters.

"The hell," the hood with the .45 said, "can't see shit." He waved his hand before his face seeking to part the pall. The ice axe whistled through the dissipating cloud, sailing end over end, until the blade sunk into the center of his forehead. Eyes rolling back, his brain ceased functioning by the time he collapsed to the floor. The smoke lifted from around the fresh corpse, crawling upward to the ceiling like ghostly tendrils. The occupants of the apartment were revealed. Water could be heard dripping into the pan beneath the ice box in the kitchen. Henson stood stock still on the plain carpet.

Eddie, positioned just beyond the archway of the open pocket door, pressed the barrel of his weapon against the side of a pretty woman in a fashionable skirt and midday blouse. "You go back and tell Daddy Paradise you failed, shine. Take another step and this here fine brown gal gets ventilated like Swiss cheese." The girl looked nervous but not overly so, Henson noted, cool-headed.

"They hurt you any, Destiny?" Henson asked.

"Oh, they crowed and strutted like roosters do, but nothing that'll give me nightmares."

"Hey, cut it out." He jabbed the barrel into her for emphasis.

11

"You got any idea who I work for, huh?"

Henson said, "I know exactly who you work for."

"Then you best skedaddle. You messin' in white folks' business and you already in way over your head." His gaze flitted toward the dead man then back in Henson. "You gonna pay for what you did."

"If not in this world, then the next."

"What?' he began, but didn't finish.

In a motion that confounded the thug, Henson whipped his empty hand across his body like a magician's flourish. From out of his sleeve flew a shuriken—a throwing star. Two of its five razor-sharp points embedded deep in the wrist holding the Tommy gun. More from surprise than pain, the hood reacted, his grip loosening on his prisoner though he managed to hold onto his weapon. She drove a heel into his foot and he gritted his teeth.

"Goddamn black bitch," he wailed.

He twisted, leveling the gun back on her, but Henson had already closed the distance between them. Henson grabbed the barrel as a burst of fire leapt from the Thompson. Rounds ripped into the couch, cotton stuffing erupting from the destroyed cushions.

"Let go," the hood rasped, hitting Henson in the gut, surprised his fist met packed muscle. And just that quick, Henson batted the machine gun away while taking a step back as it fell to the floor.

"You gonna get yours now, boy," the hoodlum said, his fists up in a boxer's stance. "I don't need no gat to teach you a lesson." He charged forward, swinging. In three blurry moves from Henson the criminal was down on his back on the floor, blinking hard at the man standing over him. Face blank, Henson's heel crashed down on his face, sending him under with a broken nose.

"What was that you did?" Destiny Stevenson asked Henson. "I've been to prizefights, but I've never seen boxing like that."

"It's called wing chun."

"What is that?'

"A kind of fighting technique, Chinese style of combat."

"You learned it in Chinatown?"

"China," he said tersely. He gathered up her jacket, purse, and cloche hat and handed them to her. "Like the man said, we better skedaddle." He also retrieved his axe and throwing star.

"My father sent you?"

"Yes."

They were at the door. More than one head poked out of an apartments in the hallway, then retreated.

Stevenson pointed at the throwing star Henson slipped back up his sleeve, securing it in place. "That part of that wing chop-chop?"

The throwing star was of Japanese origin, but it was better not to be too literal. "Yes," he answered. He undid a gunny sack from his tool belt and put the belt, axe, his remaining firebomb and a few other items inside. He carried it as they headed toward the rear stairwell.

"You're not part of fathers' following, are you?'

"How can you tell?"

"You don't have that glazed-over look they get when his name is mentioned."

He chuckled as they descended. "He has his ways. A lot of people respect him."

"Ain't that something."

He glanced at her, not sure how to interpret her remark. They reached the ground floor and Henson held up his hand. He cracked the service door open and scanned the thoroughfare. He signaled for her to exit and they did, staying close to the building. There was no way the gunshots hadn't been heard, and there was a smattering of people loosely bunched in front of or across the street from the building.

Henson and the woman went farther along the gloomy passageway between the buildings. Even in the near dark, he deftly guided her around trash cans and discarded pallets. They stopped at the rear door of the building opposite.

"Why aren't the police coming?" the woman wondered aloud, given the absence of a siren.

13

Henson pushed against the door, eaten around the edges from termites and rot. It gave in easily. "I'm guessing they were told to stay away. Mr. Flegenheimer has influence in certain circles."

"Oh, isn't that—"

"Yep, he's better known as Dutch Schultz. That's why your father hired me to fetch you back." The two made their way through a murky storage room filled various steamer trunks, broken furniture, and several large standing radios including Atwater Kents and Crosleys.

"I see," she said without rancor. They paused at another door and she touched his arm. "You some kind of circus strongman? But you're all sleek and move like, I don't know, a dancer." She liked his thick mustache and his chiseled face but didn't want to seem too forward.

"My ex says I got two left feet."

"Ex, is it?"

"Mm-hum. Come on.".

The storeroom took them into hallway next to a set of stairs leading up to other apartments. They left the building, the people gathered next door not paying them any attention as they walked away in the opposite direction. One block over, they were on 119th Street and Henson pointed toward Madison Avenue.

"That way, then we can walk or catch a hack. We got to get further uptown."

"You taking me to him, the deliverer his glorious dang self?" She smiled sweetly.

"He wants to see you."

She huffed but didn't say anything else.

He said, "For somebody who's just been kidnapped by a couple of mobsters, you don't seem that rattled. You handled yourself pretty well back there."

"For a girl, you mean."

"For anybody."

She regarded him.

They passed a restaurant where diners ate at tables next to a large plate glass window looking out on the street. A band played moodily over a radio from an open window of one of the overhead apartments in the building. A big man, six-three and chest like an anvil, in a suit, bowler hat, and a cigar perched on the side of his mouth, stepped out of the eatery into their path. An ostentatious diamond on his little finger caught the light from the bulb over the doorway.

"Matthew 'Polar Bear' Henson, how's the world treating you?" he said heartily. The man touched the brim of his hat nodding at Stevenson. "Ma'am."

"I can't call it, OD, you?"

Oscar Dulane hunched his broad shoulders. "Fortune smiled on me today. Tomorrow, who knows?" Among OD's pursuits was that of a bouncer brought on at clubs like Smalls' Paradise and Hayne's Oriental when the staff needed beefing up for special events.

Henson gave him a half-salute and he and the woman continued on.

"Matthew *who* did he say?" Stevenson asked as they walked, having heard his last name. "You're the one."

"That's me."

"Well I'll be. The one who was with them white fellas who discovered the North Pole?"

In a snow blind white haze, he saw the weathered faces of his friends, Ootah, his brothers Egingwah, and Seegloo, Ooqueah—even Peary appeared before him. As one the fur coated men gestured for him to join them as the snow storm nearly obliterated their forms. They were the six men who reached the North Pole. It would turn out only one of them would get lasting credit for the hard-earned goal.

"Uh-huh," was all he drawled returning to the present.

They hailed a Checker cab and rode further north into the heart of Harlem to be let off at a brownstone along Striver's Row. The cabbie, who wore a button on his lapel identifying him as a member of the Universal Negro Improvement Association, and recognizing Henson, let him stand outside on the running board as the explorer wanted to be on alert. Arriving at their destination, Henson rang the doorbell. A bronze-hued woman with almond eyes of an undetermined age opened the front door. She was dressed modestly and broke into a grin at the sight of the younger woman. A spray of lilacs and gladiolas was in a vase behind her on a stand in the foyer

"Oh my, wonderful, just wonderful," she said reaching out and hugging Stevenson. Arm around her, the other woman said into the house, "Charles, your daughter is here." She walked away with Stevenson, leaving Henson on the doorstep. But she hadn't closed the door on him, so he stepped inside, too, and followed them into a book-lined study. On a cherry-wood table was a small stack of magazines including the *Survey Graphic* and *The Messenger*.

"Destiny," a man said. He was medium height in a paisley vest and white shirt. The man modulated his usual stentorian tone. His naturally straight hair was combed back from a smooth forehead.

"Father," she said, allowing him to embrace her.

"I was worried sick."

"I know." The daughter looked past her father's shoulder at Henson. "But thankfully your lummox here sure knew what he was doing."

"I'm Miriam McNair," said the older woman, hand out to Henson.

"Pleased to meet you," he said, shaking it. He'd heard of her. She'd been an early investor in Madam C.J. Walker's haircare products for black women. The profits had resulted in her owning this brownstone, he surmised. He knew she was active with various negro self-betterment efforts in Harlem and elsewhere. She also conducted salons from time to time at this building under the auspices of her womens' group called the Bronze Orchids. These were gatherings of intellectuals, writers, poets, and the likes—personnel of equal rights organizations who discussed various topics of interest.

"This calls for libations," McNair said. "Destiny, are you of age? Your skin is flawless, I'm so jealous."

"You mean hooch?" she grinned.

16

"My supplier only gets the best. Is that okay, Charles?"

Her father waved his hand. "Considering what she's been through, I'm sure her late mother would understand." His nails were long for a man's and an ornate silver or gold ring was on his fingers on either hand. His given name was Charles Theodore Toliver, but many knew him as Daddy Paradise, the well-known spiritual leader.

McNair excused herself and Stevenson sat on the couch. The two men remained standing.

Toliver put a hand on Henson's shoulder. "I can't thank you enough for what you've done, Matthew. Let me add, it's a damn shame you aren't recognized more for the brave and unflinching man you are. I intend to do what I can to undo the disservice that Peary and Washington have done to you."

"That's not necessary, Charles. I prefer the life I have now. History may yet prove to be the arbiter of the truth. But I see no need to rush it."

"Do you ever take off the cloth of humbleness, Mr. Henson?" Stevenson said, crossing her legs.

"Maybe I spend too much time with my own counsel," he admitted. Among his travels years ago he'd studied martial arts not only in China, but also Zen teachings with the Buddhist abbot, the hunchbacked Master Hiroki Kodama in Japan. He was quite content to be alone.

"Growing up on the seas will do that, it seems," Toliver said. He sat near his daughter. "But now that my baby is returned, and I'm taking steps to ensure her continued safety, what can stand in my way?" He made a flourish with his ringed fingers.

McNair returned with a tray with a bottle and cylindrical glasses. She sat the refreshments on a sideboard and began pouring the drinks. The label proclaimed the bottle to be Canadian whiskey. Not the bathtub swill that often masqueraded as the real stuff, Henson noted. Taste would tell.

"Ladies first," she said, handing a glass to the younger woman who remained seated. Once everyone had a drink, McNair raised hers.

"Here's to success in all our ventures—and the progress of our people."

"Hear, hear," Toliver said, clinking his glass against hers.

Toliver, standing again, set his glass aside after taking a small sip. "Matthew, I know you're something of a freebooter, but I would like to keep you on a retainer, if you will. Helping keep tabs on the apple of my eye as well as checking in on my well-being while I'm in town. It wouldn't have to be around the clock, as I said, I'll take steps in that vein. But a man of your talents looking in on her now and then would ease my palpitations. Be assured I will compensate you as befits a man of your station."

Taking a sideways glance at his pretty daughter who was staring into her whiskey, Henson said, "That's quite the proposition, but just how long would this job take?"

"Oh, I'm a burden, am I?" Stevenson smiled at the explorer.

"Until Tolliver delivers his message," McNair piped in. She was already pouring herself another round. She held up the bottle and the others begged off.

"Message?" his daughter said.

Toliver bowed slightly toward McNair. "Miriam embellishes to make me blush. It's merely a speech."

"At Liberty Hall, which you will fill to the rafters," a joyous McNair added.

"What's it to be about?" asked Stevenson.

"Our freedom, of course." Toliver answered. "What do you say Brother Henson? The event is in less than two weeks' time."

Since he'd been approached through a mutual friend to meet with a tearful Daddy Paradise less than a handful of days ago, Henson had been wondering exactly why Dutch Schultz had put the grab on the man's daughter.

He hadn't pressed, as the advance was substantial and Toliver had been evasive. Though he did have a theory. For incompleteness had always gnawed at Henson, honed during those seven failed attempts to reach the North Pole. Once he set out on a course, he burned to see things through. And what the hell, this line of work was better than clerking behind a desk. Still, he knew better than to not learn all he could about an unknown territory.

"Tell me the truth, why did Dutch Schultz kidnap Destiny?"

"That's rather impertinent," McNair said. "You have no truck prying into this man's endeavors. Important undertakings all, I must add," she sniffed.

Toliver held up a hand. "That's all right, Miriam. I believe Mr. Henson is a man who can keep a confidence." He turned his head toward his daughter. "And she is of an age to see that one's folks have—shall we say—dimensions to them."

The daughter looked expectant as her father continued.

"As you know, Matthew, that Beer Baron of the Bronx has a large appetite, his eyes are bigger than his stomach, as my sainted mother would say. He is known to employ ruthless methods when he wants what he wants, like a tantrum-prone child."

Maybe it was the whiskey, but Henson wasn't in the mood for a long wind-up. "You have money in Queenie St. Clair's numbers operation." Stephanie "Queenie" St. Clair, of African and white French parentage, was among the high-steppers of the Harlem rackets.

Toliver nodded. "I've long been a silent partner in her policy banking."

"Me, too," McNair said, hand on her hip and jaw thrust defiantly at Henson, daring his scorn. "It's a way for our hard-working people to get a leg up given being frozen out of white-run institutions who won't loan to them. You realize how many restaurants, dress shops and who knows what all else wouldn't be around if not for this informal lending?"

Lending that demanded a healthy interest rate.

But Henson said, "I'm not passing judgement, I simply want to know what I'm getting into."

"Seems we're both pawns in a bigger game, Matt," Stevenson said.

"This is your duty as a New Negro," McNair said to Henson, taking another sip.

"Miriam," Toliver chided.

"That's okay." Henson hadn't been a follower of Marcus Garvey, or for that matter much of a follower of any negro advancement leader. He did, though, believe in self-improvement. He respected that Toliver and McNair put their money where their mouths were. Plus there was the opportunity to be around the intriguing Destiny.

"I'm in," he said, tipping his glass toward the other three. "But we'll need a crew to cover the hall that night. I'll take care of rounding up the men, but you'll have to cover their fee, understand?"

"Miriam?" Toliver said.

She shrugged in ascent.

"All right, then," Toliver said. "I knew I was hiring the right man for the job."

Destiny Stevenson stood, and bottle in hand, poured another round for herself and Henson. She leveled her gaze on him, "Indeed."

Henson was flattered by her attention and more than a little self-conscious of the grey creeping in at his temples.

Given her dusky skin tone, it wasn't noticeable that McNair flushed.

Daddy Paradise cleaned one of his long nails with the end of an ivory plated pen knife, smiling at the others.

Elsewhere, in a darkened room in a fleabag hotel on the lower east side, a gaunt white man in his late sixties with a shock of white hair moaned and sweat atop a thin mattress. Laying on its side on the floorboards was an empty unmarked bottle, cork nearby. Until recently, it had contained what was left of his laudanum. He was in wrinkled pants and a dirty undershirt and the effects of his opium-laced alcohol ignited the fevered dreams he so looked forward to each night. For it was in those mindscapes of his imagination that the answers came to him in many forms—from his beloved Elyce, to a talking frog squatting on a jade stone.

He stopped thrashing and bolted upright in the dark.

Hands gripping the side of the bed, he muttered, "The daughter… yes, Henson is the key."

CHAPTER TWO

"You know about this darkie?" Arthur "Dutch Schultz" Flegenheimer said, nearly biting the end of his cigar off as he gritted his teeth. Schultz had a flattened nose and big ears sticking out from his head. "Killed one of my boys and put the other one in a hospital. And on top of that, you expect me to just sit on my hands? Not to mention that greedy kraut bastard Hoffman upping the ante on me to keep a lid on this."

"You won't have to keep in check for long," his companion Fremont Davis said. "Though, I'll grant you, I should have foreseen the possibility of his involvement. Mr. Henson does move in interesting orbits." Davis had close-cropped steel grey hair and a trim goatee.

"Uh-huh," Schultz said, unimpressed, settling back in his chair. Above him was the mounted head of a stag, indifferent in death to his surroundings. In a corner was an Egyptian New Kingdom sarcophagus. He finished his drink and sat the glass down carelessly. It tipped over. Face contorted in barely contained anger, he pointed a finger at the man sitting opposite. "You better not be trying to pull the wool over my eyes. Bad enough I got Queenie and Holstein to contend with, now this...swartze Tarzan comes swinging in bumping off white men like he pleases. Shit."

Davis suppressed a chuckle. "This is but a minor setback, partner."

"Yeah, well, don't you forget that. Think I'm all weak-kneed sitting in all this?" he indicated the room they were in, "Drinking your fine booze and enjoying your Cubans? I can afford my own cigars." He tapped twin fingers against his chest. "You got me putting my men at risk."

"We are, all of us, taking risks, Dutch. But the payoff—as you would say—will be well worth it."

As he rose, he pointed a finger at the other man who remained sitting. "It better be." Shultz left.

Outside, the night air bracing him was cool. At the curb one of his men leaned against the gangster's spotless Packard Phaeton. Vincent "Vin" O'Hara was ruggedly handsome with high cheekbones, hazel eyes and a half moon scar on the side of one eye. He wore a straw hat over his brown hair. Several cigarettes littered the sidewalk near his square toe Oxfords.

"Let's get out of here, Vin," Schultz said.

"Sure, boss," said the other, opening the rear door for the bootlegger. The Packard's eight-cylinder engine caught on the second turn of the crankshaft and headlights springing on, off they went.

Upstairs, Davis stood at the window of his corner office watching the other one drive away. He let the drape he'd pushed aside fall back into place, blowing cigar smoke toward the ceiling, thoughtfully watching the vapor trail filter upward. He'd told the gangster only what he needed to motivate him to do his bidding. But it wouldn't do for him to enact his vendetta against Matthew Henson—at least not yet. He needed the first man to reach the North Pole alive a little longer.

CHAPTER THREE

Matthew Henson awoke early despite having been up past midnight. He lay under a sheet in his flannel long johns, but his chest was bare. As was usual, he'd left his bedroom window wide open for the bracing night air, just as he'd done since he was young. This adoration for the cold hadn't begun on his Arctic expeditions. It was from years of seagoing in rugged climes and often having to sleep in the open on the deck.

Finishing the sixth grade in Washington D.C., and yearning for he didn't know what then, he'd signed on as a cabin boy off the docks of Baltimore. This was a merchant ship, *Katie Hines,* bound for China under the command of Captain Childs. That would be his first time experiencing a foreign land but not his last. Over the course of his time as a seaman, he would travel back to China, go to Japan, Manila, North Africa, France, Nicaragua, the Black Sea and on into southern Russia and the northwest Murmansk area.

Though he only had a grade school education, it turned out Henson had a facility for languages. While not proficient in many tongues, his Spanish and Mandarin were more than passable. Later, when in northwest Greenland, that facility was helpful in learning more than one of the Inuit dialects. He was the only member of the eight Arctic expeditions to do so.

Various masks, items and totems sprinkled about the spacious apartment attested to his journeys and sometimes stays in these foreign lands. Several of his artifacts—an original Kiyonaga wood block print and a Yoruba orisha sculpture—would be the envy of a museum curator. But the monetary value of his possessions was always far from his mind.

Getting dressed, Henson reviewed the matters at hand. Like being able to sense the difference between a patch of ice he could step on and one that only *looked* solid, he was of the mind that Daddy Paradise and Miriam McNair hadn't been completely leveling with him.

It was no secret that Dutch Schultz was seeking to take over the lucrative Harlem numbers trade. Certainly to that end what with his volatile nature, he'd use kidnapping, gun play and any and all other forms of intimidation to get what he wanted. And presumably the opportunity had presented itself when Toliver came to town for this talk as he wasn't headquartered in Manhattan but Chicago. But Henson had also known the Daughter lived in town, had been here for more than four years running a music shop. It was only recently Toliver publicly admitted she was blood, having been raised by the mother. Could be Schultz waited until Toliver was in the vicinity. Could be he had been planning this for some time. But two and two weren't quite adding up in his head.

"Breakfast first," he determined, traipsing into the kitchenette to brew a pot of coffee and fix up some bacon and eggs. Many a Harlemite assumed he only ate whale blubber or sled dog—and he'd gladly eaten both with relish in the past. Mostly, in those days, Peary's crew would eat as the Eskimos did, fish and pemmican, with tea, condensed milk and biscuits the American additions to such a diet. His apartment had come furnished, but in addition to his keepsakes, he'd added things like the 19th century Mongolian area rug he walked bare-footed across and a slim Russian Empire era bureau made of mahogany and brass.

After dinner, he put several tools and devices on a round table near a window overlooking the street below. All on top of a letter he'd started that began with, "My Dear Anaukaq."

It was a letter he was having a hard time writing.

He paused momentarily, his fingers touching the paper then he put the sheet aside so as not to get it soiled. He took a deep breath and resumed the maintenance of his devices.

He'd rigged up a metal apparatus that clamped around his lower arm holding the shuriken in place by hinged steel fingers. By twisting his forearm, the star would release and drop down into his waiting hand. But he had to be careful, as more than once, the tension would be off and the star would shake loose and cut into his palm or drop to the ground. He adjusted the tension in the fingers, hoping that this time it would work. Using a stone, he sharpened the edges of his ice axes and checked the pull pins of his smoke bombs—which were roughly the size of handballs.

Once done, he returned the smoke bombs to his closet, nestled in a shoebox lined with cotton swabbing and crumpled newspapers. He didn't keep any incendiary grenades as they were volatile, and he certainly didn't want to burn up his apartment or harm anyone else. Though his were not the old-fashioned kind, filled with kerosene and oil, it was the casing itself, made of magnesium and alloy, that burned when ignited by a thermite charge. It was illegal to possess them, and for that reason and safety, Henson kept those grenades secured elsewhere.

He left his building on 130th and walked toward St. Nicholas Park, intending to cut diagonally through it toward his destination. He needed some dope on St. Clair and Daddy Paradise and had a person in mind as he checked the time on his wrist watch, a gift from Booker T. Washington who'd written the introduction to his *A Negro Explorer at the North Pole*. It was early, and the working men and women of Harlem were out on their way to their jobs be it nanny, cook, brick layer or soda jerk. Passing behind him as he crossed the street was a hearse from the Palmetto Ambulance and Funeral Service, a company owned by Queenie St. Clair. Entering the park, there was a serious-eyed young woman on the edge handing out informational handbills about the Laundry Workers Union of the Congress of Industrial

Organizations.

Crossing into the shadow of a large oak tree, Henson was certain he was being followed. The man had come out of an Helmbold drugstore doorway three blocks back and though keeping a distance between them, his presence was more evident as they went through the expanse of the park. The man was black, in plain clothes but his hat was expensive, Henson noted. This suggested to him the clothes had been put on to blend in, but the hat no doubt went with the suits this fella normally wore. Walking on, Henson quickly ascended a set of terraced steps. The Grange, Alexander Hamilton's house which was on the grounds, was visible through the foliage in the distance

The man on his tail had to speed up or risk losing Henson who'd already crested the top of the steps and was now out of view on the other side of the rise. He breathed through his open mouth, looking around. Off to the side in a semi-isolated section of shrubbery and trees, an old man with a full mane of grey hair like the abolitionist Fredrick Douglass sat on a bench in baggy pants and wrinkled shirt. He threw pieces of bread on the ground for the pigeons gathered about him. There was a book about mathematics beside him on the bench

"Hey, old timer," the man said as he approached the elderly resident, "you seen a guy in grey pants and dark shirt?" He flashed a fifty-cent piece. "I can make it worth your time."

"The gentleman you're looking for is right behind you," the old man said in a surprisingly clear voice.

"The hell," the man said, turning to see Henson there with his hands on his hips.

"Who sent you?" Henson said.

"Back off," his shadower said.

Henson came toward him, stirring some of the cooing pigeons into the air. "Maybe you didn't hear me."

The man who'd tailed Henson produced a folding knife from his back pocket that opened with a practiced flick of his wrist. "Let me make another hole in your head so you can hear me better, chump."

"There's no need for violence, young man. Merely an inquiry as to your employer."

He turned his head slightly to say, "Stay out of this, grey head, go back to feeding them flying rats."

"Would that I could," the older man said, bowing his head slightly. "But you're having a profound negative effect on them." He shook his head, sighing. "He indeed proves to be an obstreperous sort, Matthew, as befits one of his rung in our society."

"Hey, what gives, you two know each other?"

"Most assuredly," said the older man.

The man with the knife took a step back and turned in such a way to keep the two of them in sight. He jiggled the blade at the sitting older man. "On your feet."

"Where do you intend to take us?" the older man said.

"Never you mind. Up," he signaled with the knife.

As the older man rose he hesitated, pausing in a hunched over position. He breathed raggedly, his face was sweating, and he looked paler. "Oh my," he gasped, rocking backward and forward.

"What's going on with him?" The knife man said, panic coloring his voice.

"He's having one of his attacks. He's got a bum ticker," Henson said

"Help me," the older gent said hoarsely. "I, I…" he tottered on his feet and his collapse seemed imminent.

"Dammit, get this sonofabitch up," he barked at Henson. "And if you have to carry him, you better."

Henson came over his friend. "Yes, sir." He got an arm around the older man's chest and in this way held him upright on shaky legs.

"This way." He gestured in a direction with the tip of the knife and the three began walking. He fell in behind the two along a pathway through the park. But as they were now entering a more populated area, he put the knife back in his coat pocket, holding it there.

"Where you taking us?" Henson asked over his shoulder. "I should get him to a sawbones."

"Keep walking," the man said.

A woman pushing a baby stroller approached from the opposite direction. She smiled at the trio.

The three men moved to one side as the woman and baby passed. The older man abruptly stopped, and the knife man came up short behind him.

"Watch it," he said, between clenched teeth.

Henson rearranged his grip around the older man, who was sagging. But Henson spun him around, the old man thrusting his leg out, striking the knife man. Onlookers gaped.

The man was removing the knife from his pocket when Henson latched onto him. He had a hand on the other man's forearm, jamming the hand in the pocket. With his free arm, Henson threw an elbow into the man's Adam's apple.

The knife man hacked and coughed as he sought to get air down his throat again. Henson punched him in the stomach and doubling over, he socked him in the jaw. He staggered back, wobbly on his feet.

"Somebody help that man," a woman declared. "he's being attacked."

Henson's suddenly healthy older associate held up both his hands and in a decisive voice said, "Be assured, my dear citizens, Matthew Henson is doing yeoman's work in the service of us here in Harlem."

The one with the knife recovered, and running, grabbed a hold of the woman and her stroller. He had the knife to her throat. The woman began to cry. Henson and the old man came forward.

"Please don't hurt my baby."

"All right Amos n' Andy, back the hell off or the frail gets it, got me?"

"Okay, take it easy," Henson said, a hand up.

His blade pressed against the woman's breastbone, he backed up with her, his other hand pulling her stroller. He kept backing up, Henson, the old man and a few others following at several paces. They reached the sidewalk, a streetcar clanging as it approached along the adjacent thoroughfare. The roughneck shoved the woman hard to the pavement. The baby carriage rolled lopsided on two wheels and crashed over on its side. The baby tumbled out, wailing, and at the same time the knife flew at Henson, who dived out of the way. In three bounds the hood had leapt onto the back of the streetcar and rolled away.

"It's okay, it's all right," the old man said, cradling the frightened baby. He gently squeezed the child's pudgy arms and legs, checking of any broken bones. He handed the baby to his equally frightened mother.

"I believe other than a little shook up, he's fine," he said.

Tears on her cheeks, she stared lovingly at her child.

"When you need a cop, there's never one around," she said, earning nervous laughter from passerby.

As the people returned to their normal day, Henson and the old man talked, walking toward another park bench.

"What was that all about, Matthew?" The older man, Lionel "Slip" Latimore asked.

"Roundaboutly, I think it has to do with what I was coming to see you about."

Latimore had done some freelance work for Queenie St. Clair, obtaining hard-to-get information on a few of her adversaries. He was a master pickpocket, a known consort of underworld types, a safecracker of some adeptness, and had the curious ability to appear deathly ill. This latter oddity added to his other skills had earned him his nickname long ago. He'd even escaped a lynching once, or so he proclaimed.

"Well let's feed a few pigeons and hear what you have to say." He produced more bread from a pocket and the two sat and talked and threw pieces of bread the birds pecked at as they did so.

Meanwhile, another friend of Matthew Henson was putting an experimental airplane through its paces over the Central Valley wetlands near Newark, New Jersey. Aviatrix Bessie Coleman had just come out of a barrel roll when the silver-plated plane's engines stalled and the craft, the "Skahti", started freefalling out of the clear sky.

CHAPTER FOUR

"Bessie, Bessie, are you in trouble?" The man's worried voice crackled through the radio's mesh grill in the cockpit. "Bail out, bail out!" he pleaded.

Eyes on her controls, she said, "Don't get your blood pressure elevated, Hugo. I expected this."

"*Expected*? You expected to crash the plane?"

"I expected there was a problem with the induction vents adjusting properly should you have to make an evasive maneuver." Coleman's gauges informed her the aircraft's systems were functioning as they should, so she pressed the ignition button. The propellers cranked, but the engines didn't catch. Still, she pulled back on the stick, trying to get the nose of the craft. The Skathi, named for one of the moons of Saturn, shook and rattled, but Coleman kept cool as the plane swopped through a cloud bank and as it exited, began to assume a more normal flight profile.

"What?' Hugo Renwick said from the control tower below. "Bessie, please, for God's sake, get out of that death trap."

"I thought you were a Buddhist."

"Bessie, please. It's not worth it."

"Hold on, I'm not done yet."

Due to the advanced aero design of the Skathi, including innovations in its aluminum hull that made it lightweight yet resilient,

Coleman had righted the plane. But even in glide mode, she was still losing altitude too fast. Taking her hands off the controls, Coleman reached under the control panel and grasped the wires leading to the ignition. She pulled these free as Renwick yelled over the radio.

"Bessie, you're getting awfully close to the ground."

"Thank you, Hugo, my altimeter is working perfectly."

Getting enough of the wiring exposed beyond its casing, Coleman wrapped the two exposed wires together, a spark singeing her fingers. The propellers turned again, coughing and belching black oil-soaked smoke from the exhausts. There was also a propeller mounted on the rear of the fuselage, but that was for stability and only operated at specific times.

"Come on…" she urged. Air whooshed past the cabin. Yet because it was an advanced aircraft and soundproofed accordingly, she barely heard this as she continued dropping.

"Bessie, what's happening?" came Renwick over the radio.

"Come on…" she took the controls again, and calculated how badly the plane—and her— would crack up making a dead-stick landing. She pressed the ignition. First the starboard side engine coughed and caught, then the one opposite.

"Holy smokes," she laughed.

"I can't take this," Renwick said over the radio.

An elated Coleman flew across the landing field where her mechanic Shorty Duggan waved his arm at her. She banked around the squat two-story control tower, climbed the Skathi back into the air, then circled around to bring the craft in on the runway. Her intent wasn't a traditional landing.

"That lass sure is something, ain't she?" Duggan said, as Renwick fell in step beside him as the two headed toward the descending aircraft. The seasoned mechanic was pot-bellied, perpetually whiskered, in his fifties and bow-legged. The forty-six year old Renwick was rangy, high cheekboned with combed back black hair and round, rimless glasses.

"Careful, Shorty, Bessie would eat you up and spit you out for breakfast."

Duggan smiled yellowed teeth. "Ah, what a time it would be. But you rest easy, Mister Tycoon, I think of 'er as the daughter I never had, don't you know?"

"Yes, I do," Renwick said solemnly.

Duggan took out a well-worn pipe from his pocket and stuck it between his teeth on the side of his mouth. He made no effort to light it as he and the man financing this operation watched Coleman bring the craft the ground, for it was unlike any other plane currently in existence.

The wings of the craft tilted upward. Coleman was thankful those switches weren't malfunctioning. The rear rotor simultaneously turned in sync with the twin modified Pratt & Whitneys which were now pointing straight up. In this way, the plane hovered in midair much like an autogyro, but not requiring a massive overhead propeller suspended over the cockpit. The craft touched down vertically on the runway and she cut the engines. The gearing in the wings whined as they lowered in place horizontally for takeoff.

"You nearly gave me a heart attack," Renwick said as she came out of the cockpit onto the built-in rungs.

"What happened?" Duggan said, concerned for her, but also anxious his work had been inferior and the reason for the engines quitting.

She repeated what she'd told Renwick.

"Ah, well," a relieved Duggan said, "damn engineers." He took his pipe out and pointed the much-chewed stem at the two of them. "Didn't I say fiddlin' with those louvres to gain more speed in the lift would have consequences?"

"You did, Shorty," Renwick admitted. "But we're pushing the boundaries."

"Physics is still physics, Mr. Renwick, and it's fair Bessie's gorgeous hide on the line when you push them there boundaries."

"I know what I've signed on for," Coleman said, carrying her leather helmet and goggles in her hands, radio wire dangling from it. "And, anyway, the engines would have started right up again if not for the ignition switch."

Duggan stopped. "It failed?"

She shrugged. "These things happen."

"I put that switch in the Scotty meself last week, Bessie." Biting down hard on his pipe he marched back toward the experimental craft and inside the cockpit.

Standing several feet back from the craft, an observer might mistake it for a Ford Tri-Motor, though its body was more of a tapered design. The plane had a motor mounted under each side of its hinged wing but instead of a propeller in the center there was an oval. Set inside of that was a row of circular louvers that fronted an axial-flow turbojet based on a design by the French engineer Maxime Guillaume. The Frenchman had been paid for use of his patent, which existed as drawings only, no prototype. He hadn't yet solved the problem of making compressors that didn't fail due to fluctuations in air pressure. Renwick's brain trust had made progress in that regard, at least to the extent that the turbojet bestowed greater speed to the plane. But most importantly, when the plane was switched over to land vertically, the center turbine helped keep the craft aloft in a temporary stationary position.

Inside the hanger, they walked past various internal and external pieces of aircraft as well as a DC and gas-powered electrical generators. On a workbench Duggan took the switch apart and stared at it. He pointed the tip of his screwdriver at the insides. "The contact points have been removed. When I put the switch in last week, I tested it, and it worked fine."

"None of us doubt you, Shorty," Renwick said.

Bessie Coleman folded her arms. "Sabotage. But subtle-like. Done by someone who counted on us always tinkering with the Skathi."

"Easy enough to observe us from the woods around here,"

35

Duggan noted. The private airfield was in a bulldozer cleared area in the wetlands.

"You don't exactly lack for enemies, Hugo," Coleman observed.

"Cutthroat usually has other meanings from the boardroom types," Renwick said. "They use their lawyers to entangle you through legal maneuvers."

"Maybe they don't have time for that. Or maybe they simply like the more direct method," Coleman said.

"And let's not forget there are plenty of flyboys who feel a woman—especially a colored gal—ain't got no business in the air," Duggan wryly noted.

She'd received her pilot's license two years before Amelia Earhart. Though Earhart had gained additional notoriety as the first woman to fly across the Atlantic, it was as a passenger and not lead or co-pilot. A French speaker, Coleman was the one who knew about Guillaume's pioneering theories.

Renwick said, tapping the switch, "There's plenty of my rivals would love to derail this effort. Aviation is a field with vast potential and to be the first with this kind of airship, well, one's reputation would be made."

"Aye, like Cook versus Peary?" Duggan said, looking at Renwick. "Who gets their first or can make his claims stick, is all that counts."

The man gave him a wan smile. "Still, I assumed our isolated location would be protective cover, but I see I better bring on some guards for all concerned," the industrialist added.

"I hope you're not talking about Pinks," Duggan said. "Just 'cause it was a silver-tongued Scotsman who started them, I don't hold much truck with them railroad boss siding, strike breaking bastards."

"Amen, Comrade," Coleman said straight-faced.

"They'll be hand-selected by me," Renwick said.

"Okay. Let's go over the Scotty to make sure nothing else is amiss."

"You read my mind."

"I'll see you two a little later," Renwick said.

The pilot and the mechanic said their goodbyes and walked back to the experimental craft. Renwick drove away in his Chrysler roadster. He stopped in town to get an egg cream and use a pay phone in a drugstore as there were no phone lines out where the airfield was.

"Hello, Dash, is that you?" he said, after he'd settled in the booth and got the operator to dial the number he wanted after consulting his pocket address book. "It's Hugo Renwick...yes, that's right, how are things? What are you working on now?' He listened for several seconds then spoke again, "Huh, all about a black falcon statue you say, sounds damn interesting. Look, I wanted to pick your brain for some thick necked chaps for a spot of guard duty. Hush, hush stuff. But that must be reliable. Right, no, they don't have to have been in harness."

Renwick took another sip of his soda and began jotting down a few names offered by former Pinkerton detective, and current teller of hardboiled tales, Dashiell Hammett.

CHAPTER FIVE

The gaunt white man had slept longer than he'd intended. Though not heavy, the rusty springs squeaked as he swung his legs over the side and, his rather long feet on the floor, he got his bearings. He'd run out of laudanum the day before and had told himself that he didn't need the drug to get his work done. That, really, he should do his best to keep clear-headed and able-bodied. This was not a new argument. But no more. Too much was at stake.

Dr. Henrik Ellsmere, product of an Old-World upbringing and education in his native Austria at the University of Vienna and the Graz University of Technology, lecturer at Cambridge and Princeton, rose in his ratty pajama bottoms and undershirt, scratching at himself. He bent down to the mattress, turning his head this way and that, sure there were bedbugs, but like every morning, saw no evidence save the little red bites on his body. There were a lot of cats prowling around here—it had to be fleas, he glumly concluded. In the small room was one table. On this was a raft of loose sheets of paper, spilling onto the floor. The pages were filled with Ellsmere's calculations and projections in his precise numbers and letters in pencil.

After a trip to the bathroom at the end of the hall, he picked up his notes, seeking to put them in rough order. Maybe next week he'd give up laudanum, as he felt a belt or two of the wonderful elixir might provide the key to his formulations. No, he resolved yet again, he must be strong. A sound caused him to look up from his papers. The sash in the window leading to the fire escape was being raised by a tiger.

He blinked hard, worried that the hangover from the laudanum was playing with his mind. Ellsmere realized it was a man in a coat and hat, wearing a tiger mask, bright orange with black stripes like what would be worn at a Halloween party, held in place by a rubber band attached to either side. The hat was pushed up on his head. The Tiger Man came into the room

"All right, prof, you're coming with me, and don't give me no guff." He was large, over six-two, and the bunching around the material of his coat sleeves told Ellsmere this was a muscular individual indeed. He advanced on the older man, blocking the window. The only other way out was the door, and the man would be on him in two bounds should he try and run. And how far would he get anyway? He was old and had arthritis in a knee. This man would be on him like a fish monger's cat on a mouse. The Tiger Man had worn a prophetic disguise.

"Look here, my good man," he began, realizing he was speaking in German—he tended to revert to his native language under stress. Continuing in English, he said, "I'm in the middle of most important work and have no time for circus hijinks or whatever this is."

"Come on, big brain, this won't hurt a bit. It'll be over before you know it."

"Let me get dressed first, please."

"Okay, you do that. But no funny business." He glanced around the room. "Jeez, what a dump. I'm doing you a favor taking you out of here."

"Yes, sir." His pants were draped over a chair, as was his shirt. He dressed, put on his shoes and then stepped to the chesterfield, picking up a hair brush.

"Okay, Casanova, let's go," the Tiger Man said impatiently. "Ain't no chorus girls where I'm taking you." A cigarette he'd lit dangled from the slot in his feline mask. He ground it out on the floor to join other black spots there.

Ellsmere had combed back his tangle of hair, regarding himself in the mirror as if he cared about this appearance. He turned from the dresser toward the door.

"This way," said the masked man, jabbing a thumb at the window. My jalopy's in the alley."

Ellsmere walked up, breaking a glass capsule he'd taken from the dresser against the man's cheek. A plume of green smoke arose from the shards, briefly enveloping the Tiger Man's head

"The hell," the masked man yelled. "You want it rough, you got it, chump. He grabbed the smaller man by the shoulders in his meaty hands. "I gotta bring you back alive, but you're gonna be minus a couple of teeth for acting smart." As he said this, a weakness spread through his arms. His grip went lax.

"Hey, what gives?" he wobbled as he tried to get closer to the retreating Dr. Ellsmere. But try as he might, his limbs were suddenly incapable of use.

"I keep a few of my prototypes around," the older man crowed. "This is a tough neighborhood, after all."

"You lousy little…come back here." Tiger Man tried to get his arms up, but they only flopped at his sides. He took a step and went down face-first. He managed to raise his head, the pieces of his cracked mask held in place by his sweat. "I'm gonna fix you good," he promised, wiggling his upper body in an effort to ris—but to no effect.

It was like watching the contortions of an armless bear, Ellsmere noted, chuckling nervously. "Of that I have no doubt my large friend, if I were to wait around for my concoction to wear off." He gathered several more items from the dresser and put them in his pockets. Notes in hand, he rushed out of the door, Tiger Man cursing at him. A man that size and weight, the paralyzing gas would soon wear off. But he was grateful this forced field test showed it worked as he'd estimated. He wasn't quite ready yet, but he had to find Matthew Henson.

Down in the street, Ellsmere walked briskly away from the Beaumont. He crossed the alley, seeing the Tiger Man's car parked

40

there. He chided himself for not taking the keys from the thug's pocket, but didn't think it was a good idea to double back now. Maybe the goon was still immobile, but he could also possibly have use of his big arms and fists this time on him. He caught a streetcar and headed to Harlem.

Elsewhere Queenie St. Clair and Venus Melenaux got out of a silver and grey Duesenberg in front of the Palmetto Ambulance and Funeral Service on Seventh Avenue—what some called the Black Broadway of Harlem. The Service occupied a garage where the vehicles were stored and maintained, as well as a two-story structure to the side where the funeral parlor, its display and prep rooms and such, occupied the ground floor. There were offices and a private apartment on the second floor.

Upstairs the two entered the main office. Set on St. Clair's desk was a tray containing a pot of steaming tea and two china cups. Melenaux poured for both as St. Clair removed her toque and hung it from a hook on the standing coat rack. Meleneaux wore stylish men's cuffed pants, a sweater and a beret which she did not remove. She also had a desk in the office, and took her tea over to that one. There was a phone on each desk—each an unlisted number was not widely known. The morning totals from their collectors, those who took in the monies from runners, were already starting to come in and it was only a little after eight. The runners had regular routes and took money, coins and the occasional dollar bill, and wrote down the numbers from the bricklayers, maids, seamstresses, cake makers and bellhops on their way to their jobs. The previous day's figures would be posted in the newspapers by 10 A.M.

While some policy chieftains wanted to know the initial takes, and had their collectors use the phone, calling in using worked-out code words in place of numbers, St. Clair knew from her police contacts that the cops could listen in on such conversations. Codes were meant to be cracked. She relied on her collectors, who might be the bootblack

41

in a barbershop or operating a cigar and candy stand in the lobby of a hotel, secreting the money away under the floor and what have you. They did not write down sums on slips of paper, and therefore did not have to memorize them or be prepared to eat the paper should the cops approach. The collectors, in turn, would wait until the late afternoon and turn in their money at specific locations where the finals were counted by a coterie of middle-aged women overseen by Meleneaux.

The women, some of them widows, some of them having been injured doing factory work, had been recruited through personal contacts, garden clubs and even artistic appreciation associations. It was a safe way for them to make some earnings, or raise money for their groups. Each location was under the direct auspices of one of her hoods to ensure the peace. St. Clair understood everyone enjoyed a little larceny. To ensure that her collectors weren't skimming off the top, St. Clair would randomly tell a certain number of runners each week to write down the amounts they turned in to any one collector.

As all this required organization, including paying off patrolmen and their higher-ups to keep looking the other way. There was also keeping track of things like peoples' birthdays—small things like that kept her employees happy. So, the two women were busy at their respective desks with paperwork, notes, directing this or that person over the phone to follow through on a particular task and the like. At one point the assistant funeral director, a pudgy individual with a balding pate, came in with the morning mail for St. Clair. "Thank you, Herman," she said to him. "After lunch Mr. Riordan will be stopping by."

"Yes, ma'am," he said departing.

Reaching the part of town where he knew Henson resided, Ellsmere realized he didn't have an address for him. "Once again, getting my carts before the horses," he muttered, shaking his head. He found a phone booth in the lobby of a theater.

"Dammit," he muttered, not finding a listing for Henson in the phone book. Back on the street, he saw two men laughing and talking in front of a luggage shop and interrupted them.

"Excuse me, gentlemen, but I'm trying to find Matthew Henson."

"That explorer fella?" One asked. He was smoking a cigarette.

"Yes, do you know where he lives?"

He looked at his companion who stared blankly back at him. "No, can't say I do." He blew smoke into the air.

"Say," the other one said, snapping his fingers. "Don't he have that radio show he does?"

"Yeah, that's right," his friend agreed. "Talks about different places he's been and what not. What do you call it, aw, my old lady listens to it."

"Where does he broadcast this show?" Ellsmere asked. A car screeched around the near corner and he looked at it approach anxiously. It went past without incident.

"Ah," began the other one, "I think it only comes on once a week or something like that."

"Where?" Ellsmere repeated impatiently.

The man with the cigarette narrowed his eyes as smoke clouded them. "Why you so eager to find Henson, huh? You, what do you call it, anarchist?"

"I believe that is *my* concern, sir."

"Go on with you, old man," cigarette man's friend said, swiping his hand through the air.

Ellsmere grunted, departing and talking to himself "Don't get agitated, keep your head," he said. "These fools don't know what I know."

The professor was overheard by a woman who was placing oranges in their display tray in front of her and her husband's tidy grocery store. She glared at the gaunt white man whose longish white hair was once again haloing about his head. The woman had just had an argument wither husband over his indulgence in playing the numbers, and not winning, and she was not in a good mood.

"Who you callin' fool?"

Ellsmere ignored her and kept walking. She wasn't satisfied and followed him down the street, pointing a finger at him, an orange in her other hand. "I said, who you callin' a fool?"

The scientist looked around, frowning. "Madam, I have much more important matters to attend to than your prattling. That is unless you can tell me where Matthew Henson can be found. If not, please be away with you."

"Me, gone?" she yelled. "Seems to me *you* the one who should be gone."

Their elevated conversation garnered attention from several people as the woman got closer, gesticulating at Ellsmere. "Who are you to come around here disrupting business and commerce? Why you want with Mr. Henson, huh? What's he to you? You working for that backstabbing Admiral Peary?"

Wearily, Ellsmere said, "Robert Peary has been dead some eight years, madam, and he was not an admiral. Now really, be off with you."

"What did you say to me?"

"Be away with you, woman," he said, raising his voice, too. "Business you say? I am on important business that is far beyond your comprehension."

"Oh, I'm stupid, am I?"

Ellsmere had already turned back and said over his shoulder, "You said it, not me."

A man in rolled up sleeves stepped in front of Ellsmere as murmuring rose around him.

"Maybe you figure we're all stupid up here, with your high and mighty ways?"

"Sir, I implore you, I must be allowed to get on with my task at hand."

"Oh, I got a task for you."

"Okay, break it up," demanded a new voice.

Heads turned toward a black patrolman making his way through the knot of people. The rows of brass buttons prominent on his dark blue tunic. His billy club remained sheathed.

"Office Rodgers, this man obviously isn't from here, and is spouting insults and nonsense," the grocer said.

"That is not so," Ellsmere said. "I have merely come to this community—as I said—to find Matthew Henson. An old acquaintance of mine, I might add."

"Hmph," the woman huffed. "Yet you don't seem to know where your old friend is, do you?"

"A minor molehill you are turning into a mountain," he retorted.

She stepped toward him and Rodgers got his hand between them. "Look, you come with me, and we'll see about you and Matthew Henson."

"Are you arresting me, officer?"

"I'm cooling things off, mister. Now come on." Rodgers was a good-sized individual, grey eyes in a brown-skinned face. His cap sat square over his close-cropped black hair.

Ellsmere hesitated but what choice did he have he decided. "Very well."

"And don't come back," the grocer said, earning a few chuckles.

"Do you know about Matthew Henson's radio broadcast?" he asked the cop as they walked away.

"Yeah, he does it from Smalls' Paradise on Thursdays."

They passed a newsie hawking copies of the *Herald*. "Extree, extree, grandmother kills burglar with ice pick. Extree, extree, grandma kills burglar with ice pick. *Herald*, get yer *Herald* right here." He shouted, waving a folded over newspaper over his head.

How's it going Henry?" the cop asked the newsie.

Okay, Officer Rodgers," young Henry Davenport said as he continued selling his papers.

"Oh dear, I'm afraid I can't wait that long for him to show up there."

"You won't have to. I'm taking you to May-May's."

"What would that be?'

"A hash house where he often has his lunch." Henson also got his messages there but he didn't add that.

"Ah, well then."

Rodgers regarded the odd white man, but this wasn't the first time some outsider had come uptown in search of the explorer. Less than a month ago, he'd directed a writer doing a "where are they now" story for *Look* magazine to May-May's. But this fried egg, he figured it better to escort him personally least he start a ruckus.

On Lenox Avenue near 132rd Street, past a narrow doorway where a placard in the window announced the services of herbalist and spiritualist Brother Morris, an unlit neon sign read in big script "May-May's Downhome Diner", and in smaller lettering, "Savory Cooking". As it was still before lunch, there was only a handful of customers inside the establishment.

"My, that smells good," Ellsmere said, taking in the aroma.

"Uh-huh," Rodgers said, wondering if maybe this guy wasn't a hobo on the make. He stirred him toward the horseshow-shaped counter. "Have a seat."

"Will Henson be coming in soon?"

"I have no idea, but I'm going to get the proprietor over here. Sit tight."

Ellsmere sat, and the patrolman went around the far end of the counter out of sight. Momentarily, he returned with a handsome copper-skinned woman in an apron walking on the inside of the counter area.

At a table in the corner, two men enthusiastically discussed why the Yankees starting lineup didn't hold a candle to the likes of Satchel Paige and Josh Gibson of the Negro Leagues' Black Barons and Homestead Grays.

"Shame they don't let 'em play in the majors," one lamented.

The other man concurred, pouring even more sugar in his

lukewarm coffee. "You know some of our boys have been going down to Mexico to play. Got an owner down there don't mind the color."

"Yeah?" his companion said.

"May, this here gent says he's a professor and has to see Matthew," Rodgers said back at the counter.

"He does, does he?" May Maynard asked. She was tall, dark-skinned and sharp eyed.

"I was on one of his expeditions," Ellsmere said, telling her his name. Yet, despite his eagerness to prove himself, he held back from mentioning it had been the second expedition, the one to retrieve the largest of the meteorites in Greenland. *Keep your tongue still*, he admonished himself.

She crossed her arms. "Like we haven't heard that before." She looked over at Rodgers. "Remember that one who said the ghost of the admiral had sent him with a message for Matthew?"

"I am in full possession of my faculties, Miss May."

She and the cop exchanged a look. Then, "Let me make a call or two." Pointing a short-nailed finger at Ellsmere she said, "But if you act up, bother any of my customers, I'll put a rolling pin upside your head, understand?"

He dipped his head slightly. "Most assuredly, my dear Madam."

"My dear indeed," she said, turning about and walking back to the swing doors fronting the kitchen.

"I'll leave you to it." Rodgers touched the brim of his cap and left the restaurant.

Not far away, Henson entered a cramped space where several gamblers were engaged in a boisterous game of craps. Sweat, stale food and sour breaths made the air in here eye-watering.

"Six is the point," said a man in a gabardine coat.

"Six you mother, six," said another, a burly individual jiggling a pair of dice in his hand. In his other, he held several dollar bills tighter than he'd hold his hand around the waist of his sweetheart. He blew on his hand and rolled the dice across a green felt table. Double threes came up amid cries of joy and disappointment.

"Come to Papa," the shooter said, scooping up money that was thrown onto the table.

"While you're in a good mood, Oscar..." Henson interrupted.

"Well, well, look who's slumming," Oscar Dulane otherwise known as OD cracked, handing the dice off to the man next to him. The two walked over to a quiet corner.

"Got a paying prospect for you," Henson told Dulane. In addition to his being a bouncer, he also did work as—what was euphemistically termed—a "home defense officer", rugged types employed by the ones who put on rent parties where back rooms were available for husbands tipping out on the missus. This often meant gambling was part of the attraction, and his job was to keep the peace if a tipsy patron acted out.

Henson explained he needed some men to do guard duty at Daddy Paradise's upcoming talk at Liberty Hall.

OD said, "I can get some boys for the job. But it'd be good to go over the place, right?"

"For sure. I'll make the arrangements. Figure three days out."

"Sounds good to me."

They discussed the job some more then Henson left. Back on the avenues, the newsie, Henry, told him Officer Rodgers was looking for him.

Ellsmere was on his second cup of coffee when Henson arrived. Several of the diner's patrons said hello to him as he stepped inside. The professor brightened at seeing him. "There he is, he who looked the Grim Destroyer in the face and didn't blink."

Henson smiled sheepishly. "Good to see you too, Prof. It's been awhile."

He rose from his stool, each had their hands on the other's shoulders. "My Lord, Matthew, seems you haven't aged a day."

"I wish that was true."

"We have a matter of much import to discuss, my lad. Where

might we have such a discussion?'"

"There's a booth in the back." Henson took notice of the folded-over notes Ellsmere had with him.

Ellsmere followed his gaze. "I suppose that will have to do."

Once they were seated, a waitress came over, refilling Ellsmere's cup. She sat an empty cup down for Henson and filled that, too, from her tin pot. "Hi, Matt, breakfast or lunch usual?"

"Guess I'll have myself a late breakfast, Florence," he said. "What about you, Prof?"

"What's your usual, Matthew?"

"Eggs over easy, grits, bacon, coffee and sourdough toast," Florence Brown said. "He's got to keep his strength up," she deadpanned.

"Heh, well that's more than I can handle," Ellsmere said, patting his stomach. "But I could go for some eggs and bacon."

"Got it," she said and walked away.

Henson sampled his coffee. "So, what's on your mind, Henrik?"

He looked over his shoulder conspiratorially, then leaned forward. "The Daughter."

For a second Henson wondered how Ellsmere had heard about Destiny Stevenson. But then he got his bearings. "What about it?"

"They're looking for it."

Like when he was sledding and would halt the dogs to determine if a stretch of ice might be thinner than it looked, a familiar ball of wariness formed in his stomach. "Who is 'they', professor?"

He plopped his sheets of calculations onto the tabletop. "As you may know, I've experienced something of a vagabond life since, well, since my troubles."

Henson had been the one to deliver Ellsmere to the sanitarium after the return to New York on the whale ship the Hope, bearing the largest of the Cape York meteorites, the thirty-four ton Tent, Saviksoah. The "Great Iron" as the Eskimos had nicknamed it. Eleven feet long and seven feet high. It took many hours, several hydraulic jacks and other engineering adaptations to load it onto the ship Previously, two other ancient meteorites had been brought back from the north shore of Melville Bay, the Mother, Ahnahnna, and the Dog, Kim-milk, both of which were much smaller than the Tent.

Henson lowered his voice. "You didn't tell anyone anything, did you?"

"Of course not. All this time, even at my most..." he gestured, "untethered, I have not given that confidence away. But I must admit, through all my travails, unlocking the secrets of the Daughter has been the one beacon focusing my mind. Helping to keep me on task, I suppose one might say."

Henson nodded, staring into the depths of his coffee.

Their food came, and both remained silent until the waitress departed again. Ellsmere spoke, "In my wanderings after my incident, in my travels, I might take a research job or lab work, what with teaching posts not available to me given, well you know..."

Henson started in on his breakfast. "No rush, prof, but about the Daughter..."

"Yes," Ellsmere said over a mouthful of food. He swallowed, looking down at his meal, grinning. "I see why you frequent this place."

Henson smiled, "Beats roasted seal, don't it?"

"Oh, we got used to a lot of things out there, didn't we? Anyway, as I was saying, I've been living in an itinerant manner. Even went out to Los Angeles for a time, a place called Pasadena actually. The one time I almost got a post again." He forked in more of his breakfast, looking off, then refocused. "Anyway, making my way east again, I was approached by an interesting woman, herself part Inuit I'm pretty certain, with an interesting proposition. This was oh, four or so months ago."

"And what was the job?"

"That's just it, her finding me was a dream. I was paid handsomely, provided rooms and pertinent books, and all I had to do was further pursue avenues previously abandoned. Every two weeks or so she'd drop by and ask about my progress."

Henson took a few steps onto that ice. "But she was a ringer?"

"As the colloquialism goes," Ellsmere said in German, knowing that Henson would understand. He switched back to English. "About three weeks ago she asked me pointedly about my time at Princeton."

"Why did that raise your hackles?"

"The light bulb finally went off in my head, Matthew. So hungry was I for being appreciated. But I suddenly understood, given her follow-up attempts at deflection, that the previous scientific inquiry for the sake of inquiry was just to butter me up you see. To draw me in and have me lower my guard. Her real interests, and that of her backers, I surmised, was what we are calling quantum physics that Dr. Einstein has gotten so much attention advancing."

Henson detected the envy in his voice. "What does that mean, quantum physics?

"In 1919, astronomer Edwin Powell Hubble advanced the theory that our universe is constantly expanding, my friend. That it is not fixed, since the science of astronomy was established. This changed everything."

Henson chewed and recalled that more than once he'd been in an Arctic storm at night and the only way to find his way back was sighting specific star formations. Still, he didn't have a PhD, let alone two of them. "How does that relate to what happened to you?"

"I could go into what all that means via Hubble's and Bohr's theories. But to be succinct, it's about the energy that is all around us, my rugged fellow. Untapped and unseen. But there nonetheless. It's about unlocking the potential of the atom."

Now the ice began to crack beneath his feet. "Or objects from space."

Ellsmere stopped eating and sipped his coffee, eyeing his companion over the rim of the cup.

"Did she mention the Daughter?"

Ellsmere was chewing again. He paused and put his fork down.

"Not directly, but I sensed that's where she was going. As I said, she soon took the conversation elsewhere, but two days later, wound back around to my thoughts on this branch of physics."

"I don't know, that seems natural as it relates to you. There's a lot you have your finger in."

"Believe me, Matthew, I am not imagining this. I'm not hearing voices or seeing little green men. I didn't even during my breakdown. My memory has always been quite intact. Which reminds me, when was the last time you've seen your son?"

"Longer than it should be," he admitted.

Ellsmere started at him. "Take it from a man with no family, Matthew. Don't let it go too much longer."

"You're right."

Ellsmere held a piece of bacon near his mouth. "To continue, my rooms, if you will, were part of a larger mansion in Poughkeepsie. Mind you, I had relatively free run of the place until that evening when she broached that particular subject matter."

"You know where this mansion is?"

"Not exactly. It was near a park though, and not far from the main highway. Along a kind of second floor landing was a row of stained glass windows, religious scenes."

"You were locked in that night?"

"Yes, but overcoming a mortise lock was not hard," he said proudly. "Prowling around, alert after those remarks about my atomic work, I overheard my beautiful captor talking to someone on the phone. I did not gather all of it, but I distinctly heard her mention the Daughter. Also, I understood they would be resorting to more… direct methods to get me to cooperate."

"You figured to lam it out?"

Ellsmere frowned.

"Escape?"

"Here I am."

"But if the Daughter's been found, I'm sure I would have gotten word," Henson said, tamping down any urgency in his voice. No one knew he possessed the Daughter, a dangerous piece of space rock that scared him.

"Unless the resourceful Ootah is dead. For this is something those of that ilk would kill for to possess."

"You think she worked for some oil or coal outfit? This part-Inuit woman?"

"That is a possibility. At any rate, I've been hiding out near the Bowery. Frankly, and I suppose the psychiatrists at Dunwich would say this was a diversionary tactic on my part, I allowed myself to become immersed in what would it take to tap the Daughter's potential."

"That ciphering of yours?" Henson said.

"Yes."

The lunch crowd began entering, a mix of working men and women and others in snappier clothes. Henson keenly aware of the presence of more eyes and ears. "Let me settle up and we'll go back to my place."

"Very good." Stepping to the counter to pay, a portly man in glasses and a striped shirt looked over at him from his stool there. He took hold of his copy of *The New York Amsterdam News* he'd been reading with his meal.

"Would you mind autographing this, Mr. Henson?" the man said.

Henson smiled at the coffee-stained newspaper which was folded to a print ad. The ad depicted a drawing of a smiling Henson's face, a fur hood over his head. In big letters the wording read: "There's only one discovery for me, Clicquot Club Pale Dry Ginger Ale." Smaller type went on attest that the product was made from the purest spring water, fresh juices of lemons and limes, pure cane sugar, and only the best in Jamaican ginger.

"Here you go, glamor boy." Mayfield handed Henson a pencil from behind her ear and he signed the advertisement. Handing the newspaper back, he noted on the flip side was a brief article about Daddy Paradise's upcoming talk at Liberty Hall.

Henson paid, and the two men stepped out onto the thoroughfare. As he'd told Destiny Stevenson, there hadn't been anything in print or radio about the escapade from the other night. At a corner newsstand, a man with several days' growth of whiskers and a balding head stood behind the array of newspapers, slicks and pulps such as *Argosy* and *Weird Tales* prominent. Despite the warmth of the day, he wore a threadbare sweater buttoned to his breastbone. He nodded at Henson, who nodded back.

"Mr. Greene, how goes it?"

"Same old sixes and sevens."

"I hear you."

A car with a canvas top screeched into view, nearly running down a woman crossing the street who made her objections known.

"Get down," Henson yelled, the glint of sunlight on the end of a Thompson gun's barrel filling his vision. The gun rattled rounds at them, the spray of high-pitched bullets sending up a blizzard of newsprint and lurid color covers. Henson grabbed Ellsmere and they plunged behind a parked car. People screamed and ran and dived for cover all around him. A man, praying loudly, dove with his arms in front of his face through a plate glass window of a bakery.

"Are you hit?" Henson asked.

"I believe I'm whole, for now," Ellsmere replied.

The machine gunner was not the one called Eddie Henson had encountered the other night. These Chicago Typewriters were too damn plentiful. And that didn't mean these men didn't work for the Dutchman, too. Though could be they were working for whoever put the snatch on the professor, as he didn't figure that to be Schultz.

The canvas-topped car drove past, then, tires smoking, made a U-turn to roar back toward the two.

"Stay put," he told the scientist, getting into a crouch.

"Just what is it you intend to do, Matthew?"

"See if I can get us out of this." Normally he didn't go around armed, but since taking the job to protect Daddy Paradise's daughter, he'd been keeping a couple of his throwing stars on him. He'd have to get close enough to use them—and stay alive in the process.

On the passenger side of the car, a man rode the running board, pistol in his hand. He was in a suit and hat, a lion's mask like something for a Halloween party covering his face. The car slowed, and he leapt off. On the other side, the one with the machine gun also got out of the car. He was dressed similarly, a rhino mask covering his face. The driver, in a cheetah mask, remained behind the wheel, engine idling. The lion with the handgun grabbed a small man who'd ducked behind his pushcart. The handgun's muzzle was put against this man's head.

"Okay, Henson, give us the bookworm and I'll let this poor bastard keep breathing. If you don't, he's the first one I kill—but not the last."

Hands up, Henson took several steps toward the two. "Maybe we can talk this over." The machine gunner in his rhino mask was flanking him to the left. Even if he could plant a star in the head of the lion, the other one would cut him down in a blink.

"You're in no position to dicker," the lion said.

Henson chanced more steps. "Maybe I got money to make a counter-offer."

Lion snickered. "Where'd you get money?"

"What do you think we bought back from the North Pole? Gold." He calculated he might be able to throw both stars at once, strike his twin targets.

"Bullshit."

"Yeah?" He stopped, stiffening. He knew he was going to be too slow in trying to fling one of his flying stars. Rhino Mask had sensed something was up and was leveling his weapon on Henson, about to riddle him with bullets.

CHAPTER SIX

"Drop it," a voice growled.

Rhino Man turned around, but before he could trigger the machine gun, a shot lanced from Patrolman Cole Rodger's revolver. Rhino Man's eyes widened behind the slits of his mask.

Henson didn't hesitate; his arm snaking out like a fakir hypnotizing a cobra, he flung one of his throwing stars. But Lion Man had pushed his hostage down, jumping out of the way of the five-pointed ninja weapon. It nicked his coat arm but whisked past. He shot at Henson who was already in motion, not exactly going for cover but up and over the pushcart, which got knocked on end. A bullet pinged off the corner of the metal cart as Henson landed in a crouch. Henson threw a steak knife he'd plucked from the cart, and it sank into the middle of the Lion Man's chest, pinning his tie to him.

The car sped away, Officer Rodgers didn't want to risk shooting at it lest he miss and hit an innocent. He put handcuffs on the wounded Rhino Man, whose machine gun lay nearby.

"Get these off me, nigger," the wounded man demanded.

"Shut the hell up." Rodgers tore off his mask, and then that of the dead man. He took out his notebook and called over several passerby who'd ran for cover, getting names of potential witnesses.

Henson, several feet away from the busy cop, got closer to Ellsmere who'd remained hunkered down behind the parked car. "Give me your papers," he said quietly.

The older man did. Henson went to shot-up newsstand. The proprietor had been grazed in the arm, but was otherwise unhurt. Henson folded up the notes and stuck them below the newsstand's counter. He then winked at Mr. Greene, who dipped his head.

A police car roared up, followed by another, each sporting the new colors recently adopted by the police department—green bodies, white roofs, and black bumpers. The second one was a late Ford Model A, and one of the cops rode the running board, cranking the siren as they approached. White officers spilled out onto the street, guns and nightsticks out. Henson stood next to Rodgers, making sure they could see his outstretched hands. That this colored policeman seemed to have matters in hand sent a ripple of restraint through the policemen. One of them came forward, a dead stump of a cigar in the corner of his mouth. He was a sergeant.

"What the hell's going on here, Patrolman?"

"These here jungle mask fellas tried to kill Mister Matthew Henson. I have a description of the car they came in and a license plate number."

The sergeant rolled the cigar around on his thin lips, eyeballing the explorer and the knife sticking out of one of the hoodlums. "Henson… the butler for that bird who discovered the North Pole?"

"Hardly," Ellsmere said, having gotten up.

"Who are you?"

Henson answered, "He's a colleague of mine."

"*Colleague* is it?" The cop looked from one to the other. "Okay, we'll straighten this out at the precinct." To Henson, "Gimme your hands."

"That's not necessary, Sarge," Rodgers said.

"I'll be the judge of that," he said, clinking the cuffs on.

They took Henson in one patrol car, and an uncuffed Ellsmere in the other. An ambulance came, collecting the wounded man and the dead one. Rodgers made sure to ride in the vehicle with Henson so he'd arrive at the precinct unharmed—or arrive at all.

At the 28th Precinct, the sergeant addressed Rodgers as they took Henson toward an interrogation room.

"Write out your report, Patrolman," he said.

"What about Mr. Henson?"

"You on the detectives' squad now, Rodgers?" he huffed.

"I just meant, don't you want me to corroborate his statement?"

"Get that report done," the sergeant repeated icily. "Then go the hell home. You're not clocking overtime babysitting this egg."

"I'll be okay, Cole," Henson told his friend.

"See?" the other officer said, "Henson here is going to do his duty as a citizen and convince us why he shouldn't have a one-way ticket to the electric chair for putting knives in our other citizens."

"Plenty of witnesses saw the dead man shooting at him," Rodgers said. "I've got a few names. I'll make sure they're in my report."

"You do that, Frank Merriwell. Come on," he pushed Henson toward a hallway. At a door inset with a rectangular window, the sergeant unclipped a ring of keys from his belt and unlocked it.

"In you go."

Henson walked in, hands still cuffed behind his back. There was a small desk, two chairs, and an overhead bulb with a cowl. There was also a door on one side of the room and Henson figured it was from there detectives would come and go. He sat on one of the chairs and the sergeant left, locking the door to the hallway again.

At the funeral parlor St. Clair and Melenaux were brought in a lunch of oxtails, rice with gravy and green beans. A little after 1:30, Tommy Riordan arrived at the facility. He came upstairs and shook both their offered hands. In a side room that was laid out like a lounge, they sat and had wine.

"Looking fit, Tommy," Melenaux said.

"And you, yourself, Venus…Miss Queenie."

Riordan was one of the captains of The Forty Thieves gang.

They were an old Irish outfit originating in Five Points during the last century. The fiftyish Riordan was dressed in a grey suit and his flat-brimmed hat lay on a table near them. While the gang had been used to crack down on black shopkeepers as negroes settled into Harlem in 1919 and 1920, times had necessitated a different outlook. The Thieves and St. Clair were allied in their efforts to keep the hands of the Dutchman and his Italian mobster friends off their respective territories. Also, arrests of numbers runners had gone way up, some of the pressure coming from the straight-laced black press to crack down on crime. Having a pipeline into Irish-dominated Tammany Hall was good for St. Clair's interests as well. To that end, a stuffed envelope was also placed on the table. With a flourish, Riordan lifted his hat and plunked it down over the envelope.

The two discussed various topics of mutual interest, including St. Clair's investment in the liquor The Forty Thieves controlled in other parts of Manhattan, Brooklyn and Queens. In this way, unlike typical numbers' barons or baronesses who might have twenty-five or so square blocks of Harlem as their purview, St. Clair's reach was wide-spread.

Adjusting his tie as he prepared to leave, Riordan said, "I understand that Mr. Holstein has gone missing."

Melenaux and St. Clair exchanged a look. "That's news to us," Melenaux said. "This Schultz's doing?"

"He left his club last night and had his man drive him to see a lady friend around midnight. He did not make it upstairs. Now, I've heard the name of a certain fellow associated with moving Dutch's beer come up."

"A crony of the Dutchman," St. Clair noted.

"Well, you might look into it. I'd hate to see that bastard get a leg up." He stood, slipped the envelope inside his jacket, and, touching the brim of his hat, walked out of the offices of the Palmetto Ambulance and Funeral Services.

At one point as Henson sat and waited in the precinct, a beefy, florid face appeared at the rectangular window. This man regarded him with dispassionate disdain. The face went away. About an hour later, the side door opened and the face from the hallway came in. The detective was burly, and his sleeves were rolled up exposing hairy forearms. He had big ears and a paunch, but there was muscle across his chest and into his arms. He smelled of cigarettes and hooch, though this was mixed with a coffee overlay. He no doubt had an eye opener in the mornings. After years of having to be quick-witted in the wild, Henson had developed a keen sense of smell. The detective had a file folder with him.

For several moments he stood, regarding his prisoner, tapping the folder against a thick hand. He then undid the cuffs, dragged the chair by its back legs across the linoleum, and sat on opposite Henson.

"You're something of a figure here in Harlem, aren't you?" he said.

"I suppose."

"Who were those men you had a run in with?"

"I don't know." He was going to add that there were after Professor Ellsmere, but no sense volunteering information he wasn't directly asked. "I'm pretty sure they were known criminal types."

The detective showed no emotion. "You normally consort with those types, do you, Henson?"

"As it happens, I seem to encounter members of the underworld from time to time. But no, I don't pal around with them, if that's what you mean."

"And what is it you do for a living?"

"I give talks about my explorations and travels. I also have a weekly radio show on WGJZ."

"If that's so, why would these underworld types— to use your words—be involved?"

He shrugged a shoulder. "I can't say."

"Or won't." He resumed, "Isn't it the case you help some of the residents of our fine city now and then for money? You see yourself as some kind of colored Nick Carter, Henson?"

"You got that in your file there or from Dr. Ellsmere?"

"I ask the questions, Henson."

"Yes, sir."

The plainclothesman let a silence settle between them. He leaned back, opening the file folder and leafed through the papers in there. His mouth was set in a line as he scanned. He closed the folder. "You're looking at murder charges, Henson. You better come clean with me or I won't be able to help you."

"I was defending myself."

"That's what they all say."

"It's the truth."

"We know how to get to the truth around here."

Henson regarded him unblinking. "I can take it. Rubber hoses and all."

The detective was about to say something but there came a soft knock on the side door and a uniformed cop stuck his head inside. "Detective Hoffman, Captain said to fetch you."

Kevin Hoffman rose and left, taking his file folder with him.

In civilian attire, a tired Cole Rodgers walked up the steps to his apartment in the San Juan Hill neighborhood. The widow Mrs. Stokes nodded at him from her first-floor window seat overlooking the avenue. He had a copy of the *New York Age* newspaper folded over in his hand.

"That daughter of yours is growing like a weed," she said as he reached the outer door.

"Yeah, she's something all right," he grinned, entering the building.

Three flights up, he found his wife, Cora Rodgers, doing their daughter's hair. The pungently sweet odor of pomade permeated the room. He set the newspaper down on a table near the door. On the table was a pewter vase he'd brought back from France after the war.

"Daddy," his daughter Irene said.

"How's my girls?" He kissed his daughter on the forehead and his wife on the lips quickly, their daughter smiling up at them.

"There's some food for you on the stove," his wife said. Her husband had been on duty twelve hours.

"Thanks, honey." He stepped into the kitchen area. A plate rested on a cold burner, a piece of re-used butcher's paper wrapped over it.

"Ow, Mama," Irene said as a tangle of hair was brushed upward from her scalp.

"Hold still, okay?" Cora Rodgers replied in a soothing voice. She was sitting on a chair, the four-year-old on a stepstool in front of her, her back to her mother.

"Yeah, be thankful your mother's hair ain't got as much kink as us homegrown negroes," her father joked, forking in a piece of meatloaf. There was also fried okra and corn, his favorite.

"What's Daddy talking about, Mama?"

His wife shot him a look. "Your daddy thinks he's funny is all." Cora Rodgers, whose family hailed from Jamaica, was of mixed heritage, including a white grandmother.

Rodgers laughed, enjoying the sight of the busy mother and daughter. A domestic contrast to the craziness of the shoot out earlier. An incident he wasn't going to mention to his wife, unless she happened to see it in the newspaper.

"Have you thought more about Battle's offer?" his wife asked, hairpin between clenched teeth.

"A little," he said.

She titled her head up at him but didn't go on.

Sam Battle, the only black sergeant on the police force had been asking him to come around to his Monarch Lodge of Elks. Not only did such an association offer comradery, as there were a few other vets who belonged, but other associations as well—the kind that might come in handy when dealing with the ofays in the department. But nobody did nothing for nothing, and one way or the other, he'd have to be beholden to some preacher or political type. But then again....

"I'm not dismissing it," he said. Rodgers turned his attention to a cold pot of leftover coffee on the stove and, lighting a wooden match, he got the burner going to reheat the brew.

Hand in his pocket, he looked out the kitchen window at a brick wall. But Rodgers could see through that as he tried to envision what kind of world he was going to leave for his daughter and the other black children of this city. He'd been a Harlem Hellfighter in World War I, a Black Rattler, member of the 15th New York Colored National Guard unit, and had seen war far too up close and horrific at the battle of Belleau Woods under the banner of the French army.

In the couple's bedroom the *Tribune's* coverage that day of the veterans was framed, some in wheelchairs, some on crutches, as they marched from Fifth Avenue winding up on 145th and Lenox Avenue.

The section read: "Up the wide avenue they swung. Their smiles outshone the golden sunlight. In every line, proud chests expanded beneath the medals valor had won. The impassioned cheering of the crowds massed along the way drowned the blaring cadence of their former jazz band. The old 15th was on parade and New York turned out to tender its dark-skinned heroes a New York welcome."

But how soon the cheering soon became taunts when angry whites reacted to these negro doughboys who dared to dream that giving their bodies and blood for freedom overseas meant they could demand rights as American citizens back home. He remembered vividly that red summer of 1919, less than a decade ago, when colored veterans and other black folk were murdered by rope and gun and knife in white riots across this nation—often at the hands of fellow doughboys. Yet those events are what propelled him to join the force, to be in a position to not let that kind of slaughter happen again, if he could help it. To make sure as much as possible that negroes, be they Matthew Henson or not so famous, didn't get brutalized when in custody, that they received fair treatment like anyone else. And yes, he'd also signed up to show those crackers blacks would work to keep their communities safe just like the white ones did. The boiling pot whistling on the stove dissolved his reverie and he turned the fire off.

Later, back at the precinct, Hoffman returned, standing in the open side doorway. "I don't know what your game is, Henson, what it is you think you're doing. But let me tell you so I'm clear, you grandstanding coloreds always get your comeuppance, hear me? That struttin' white pussy lovin' Jack Johnson, the red spouting A. Philip Randolph…you think you're a symbol, don't you? The New Negro who done come to show the way to his people by his shining example."

"I'm just me, Detective Hoffman."

"Got white folks you call by their first names, having cocktails and finger sandwiches with them when you give one of your lectures, huh?"

"You find that objectionable?"

Hoffman came further into the room. "Get the fuck out of here."

"What about Henrik?" He purposefully used Ellsmere's first name just to dig at him.

"Get," Hoffman said, showing cigarette-stained teeth.

The lock on the hallway door clicked and Henson exited. Out in the main lobby area, his lawyer, Ira Kunsler, was waiting for him. He was a rangy individual in a box coat and loose tie, dark eyebrows and hair going grey. He started at his client, frowning and touching Henson's cheek.

"They didn't work you over, did they, Matt?" They shook hands.

"Handled me with kid gloves. How'd you know I was here?" Henson asked.

"May called me. She'd seen the shooting and you and Ellsmere getting trotted off. I remembered you telling me about him once."

"Remind me to tip bigger there."

"Let's get out of here, Matt."

"They tell you anything about Ellsmere?"

"Let's get out of here first," he urged.

Outside the two stood on the lower steps, police and civilians, some willingly and others unwillingly, going past them. Kunsler bent down pretending to tie his shoe. He got back up. "Don't look, but I think that mug in that sedan up the other side of the street is bird-dogging us."

"A fella like those in the masks?"

"No, G-man, I'm thinking." He put his hand on Henson's arm and they two set off down the street. "In answer to your question, I don't know exactly what's happened to your professor friend. I am of the opinion the authorities have put the grab on him. I'd noticed that fella up the street when I got to the precinct. There's a certain look those boys have," he said, solemnly. "Anyway, Ellsmere wasn't in there nor was he listed on the bail sheet. This I found out after I demanded to see you." They walked along.

"And, loath that I am to admit this, it seems your release had little to do with my formidable skills as your mouthpiece. There's a reason the cops haven't charged you with anything—at least for now."

"Despite me planting a knife into a white man in broad daylight."

Kunsler inclined his head slightly. "Yeah, bigger wheels are turning."

Henson weighed his next words. "Ira, I'm not exactly sure what's going on, myself. I'll say this, if it's what I suspect, it's dynamite. Do some digging and find out what you can, starting with those gunnies in the masks. But be, you know, discreet."

"My middle name."

"I've got some papers of the prof I need to retrieve, but going to have to shake that tail first."

"That sedan isn't following us."

"No, but there's a gent in a brown fedora who's been keeping tabs on us for about a block." Henson jutted his jaw at a stationary store. "Come on, let's go in there and make sure we're seen through the window." There was a large model of a fountain pen hanging at an angle over the front door. The two entered the shop. Back to a wall, Henson talked with Kunsler in one of the aisles, and seemed to slip the lawyer something he put in his attaché case.

Back on the street, the two split up and the man in the brown fedora followed Kunsler. Henson took a circuitous route back to the newsstand, stopping here and there and doubling back to make sure he wasn't being followed. It was closed-up, but no police presence. A padlock secured the awning, and another the plywood door to get behind the counter. While bullets had torn through the stand, the damage wasn't too bad. The destroyed newspapers and magazines had been thrown out. Workmen were already repairing shot-out shop windows nearby. It wasn't much for Henson to get the lock undone, retrieve Ellsmere's equations and leave.

He took a bus, but didn't head back to his apartment. Arriving at Columbia University, he went to the anthropology department and, descending the stairs, passed by one of the janitor's quarters. Several of the janitors here knew him, just as Henson knew the newsstand owner, bellhops, maids—the invisibles as far as the white world was concerned. Given the time of year, the boilers weren't in use. Here in the basement it was cool and cloying, like where you'd grow mushrooms. Standing in a specific spot on the floor, he counted down from the ceiling and over then walked over to one of the soot-covered bricks in the wall. Henson removed the loose brick and tucked the folded papers into the space behind. He then re-inserted the brick and departed.

His next stop was Destiny Stevenson's music shop on Amsterdam near 122nd. She sold sheet music and musical instruments from horns to violins. He entered, a buzzer sounding when he did so. In the corner was an upright piano decorated with fresh flowers. He hadn't asked, but Henson was pretty sure the put-up money for the tidy shop had come from her father.

"Here's those reeds you ordered, Jay."

"Thanks, Destiny." The musician, a saxophone player Henson

recognized from clubs around town, handed over a dollar for his purchase. He nodded at Henson on his way out. There was a copy of Eric Walrond's *Tropic Death* on the end of the glass display counter she stood behind. A bookmark was wedged halfway through.

"I tried reading that book twice," Henson said, pointing at the title. "But he's heavy on that West Indian dialect."

"Among the arty types in Harlem and Greenwich Village, the short stories in it are seen as a kind of counterpoint of sorts to *Nigger Heaven.*"

Henson's eyebrows raised. The latter book was written by the white Carl Van Vechten. As its sensationalistic title suggested, the novel portrayed negroes in ways that made many critics knock Van Vechten as a literary voyeur perpetuating and profiting from numerous stereotypes. That his soirées included whites and blacks of all stripes was really just a way for him to play street-level archeologist— observing negroes in their abandon and playing that up in his novel. The book had become a runaway bestseller.

"I know I'm not supposed to admit this, but I read that one, too. Finished it."

Theatrically, she lowered her head gazing up at Henson. "Oh, my."

"You're making progress on this one, though."

"I read each story twice, thinking about it hard in between," she said. "I'm surprised you made it by today."

"Yeah?"

"Matt, you do know your exploits of earlier today are all the talk, don't you?"

"Oh, that."

"Now I know you aren't as *aw shucks* as you pretend to be."

"You see right through me, huh?"

She straightened a stack of sheet music. "A girlfriend of mine is having a rent party tomorrow night. I might need some bodyguarding what with reds, labor agitators and wild-eyed poets falling through."

"Happy to earn my keep, Miss Stevenson."

They smiled at each other over the counter. Henson noted an unusual-looking object with wires attached on the shelf in the glass counter. "What is that?' he asked, pointing. "Looks like a little motor of some kind."

She took the object out. "It's a timer device I've been working on. The idea being it would turn on a light in the shop afterhours to discourage a burglar."

"You're full of surprises."

"My mom's side of the family were friends with Garrett A. Morgan. He was self-taught, inventor of the gas mask and the traffic signal."

"I've heard of him," Henson said.

"When other little girls were playing with dolls and shucking peas, 'Uncle' Morgan taught me how to take an electric drill motor apart and put it back together. I got hooked on tinkering."

"Wow," he said, impressed.

Stevenson cocked her head, looking past him. He followed her gaze to the door which opened again, bell jangling. Two men in suits and ties stood in the doorway. A silver and grey Duesenberg which made no more sound than a sewing machine idled at the curb.

"Queenie wants to see you, Mr. Henson." This one had the carriage of a middleweight, boxy shoulders and a crook in his nose from it being broken at some point. He enunciation was that of an English teacher.

When Queenie St. Clair sent her men for you, it was a request you were meant not to turn down, Henson observed.

CHAPTER SEVEN

After telling Destiny Stevenson he'd call her later to check in, the three men rode in silence to the E-shaped, thirteen-story, red-brick building on Edgecombe Avenue in Sugar Hill. This was where Queenie St. Clair maintained a penthouse. Walking through the lobby, Henson spotted two doormen in long dark tunics, and he had no doubt that underneath their attire were weapons in easy-to-draw rigs. The other man who'd brought him over rode up in the elevator with him. This one had uneven features, a thin mustache and eyes slightly too close together.

The elevator doors hissed open, and Henson found himself in a foyer of deeply-veined marble and jade. Against the wall opposite was a table of Rococo design, and upon that, a bust of Hannibal of Carthage.

"To the left," the man said. He rode back down in the elevator.

Henson heard a voice as he entered a converted office where there was a blend of more Rococo furnishings, complimented with Art Deco touches, like the sleek chrome and grey desk the policy queen sat behind talking on an Eiffel Tower phone. The Martinique native was speaking French into the handset and leaning back in her banker's chair. She looked at Henson to acknowledge his presence as he walked across a plush Assyrian-patterned carpet. Behind St. Clair, a window offered a view across Harlem River Drive and the river, as well as a portion of the Bronx.

Sitting in a plush chair before her desk, Henson amused himself wondering if she ever dragged out a telescope to spy on Dutch Schultz.

A pretty tan woman in a man's suit appeared near him. "Coffee, tea, or something stronger, Mr. Henson?"

"Coffee would be fine."

"One lump or two?"

"Black."

She dipped her head slightly and left. St. Clair continued on the phone, occasionally using English, but not more than a word or two at a time. The younger woman reappeared carrying a china cup and saucer and placed this on the desk before Henson. She went away again, her form swallowed into the soft gloom of a nearby hallway. St. Clair hung up, rising to greet her visitor.

"Mr. Henson, we meet again." In her accent, she pronounced his name "Hin-Son".

He stood, leaning forward to shake her extended hand. She was a good-sized woman, handsome and clear-eyed. "Good to see you again, too." Their paths had crossed a few times in the past, but this was the first time he'd been summoned to her headquarters.

"I'm going to have a little tiger's milk," she said, traipsing over to a cart with bottles of liquor and mixers on it. She poured herself a sizeable dose of scotch and came back to her desk and sat down.

"I understand you had a run in with a couple of Dutch's boys."

"I did."

"Having to do with that fine brown gal, Daddy's daughter."

She already knew all this but he replied, "Yes."

St. Clair put her drink down. "I hear you got word where Schultz's men were holed up from one of my runners."

"That's right." Toliver had told him Dutch Schultz had taken his daughter. Henson knew St. Clair made sure anybody in her employ would eyeball Schultz's men trying to poach on her territory here in Harlem.

"And you knew once they told you, they had to tell me."

70

"Of course."

"Now you're guarding her."

"Your silent partner is naturally concerned about the welfare of his child." Was St. Clair miffed that Daddy Paradise hadn't asked to have her men in on the rescue?

"And that's all you signed on to do?"

"Miss St. Clair, if there's—"

"Queenie will do."

"What do you want to know, Queenie?"

She made a face. "Just want to make sure my associates are getting what they pay for."

Henson tried his coffee. It was tepid. "You think I'm up to some kind of double cross?"

"No, no," she said. "But you know this Henrik Ellsmere, don't you? He'd been with you on one of your expeditions. The one where you brought back that big piece of rock and sold it to the Natural History Museum. But the excursion took its toll on him, didn't it? All that cold and ice and bleakness. He had some sort of breakdown, yeah?"

"He did. He's better now. How do you know about that?"

"My little Venus is quite the reader and retainer of facts. Comes in handy when you don't want to write certain things down."

Henson assumed Venus had been the woman in the man's suit. "What's your interest in Henrik?"

She gestured. "Less than two days after you fabulously rescued the girl, there's a shootout involving you that's got everyone's tongue wagging in Harlem. Knowing you were engaged by Charles, I was curious as to who this white man you were seen with could be. Though our people don't own much in the way of property uptown, we nonetheless stake claim to this territory as ours, by virtue of the bend of our backs and force of our culture, n'est-ce pas?"

"And you think Henrik tells me what to do?"

"It was said you were deferential to him."

71

"Like I was with Peary?" He meant to sound sarcastic, not bitter. She held up her hands.

"Henrik is my friend. I'm especially protective if I'm trying to avoid them getting hurt at my expense. Were those Schultz's men in the masks?"

"He is not a man given to whimsy."

"But you have an idea who they worked for?"

She sipped her drink. "What can I say?"

"I'd be curious as to your guess."

She smiled enigmatically. "I wouldn't want to speak out of turn. Was it just an old adversary looking to settle a score with you, or was it also about taking the professor?"

"Now I'm the one who has to demur." He wasn't about to let on she knew more about what was going on than he did.

She chuckled. "Very good, then." St. Clair rocked back in her chair.

He took his last sip of the coffee and stood up. "Thanks for the java."

"My man can take you back."

"I'll be okay."

"Yes, you will."

After Henson left, Venus Melenaux came back in. "What do you think, Queenie?" She sat on St. Clair's side of the desk, raking out a Gauloises cigarette and placing it in an ivory cigarette holder. She did so with a surgeon's precision.

"I think we need to determine who hasn't been dealing square with us, chérie. Better get our Irish friend on the blower."

"Sounds right."

"Certainement." The racket's boss looked up at the younger woman, who lit St. Clair's cigarette, took it from her fingers and, after taking a puff, handed it back. Their eyes lingered for several more moments then Melenaux moved away, withdrawing her hand from where it rested on the other woman's shoulder.

CHAPTER EIGHT

The following morning Henson got over to the Beaumont where Henrik Ellsmere had been staying. His lawyer Ira Kunsler had asked around, given he knew from Henson that Ellsmere had been staying on the lower east side, and what with his German accent, his previous location hadn't been too hard to pinpoint. Two dollars passed from Henson to the desk clerk told him the room number.

"You won't need no key," the haggard-looking man said. "It's already been broken into."

"Yesterday?" Henson said.

"Yeah, locksmith's coming sometime today."

"The cops?"

Shrugging, he replied, "Big shouldered gees like you."

Upstairs, Henson entered the obviously searched room, the door hung lopsided on hinges kicked loose from the frame. He stood just past the threshold for a moment, taking in what little there was to see. The drawers of the chesterfield had been pulled out and dumped, containing a few items of Ellsmere's clothing. The lone chair and table had been upturned, and the shades pulled off their rollers in case the professor had hidden anything that way. If there had been of value here, it had been taken. But the condition of the room lent credence to what Kunsler had speculated, that Ellsmere was now in the hands of the government. But the authorities were not the ones who'd held him at the mansion in Poughkeepsie.

Henson hadn't come here to look for what Ellsmere was working on —he knew what, in a general sense. What he wanted to know was who'd had him and sent masked hoods to get him back. That meant he had to backtrack to identify his quarry. Securing the door as best he could from nosy passersby, Henson went down on all fours, probing the lower quadrants like a sled dog out on the trail. He went about like that, not self-conscious at all. Behind the chesterfield which had been pulled away from the wall, below the window, then over to a far corner. He didn't turn up anything. Back over by the bed frame, the mattress having been tossed aside, he noticed the rear leg seemed slightly higher than the others.

Henson got up and, turning the frame over, saw that the tubular end of the leg could be pulled free and he did so. He then lifted the entire frame and shook it. Nothing. He assembled the leg again and put the bed back down. Mouth twisted in concentration, Henson took a last circuit around the room. He paused, then went back to the chesterfield. Several coins were on the top, some atop the others. He lifted what looked like a quarter off the other coins. It was silver— only it wasn't money. The disk was larger than a half dollar, but could easily be overlooked among the other coins if you weren't paying close attention. It was an emblem of some sort. On it was stamped a futuristic-looking cityscape and the words "Weldon Institute" arching above the image. Back and front were identical.

Whistling a sea shanty, Henson quit the room carrying the item in his pocket. Back outside, he made a call to his lawyer but got no answer. Thereafter Henson made several more inquiries by phone or in person. He stopped at a florist to have flowers delivered to May Maynard as a way to say thanks, then made a trip to a brownstone on the upper west side.

"Help is addressed at the side door," the butler sniffed after answering Henson's knock.

"Tell Lacy it's Matt."

The butler, a sallow-faced, reedy white man of maybe sixty glared at this upstart negro. "Be gone with you." He started to close the door.

Henson stiff armed the door. "You best tell Miss DeHavilin I'm here or it'll be your hide. You know how she tolerates us dusky bohemians." He laughed heartily.

Unsure of what to do, but recognizing the accuracy of what Henson had said, the butler relented. "Remain where you are." He closed the door, footsteps retreating through the foyer. Soon, through the frosted glass of the front door, Henson noted a shadow approaching. The door was flung open.

"Matt, darling," Lacy DeHavilin said, a toothy smile on her face. She was a fifty-plus zaftig white woman who dressed in swirls of scarfs, shawls and bursts of color. She put her arms around his neck and hugged him tight.

"Come in, come in." She pulled him in. The butler stood to one side, stone-faced yet somehow managing to suggest a sneer.

"Bring us some refreshments, Solworth. Some of that chicken with asparagus and dill from last night will be fine. You like it cold, right, Matt?"

"Sure," he said.

"And white wine, of course."

"Of course, madam," Solworth said.

"We'll take it in the study." She led the way, taking Henson by the hand.

The two walked deeper into the house, original paintings by Jacob Lawrence elbowing for space next to a Pablo Picasso, these over sculptures by up and comers like Augusta Savage and collections of surrealistic works. In her study, one wall was filled with first editions and another wall was adorned with various totems and symbols of the occult. They sat on the couch, DeHavilin tucking a leg under.

"Matt, you've stayed away too long, you must bring me up to date on your activities. I was just at a meeting of the editorial board of *Opportunity* the other night and damned if your name didn't come up." *Opportunity Magazine* was published by the Urban League.

"I've been meaning to get back in touch, Lacy."

"Liar," she said, "but I forgive you."

The door opened, and the butler wheeled in cold roasted chicken, red potatoes—also unheated—and drinks. He looked at neither Henson nor his employer as he served portions on their plates and left. They ate, plates on their laps. She nibbled, and Henson, hungrier than he realized, ate with vigor.

"But I know you too well, Mr. Henson. You didn't simply drop by to renew old acquaintances."

"I'm afraid you got me, Lacy."

"We'll see."

"I might be wading into the thickets on something and came to find out what you know about the Weldon Institute. Word is you were invited to one of their soirées a few months ago." He munched heartily on his food.

DeHavilin was filing her empty wine glass. "In a nutshell, it's a utopian enterprise run by Hugo Renwick." She paused. "No, I'm being too dismissive. Hugo is more grounded than that, though he did back a project called Llano del Rio in the California desert several years ago. It was an attempt at a socialist commune that, sadly, didn't succeed."

"I know that name," he said. "Renwick was one of the backers of a Fred Cook expedition."

"You hold a grudge?"

"No," he said. "But is he a kind of socialist, like Asa?" He referred to their mutual friend A. Philip Randolph, the radical head of the Brotherhood of Sleeping Car Porters. The largest black labor union in the country.

"Oh, I think your gorgeous self makes you the most dangerous negro in America. Or at least, in my boudoir when I can get you in it."

"You can't tell, I'm blushing."

Smiling, she continued. "Hugo's a capitalist, but one with vision, a futurist to borrow that term from the painters. Our version of a Fabianist I suppose."

"He wants to better our country for all."

"Technology being the tip of the spear to accomplish that," DeHavilin added.

She sat back holding her glass, taking him in. "Among other things, he employs an old friend of yours, Bessie Coleman."

"Doing what?"

"Apparently test flying some sort of science plane of his."

"He has real money, then."

"Indeed he does. Steel, tires, and construction. And he has a degree in engineering."

"What else do you know about his institute?"

She drank him in deep. "You'll have to force that out of me."

"Lacy…"

"Matt…" She leaned over and gave him a quick kiss and got up.

DeHavilin went to an assortment of records in a free-standing walnut cabinet that housed her gramophone. She selected a 78 platter, removed it from its sleeve and placed the record on the turntable after powering up the machine. She deftly set the needle in place, a minimum of hisses and pops accompanying the revolving disk as the music played. He expected to hear a swing jazz tune as such was a favorite of hers. But rather than an up-tempo blast from a clarinet, he heard chimes, cymbals, an organ and, coming in and out, an instrument he couldn't identify.

"What is that?" Henson said. "It sounds like electric wind."

"The inventor named it after himself, a thereminophone by Leon Theremin. Isn't it simply transcendent?" DeHavilin sprayed some perfume on from an atomizer. "The organ player is an Indian gentleman named Chandra Mutrhraji, and you simply must accompany me when he comes back to town for a concert." She walked to the study door and turned the lock. She closed the drapes and lit some candles and incense, humming a tune. Then without further preamble, DeHavilin began undressing.

Well, Henson concluded, unbuttoning his shirt, he had known this might happen if he came to see her. His duty required much of him, he reasoned with a crooked grin. DeHavilin was now only wearing one of her long scarves she'd wrapped partly around her, waving an end at Henson as she came over and let him take her in his strong arms. She nibbled his bare chest.

They made athletic love on and off the couch. On a wall behind them was a photo of Henson, Commander Peary, two of his Eskimo friends and fellow explorers, Ootah and his brother Egingwah, a now deceased man named Jason Leeward, and DeHavilin. They were all dressed in furs and standing before an outcropping of ice. It appeared that snow was falling. The photo was a fake, taken at a photographer's studio in Brooklyn against a backdrop. DeHavilin, a coal and gas robber baron's widow, had been an investor in one of the North Pole attempts. Everyone was smiling in the picture, in on the joke.

Sometime later as they lounged, Henson picked up a medallion that was a twin to the one he'd found in Ellsmere's room. It was sticking out from underneath a magazine. "You've got one of these, too?"

"Yes, Hugo gave those out as party favors at that function I was at."

"You remember seeing the professor there?" He described him and the self-same medallion he'd found.

"Can't say I do, but that doesn't mean anything. There was any number of people there that evening. One of the Rothschilds, my friend Elaine from the Carnegie Foundation, even that flamboyant Daddy Paradise made an appearance."

"Did he, now?" The two were clothed again and the drapes were open. Sunlight slanted across their forms through the large windows. "You know him?"

"A little, why?" She chewed on a strawberry and had more wine.

"He's back in town to give a big speech at Liberty Hall."

78

"Yes, someone from the magazine is going to interview him afterward."

"Are you going to the talk?"

"'Fraid not, my sweet. I've been invited to an excursion to Cuba with Ernest Hemingway, among others, and we're leaving Thursday. You're more than welcome to come along. I won't smother you too much."

"Can't get away."

She narrowed her eyes at him. "You wouldn't be thinking about renewing your acquaintance with that fly girl now that me and my big mouth mentioned she was around?"

"Me and Bessie don't know each other like that." He wondered if DeHavilin knew about Daddy Paradise's involvement with Queenie St. Clair. But he decided to confine his conversation to the institute.

"Does Renwick's outfit have an office?"

"No, but do you want me to see if I can get you an introduction?"

"Not at the moment, but thanks." He didn't want to be too beholden to her. Not that he minded their occasional rolls in the hay, but Lacy DeHavilin had a habit of taking up hobbies and soon getting bored with them. He didn't want to put himself in that kind of position. Then, too, it was probably better to see if he could come at the institute and they were unaware of him.

"This party Renwick had, was that to raise money?"

She stretched and yawned. "One isn't so crass in certain circles my dear fellow," she teased, putting on a British accent. "You don't put the bite on, as it were. These things are done to float projects out there and see who among your fellow swells might call you later, invite you to the club to discuss these notions more, you see."

"Hmm," he mused.

"That's why he had Mr. Tesla there. He was speaking about some of his ideas and how they could benefit society."

"Nikola Tesla?"

"The one and only."

She'd made coffee and Henson finished his cup. "This has been very enlightening, Lacy." He quickly added, winking at her, "And enjoyable."

"Don't be a stranger." She leaned over to take his face in her hands and kiss him.

"Never."

He rose and, kissing her good-bye, left the brownstone. It was past two in the afternoon and it was if he had been in a cocoon of bliss and was now tossed back into the harsh world. The sounds of cars and trucks motoring, their horns bleating, street cars clanging and a jackhammer pulverizing concrete at the end of the block greeted him. Maybe he should rethink things and see what it would be like to be a kept man for a while.

"Aw, where would the fun be in that?" He chuckled and walked away.

At a diagonal from his receding form, a golden-hued young woman with pronounced cheekbones and almond-shaped eyes watched him as he walked away. Thereafter she returned to her car. Built into the dash of the otherwise unremarkable car was a radio. This wasn't unusual, Chevrolet had introduced a car radio for listening to what few radio stations there were several years prior. And the police in Detroit had been experimenting with radios where crimes in progress could be broadcast from the precinct on a narrow bandwidth to patrol cars, thus ensuring a speedy response in the efforts to apprehend lawbreakers.

This radio, though, was much different. It was ahead of its time. Like in an aircraft, it allowed for two-way communication but didn't require a row of batteries under the seats, though the car did have a long antenna on a spring attached to the rear bumper. From the glovebox she produced a portable microphone, which looked like a smaller version of a stage microphone with a thick wire leading from it. She plugged this into an outlet on the radio. The woman turned it on and when it warmed up, tuned to a specific frequency and spoke into it.

"Come in, Naygoohock, come in," said the woman, depressing a button on the radio panel. "This is Petersen. Come in. This is Petersen." She released the button to receive.

"Yes, it's me," came a crackly voice.

"I've been stationed at Lacy DeHavilin's as advised. Matthew Henson came to see her today." She hesitated, then went on, "He stayed there some time. I believe we'll have an opportunity to get in her house as she's made arrangements to leave town this Thursday."

"Very good. I'll let Jimmy know. Return to your first assignment, please."

"Very well, Naygoohock." She shut off the device and disconnected the microphone. She placed it back in the glovebox, next to a revolver, and closed the lid.

That evening one of the swells who'd attended the dinner party for the Weldon Institute and an acquaintance of Lacy DeHavilin's was out on the town. One of his stops was the Cotton Club. This gentleman, scion of a Canadian timber fortune, liked it that the Club was strict in its Black Code policies—the way things should be, to his way of thinking. He could clap and enjoy the fevered antics of black dancers and musicians, but not have to rub elbows with the likes of them at the tables. The finest in black entertainment presented in a place designed along the lines of a grand southern plantation. Terrific. You could be in Harlem but not have to really be *in* Harlem. He could let loose and not have to worry about conversing with one of them. Oh, he probably could find something of interest to talk to a Langston Hughes or an Aaron Douglas—it wasn't as if he didn't enjoy their work. But it was so tiresome to invariably have to hear some variation of the Negro Problem as such conversing always seemed to wind around to. That had certainly been his experience in the couple of soirées he'd attended put on by that Van Vechten chap.

The man smiled, slipping his arm around the waist of an intriguing young woman named Myra something or another. Duke Ellington's band was playing a rendition of "Love Me or Leave Me," a rather tall woman with honey-colored skin on the vocals. He'd met this Myra before at some function and recalled she'd spent time in the Orient. Spoke Chinese if his memory served. Her hair smelled great.

Not too far away, his brownstone was in the process of being burglarized. The thief was in dark clothes and climbed the side of the building like a human spider. Closer examination revealed he was wearing specially-designed gloves where each finger and the thumb had a metal extension. These were made from hand-rolled steel and were flexibly hinged with custom made ball bearings and wiring. Drawing his hand back and then digging into the side of the red-bricked facade, he found grip in the grout between the bricks. He could accomplish this death-defying feat due to his being in tip-top physical condition aided by custom crampons strapped to his shoes. He had a lot of experience doing such at night with little or no light. Also, he'd cased the home previously during the day. The burglar quickly reached the third story. He was on the rear of the building, and from this area, had little chance of being seen given the back of another brownstone was opposite. Except for the ground floor, there were no windows on this side. He wasn't worried about leaving evidence of how he'd climbed. He wasn't going to leave finger or footprints.

He stopped at the third story—this was the riskiest part of his planned criminal entry. He had to go around to the front where there was a balcony. But as the street was a semi-private cul-de-sac, there wasn't much foot traffic at this hour. Perched at the corner of the building, he scanned the street and then, moving with quick assuredness, clambered over the front and dropped down onto the balcony. From around his chest he removed the strap to his messenger bag and dropped the gloves and crampons inside. The latch on the French windows to the balcony was easy to overcome, and the thief stepped into Levering's study. He closed the curtained windows and affixed the miner's lamp to his head, switching on the battery-powered light. The version he wore wasn't available commercially. It had been designed by his associate. In this way he was able to move about the room with both hands free. Downstairs the maid and butler had retired for the evening. He had no intention of causing them to come upstairs.

He moved silently to the standing safe, a sturdy cast-iron Marsh in the corner of the room. The safe was nearly five feet tall and looked like it could withstand a direct black from a stick of dynamite, there was no effort to disguise its presence. But the thief, a master cracksman having grown up around safes as a younger man, had an intricate knowledge of their makes and manufacturers. He wasn't going to use brute force to gain its secrets. There was a sound in the hallway. He stopped mid-stride, listening, what looked like a rubber ball suddenly in his palm. If somebody did come in, there was sleeping powder in the ball and he would squirt the stuff in their face. He also had a sap and a gun, but he didn't think it would come to that. There was no other sound and he resumed his thievery.

Taking a knee at the safe, he removed a one-of-a-kind drill from one of his hidden pockets in his coat. It was diamond-tipped and powered by batteries, made by the same inventor who'd produced his advanced headlamp. The thief, now wearing supple gloves, proceeded to drill a hole in the safe's door to the right of the dial after using a ruler to mark exactly where he wanted to drill. There was little noise as the heavy bit wormed its way into the door. The shavings fell, glittering, to the thick carpet. A part of the tumbler mechanism was revealed. His headlamp illuminated the now-exposed inner works, he began working the dial, a stethoscope with a suction cup to hold the listening end in place.

He soon had the combination and got the door open. He rummaged through stacks of cash, bonds, and a box of men's gold rings and pearls that must have been a family heirloom. These expensive items were not his target. Instead the scion who was out dancing kept certain documents detailing various holding companies, boards of directors and the like in the safe. This is what the thief had been sent to document.

Taking them might alert the men mentioned in those papers. Men who were part of a group the thief and his associate wanted as much information on as possible. The burglar took a compact box camera from his messenger bag and photographed the pages, shinning a light from his headlamp on those sheets. These he put these back where he'd gotten them, and then took the money and jewels to cover his true purpose. Before he left, he affixed a grey diamond-shaped piece of paper to the safe. His eyes twinkled with amusement.

Feeling bold, he didn't go back the way he'd come, but went to the stairs and listened. Down he went. Midway between the second floor and the first, he heard the faint creak of hinges from the kitchen. The maid exiting her quarters. A light came on, drawers opened and closed, feet shuffled across smooth tiles. A midnight snack was in the offing. From this angle, if she were at the doorway to the kitchen, and it was open, she'd see him sneak out. Taking two quick breaths, he finished going down the stairs and, taking a glance back, saw the door remain closed. He used a tiny can of oil to squirt the hinges of the door. The door opened silently, and out he went into the night and his car parked three blocks away. The vehicle was a swept wing MG J2 with the overhead camshaft eliminated in favor of a pushrod unit for greater power and torque.

The British import was not a working person's car and, truth be told, the professional at the wheel, the thief with a purpose, Jimmie Dale, had not known backbreaking labor. He had, however, put his freedom and life on the line numerous times in pursuit of justice for the common man and woman. Those who had to toil and strain in factory jobs and in the fields to make those of his ilk richer. His spite for the class into which he was born was further fueled by uncovering, in his youth, a direct ancestor who made his fortune in the north as one of the largest slave traders. A man who had essentially bought off a coastal town to cover his crimes and fabricate a false image as an industrialist. Literal blood money was passed down in the Dale family and used to start businesses, including that of the thief's father.

His father had not known the truth, but once the younger Dale knew, he couldn't ignore history. He'd found out after he'd first begin cracking safes for fun—not taking anything, because he didn't need the money. Testing himself against the reaches of the authorities. But then he was blackmailed by a woman he at first only knew as Toscin, then later, when they fell in love, as Marie LaSalle. She knew of his crimes and cajoled him into using his skill to expose a crime ring and other nefarious undertakings. Then Toscin told him about his ancestor, producing the proof. He had no moral choice but to dedicate himself to atoning for that wrong. It was through Marie that he met his recent cohort in his extra-curricular activities, Nikola Tesla. Certainly, he was an enigmatic sort. But his obsession with besting Edison had dovetailed with Dale and Marie's goal of exposing and bringing down the collaboration of the well-heeled and members of the government subverting the Constitution for their own end.

Driving home, Dale passed the St. James Club on Fifth Avenue. He was a member, as had been his late father. Several of the men on the papers he'd photographed that night were also members. He smiled ruefully, knowing he would soon be burglarizing a few of their homes and offices as well.

CHAPTER NINE

The following day at the Garden of the Redeemer Church on 135th Street a charged discussion took place. The edifice took up a good stretch of the block between Broadway and Amsterdam Avenue and had been designed by black architect Vertner Tandy. He was one of the seven founders of the Alpha Phi Alpha fraternity at Cornell University and the first registered negro architect of New York. His most famous building was arguably Madam C.J. Walker's Harlem mansion Villa Lewaro. While the church was not as opulent as the mansion, it nonetheless had its charms—from its Gothic spire reaching heavenward to the eye-catching presence of a single, hexagonal-shaped stained-glass window on the second story overlooking the thoroughfare. At the curb below various cars were parked as a meeting was taking place in the Library of Reflection. It was a large room where one wall was devoted floor-to-ceiling to books on the study of the Christian faith. There were plush chairs, couches, a conference table and a standing globe in the room, as well.

The gathering was informal, the men seated in the chairs or on the couches. The furniture having been arranged by staff so that no matter where you sat, you could see the others. There were also several teacarts which held that beverage, as well as pots of coffee and sugar cookies on bone china plates. The attendees were various clergymen of certain standing in Harlem, San Juan Hill, and a few other sections of the city there to have a sit down with Charles Toliver, aka Daddy Paradise. Ostensibly, it was about his upcoming Lift up the Race speech at Liberty Hall. But the spiritualist and the men who'd asked him here today knew what this really was about was his probable expansion into New York City. And while no women were in attendance, it was through Miriam McNair and the Garden of the Redeemer's women's auxiliary that this meeting was brokered.

"For surely there are more than enough souls to save," Toliver was saying, a smile on his composed face.

"This is not about us protecting territory, Charles, like in some wild west town," said Reverend Blake of the Second Ethological African Methodist Church farther south on Amsterdam. He was a sturdy-built individual with a mane of black hair turning silver. "It's about what you espouse."

"I'm not here to pretend to be something I'm not. I don't put on artifice as if sent directly from the heavens above." He gestured over his head. "I will tell you freely I was born of man and woman," Toliver continued. "And I, like you, will return to the dust when it's time for me to depart this mortal plane. I do not ask of my flock to ascribe to me anything more than what men can be to other men. An example in some ways and not in others. We must learn from one another. I claim no superhuman nor supernatural affectations, as do some we shall not name today."

"This is more about not putting the bullseye back on us," another reverend, T.C. Stafford, said. He was a stout man and had enjoyed more than his share of the sugar cookies. "Matters have quieted down since the Garvey situation, and that's a good thing for our people moving forward."

Toliver, who sat on the couch, crossed one leg over the other—the creases in his pant legs impeccable. "You think if your man Hoover wins the election in November, he's going to deliver the goods? Or maybe you'll see some sort of post out of your good work. This is a man who has talked openly about making the Grand Ole' Party lily white for goodness sake."

"Pshaw," Stafford said. "He was misquoted. Further, my faith in Mr. Hoover is not about me," Stafford replied. The preacher, a Republican, was working to shore up votes for Hoover in Harlem and beyond. "It's about the bigger picture."

"As is *my* mission," Toliver said. "We all want what's best for negro folk, be they in the city or in the country, in a fine home or humble abode. Indeed, what I'm about is lifting the ones of us, too many by any count, from out of those humble abodes to better living conditions. As it happens, I do believe in working for equality among the races, but not at any expense. Certainly not at the expense of losing our cultural and racial identities.

"Now let's be clear, our destinies as is our economics are intertwined. I'm not the only one in this room who consorts with supposed unsavory elements to make sure certain needs are met, such as the soup kitchen staying open or steering parishioners toward sources of loans when the white banks won't lend."

More than one reverend looked away from Toliver.

"But you would not claim to be a Christian, now do you, Mr. Toliver?" This from a third preacher who was standing in for Reverend Adam Clayton Powell Sr. of the influential Abyssinian Baptist Church. Senior had to be out of town.

"I have been very clear in this regard. In fact, you can find it in many of my printed speeches and in the book I'm looking to publish next year. I call upon the foundations of various Western, Eastern and African spiritual ways in what I teach."

"Heathen beliefs only put us further back," Blake opined. Setting near him was an elderly pastor who nodded vigorously.

"And I would counter that we can't tuck our heads in like turtles and pretend we are safe," Toliver shot back.

"Stick our necks out to get our heads chopped off?" Stafford said.

"I'm not suggesting we spit in the eye of the tiger, gentlemen. I am saying that we must be wary of that tiger and take steps to fortify ourselves. It is shortsighted to think that just because the tiger is busy elsewhere for the moment, the beast won't be turning its attention back to us at some point. Or rather simply neglect us as well. It is only united the tiger—whoever sits in Washington—will respect us, will listen to us."

"Is yours a political movement then, Mr. Toliver?' asked the third reverend.

"Whenever more than five of us are in a room at any one time, that's political," Toliver answered with a gesture. "Let's not fool ourselves, my friends. I've heard or read your sermons. Yes, you quote scripture and call for men to be good shepherds of their families and make sure you do unto others as you would have done unto you. And yes, you know the right words to speak, the emotions to summon at the funeral of yet another colored man who has died by violence from another colored citizen."

Toliver rose as he paused. "But I know what you said about justice being a bill long overdue at the funeral for the boy who died under mysterious circumstances in police custody. He pointed at one of the reverends. "It was in the negro papers that covered the funeral."

He continued, pointing at another, "And weren't you the subtle firebrand at the Urban League conference last year calling for boycotts of stores? That if they don't hire us, we don't need to shop there?"

"That's simply calling for fair play."

"You think Herbert Hoover or that other Hoover, J. Edgar, sees it like that? You think they don't hear echoes of Garvey in that? Or worse, whisperings from Moscow?"

Nervous chuckles rippled through the gathered.

"You do know one of the reasons Garvey was brought down was by one of us, yes?" Toliver had walked to one of the carts to pour some tepid tea.

"That's a fanciful rumor," Blake said.

"Is it, now?"

"I know something about this so-called negro agent referred to as

800," Blake noted. "I believe that he does exist and was used against us. Or that, like a reverse Walter Francis White, he is a Caucasian who passed for mulatto." The ironically named White, a blue-eyed and blond-haired black man, assistant secretary of the NAACP, used his coloring to infiltrate southern towns after a lynching. He did this to find out the perpetrators of these crimes, and then the perpetrators' names would be published in issues of the organization's *Crisis Magazine* and elsewhere. More than once, whites had found out about a "yellow nigra" poking around and he'd have to get out of town ahead of a lynch mob out to string him up.

"My point was," Toliver went on, "speaking out against inequality, seeding black enterprises as some of us in this room do, is enough to get us labeled subversives. We don't have to be bowler hat-wearing bomb throwers of the type found in Mr. Conrad's novel."

He got blank looks save for Stafford who was familiar with the book he'd mentioned, *The Secret Agent.*

Toliver sat again and said, "While in some respects our collective plight as colored citizens keeps us invisible to the powers that be in this country, in other ways, we stick out too much. We can't let that us paralyze us or push us to foolish and wasteful actions. I assure you, it is not my intention to blow hot air come Saturday night, inflame desires and drift away on the wind. I intend to deliver. More, I look forward to us working together for the betterment of our people and not at cross purposes."

The men in the room murmured sagely. After the meeting broke up, several were now either invited to the event or asked to say a few words from the podium. The religious leaders went their separate ways, most returning to their respective houses of worship or to visit a sick and shut-in member of their church.

Reverend Stafford drove his four-year-old Cole sedan to Blumstein's department store on 125th—which catered to black folk but didn't employ any. He parked and entered and on the third floor, the furniture department, and used one of the phone booths in the back. In the booth, door closed, he asked the operator to dial a long distance number he'd committed to memory. The line was answered on the second ring.

"Hello," said a quiet voice.

"This is Reverend Stafford."

"Yes...how'd the meeting go?"

The clergyman proceeded to tell the quiet-voiced man on the other end of the line, a Bureau of Investigation contact, what had transpired. Particularly emphasizing the threat of Daddy Paradise expanding his reach and thereby his influence.

"And he's hired that glory-hound Henson to be a kind of bodyguard," Stafford added.

"Yes, I'm aware of Henson's involvement. Go on," said the voice.

As the unidentified Agent 800 was said to be the first negro agent of the Bureau of Investigation, T.C. Stafford was one of its first paid black informants, recruited by the previously mentioned 800 less than four years ago. Stafford had provided insider knowledge to aid in the political decapitation of Garvey. The authorities —J. Edgar Hoover playing a pivotal role, had concocted a mail fraud case against Garvey for selling his Black Star Line stock. He'd been imprisoned, but pardoned by President Coolidge after considerable efforts by the United Negro Improvement Association. He was deported back to his native Jamaica.

"Thank you, Reverend. Keep up the good work," the government man said, severing the line.

Stafford went back outside. Whatever guilt he felt for informing on his peers under the guise of patriotism was offset by his jealousy of them and his desire to be the number one leader in Harlem. He would be the top dog, and the citizenry would turn to him for guidance and succor. Not to mention comforting widows and lonely housewives. There was a spring in his step as he walked away.

CHAPTER TEN

The three banjo players furiously strummed their instruments as the man on tom-toms beat out a wild rhythm with his padded mallets, his hands and arms a blur of motion and syncopation. As one, the musicians reached a crescendo and the tune climaxed with a resounding flourish. The studio audience applauded and cheered as the banjo players and the man on the drums, each costumed in big furs, stood and took a bow. Behind them, the rest of the orchestra remained seated, but nodded their heads in acknowledgement. The band was ensconced in what looked like a giant igloo, half of it cut away. There were also several penguin dolls, and a custom made polar bear prop on the stage. Numerous wires led to a control console at one side of the stage where an engineer sat.

The bandleader was a slender, tallish man in a fur hat and fur-fashioned bow tie. He walked to the standing microphone and bent slightly to speak into it. He thanked the musicians then said, "And now we're going to bring you a swinging rendition of 'Baby, I Can't Get Enough of You, Though I've Tried'."

There was applause as the band went into its final number, and louder still when they finished. "Well, ladies and gentlefolk, that brings to a close another session of the Clicquot Club Eskimos Musical Variety show here on the Blue Network out of the RCA building in the one and only New York City. But before we go, we wanted to once again bring back to the mic the man you heard earlier in our interview segment, the colored man-about-town who is known far and wide on this island of many interesting souls, the one and only Arctic explorer, Matthew Henson."

There was more applause as Henson returned to the stage. He wore a blue serge suit, white shirt and black tie.

"Matthew, before we sign off, is there anything else you'd like to add?"

"I sure would, Harry. I want to remind the listening audience they can hear my program, Strange Journeys, on WGJZ every Thursday night at seven-fifteen, broadcast from the basement at Smalls' Paradise. And when you put your stockinged feet up on your ottoman to relax, remember, my friends, to pour yourself a cool, refreshing glass of Clicquot Club Pale Dry Ginger Ale. Made from only the purest ingredients."

As Henson's pitch wound down, the band began playing a swing tune. The band leader gave the audience a half salute and shook Henson's hand. In the microphone he said, "This has been your head Eskimo, Harry Reser, goodnight and good music." A clarinet blared over this and the audience clapped again.

"All reet, Matt." Reser said, smiling and walking over to his band members.

Backstage, Destiny Stevenson intercepted him.

"That was fun," Stevenson said, giving Henson a peck on the cheek. "Glad you invited me."

"I'm happy you liked it," he said, letting his hand linger atop hers on his arm.

The stage manager came over. "Hey, Matt, while you were on the air, a call came in for you. They left a number."

"Thanks," he said taking the slip of paper.

Stevenson twisted her mouth. "Some frail wants you to explore her, huh?"

He handed her the paper. "You call the number." He gambled

there wasn't a strange woman on the other end. Though sometimes there was.

"I will." She took the paper and she used the house phone to make the call, a local exchange. Pleasantly she said, "Yes, this is Mr. Henson's assistant returning your call." She listened, glancing at Henson, her face unreadable. "Well, ah yes, I'm sure he would sir, that is, Mr. Tesla. Tomorrow, yes, uh-huh, yes, I'll make sure he gets the message and you should expect him then." She replaced the handset. Stevenson blinked hard. "That was Nikola Tesla."

"No kidding?"

"Yeah, said he wanted to talk to you about your mutual friend, Henrik Ellsmere. Said he's staying at the Service Hotel on West 27th, and could you come around eleven tomorrow for tea."

"You told him I'd be there."

"I did. Who hasn't heard of the man many said really invented radio." Arm in his she added, "Of course he'd want to see the man who really reached the North Pole first. Who is this Ellsmere?" They'd left the RCA building on the Fifth Avenue side walking toward the subway. They passed a parked tan Chrysler, the driver's side window down slightly. At the wheel was a white man, fedora pulled low on his head and slumped in his seat as if asleep. A sense of intuition that hadn't let him down from jungle bars in Nicaragua filled with drunken cutthroats to stalking Siberian snow leopards, told Henson the man was playing possum, but on they went.

"The shootout the other day had to do with him." He told her this after they were taken to the precinct, that was the last he'd seen of Ellsmere. He added he and his lawyer were of the opinion Henrik'd been secreted away by the government. If survival in the frozen wilds had taught him anything, it was never become desperate—such clouded your thinking. He'd reckoned the G-men, or whoever snatched the old prof, needed to keep him on ice until they had the Daughter and forced him to unlock her secrets. He was determined though one way or the other, he'd find the old boy.

The gunman who'd worn the rhino mask winced as he worked the wrist handcuffed to the head of the metal bed. He'd been the thug Officer Rodgers wounded. He was mortified he'd been shot, and caught, by a coon cop. There was going to be no living it down among his drinking buddies. Just thinking about it made the wound in his side hurt.

Thus far he'd clammed up when the cops had come to question him. Being in the hospital ward, they couldn't pour on the third degree, and he was getting healthier every day. But he hadn't seen no mouthpiece from his employer, so how loyal was a guy supposed to be? The gunman, like the other men in the animal masks, had been brought in from out of town. Less chance they could be traced to the boss if one got caught. That meant, at this point the cops hadn't tumbled to his record and backtracked him. He was ruminating on the best course to take when the door opened to his private room. Until this morning, he'd been in a room with three other wounded prisoners, but had been transferred to this one earlier today. On the wall next to him was a barred glass window overlooking the city beyond.

"How you doing?" One of the two newcomers said as they entered and closed the door. They positioned themselves of either side of his bed. Like that *Mutt and Jeff* comic strip, the hood reflected, one was tall and the other short, but built like a human bulldog, his muscles bulging against the fabric of his suit's sleeves.

"You two aren't regular cops," he announced. Their shoes were too shiny, and their shirts starched. He snapped the fingers of his free hand. "Government boys, ain't ya?

"Perceptive," the tall one said to the other. He had a brown fedora, the other a green snap-brim hat. Though their faces and bodies were different, their manner seemed as if they'd been stamped from one mold with individualistic variations applied by bored workers as they came off the government-issue assembly line.

"Smoke?" Snap-brim offered, shaking a cigarette free from a pack.

"Sure," he said, taking it and putting it in his mouth. The other one struck a match and lit it for him. He blew a stream toward the foot of his bed. "What can I do you fellas for?"

"Who paid you to put the grab on the professor?" Fedora asked.

"I'd like to help you, even if I knew what you were talking about, but I ain't squawking, get me?"

The two men exchanged a look. Fedora talked as snap-brim lit a cigarette. "We're going to find out sooner or later and you might as well do yourself some good, here. Or maybe you like the idea of wearing stripes in Sing Sing for the next thirty years."

The cigarette paused on its way to the hood's mouth. "Hey, I don't know what you two are trying to pull, but you got it all wrong. When my lawyer gets here, he'll straighten it out."

"Your lawyer?" Fedora said. "What makes you think you got an ambulance chaser coming?"

Snap-brim stood near the door, his back to the bed. Rivets were driven into the door holding a metal plate in place. He looked out the rectangle of glass set in it. Then back at the man in the bed.

"I just know, okay?" The thug insisted.

"Yeah, he just *knows*, you know?' Snap-brim had walked back to the foot of the bed, cigarette bobbing between his thin lips.

"Like a soothsayer?" Fedora shot back.

"Right," his companion, said, "like he can see the future."

"He see this coming?" Fedora slapped a hand over the hood's mouth. Snap-brim grabbed one of the man's ankles and pressed the tip of his lit cigarette against the sole of his bare foot. The trapped man's eyes got wide and he squirmed and thrashed as the cigarette was pulled back then stabbed onto another part of his foot, sizzling his flesh.

"Now give us the fuckin' name, punk," Fedora seethed. With his other hand he'd jerked the prisoner's free hand and wrist through the bars of the bed, wrenching on them as the calm snap-brim burned the hoodlum's feet.

On the subway heading to the rent party, Henson told Stevenson more about his friend the professor.

"Destiny, words can't accurately describe what it's like out there in the never-night, no landmarks in front of you or over your head like with the stars. Maybe a gale wailing about you, rattling your bones in a cold that seeps into your brain. And after what we'd been through, well, Henrik sort of broke down on the trip home."

"He was put away?"

"For a while. He got out though, went back to Europe as I understand it. But eventually found his way to the States." He paused. "Now and then I'd hear from him, but we lost touch."

"He was with you when you brought back a meteorite? A rock from space."

"A several ton hunk of iron ore, baby."

"Aren't you just the he-man This place was non-descript, some of its brick exposed behind missing plaster. They could hear music coming from upstairs as they entered the vestibule door, which was ajar. Up they went to the third-floor, where the hallway crowded with revelers, the smell of collard greens and a trumpet trilled from one of the open doorways.

"Two bits apiece, please," said a woman in a feathered turban and sequined dress.

Henson let a dollar bill drop into her proffered top hat. "Here you go, ma'am."

"I think you good sir and good madam. Enjoy."

She went through a nearby open doorway and as the two-stepped past, they saw people in a wide range of attire—even a tall woman in a beaded Mardi Gras mask.

"Matthew my man," a deep voice called out.

"OD, three times in one week," he responded.

"Must be fate," the big man chuckled. Oscar Dulane was wearing his bowler but missing his cigar. He was in rolled-up shirtsleeves and holding a small plate with food on it, forking it down in a steady rhythm. "I'm getting a good crew together."

"I knew you would."

Dulane nodded and turned back to continue his conversation with two other men.

"Come on, I want to introduce you to Sissy." Stevenson took Henson's hand and led him further along the hallway. They entered another apartment where a poet was standing in the center of the room in the middle of a recitation.

"Lo the journey is long, we are bred for the hardship," he was saying. The poet was stout with a nub of a head and long arms out of proportion to his short torso. "But the balance of justice tips in our favor," he added.

"This is Matt Henson," Stevenson said to a woman in knee-length plaid golf knickers. Her top was some sort of clingy material, and she wore a linen bolo jacket over that. Stevenson's friend looked Henson up and down.

"From the way people talk about you in these parts," she began, a feint Georgia accent coloring her words, "I figured you'd be seven feet tall with a blue ox."

"I shrunk some," Henson said.

She clapped him on the shoulder. There was a glass of bootleg whiskey in her other hand. "Yeah, well, any friend of my gal is a friend of mine, Mister Polar Bear. Y'all get some eats and hooch, okay? Everybody's chipped in to make this a humdinger."

She winked at Stevenson and wandered off.

"Where do you know here from?" Henson asked. "Don't tell me she was the choir leader in your daddy's church."

"You're not the only one with friends in high and low places."

In the kitchen they helped themselves to fried chicken, greens and potato salad. The food along with homemade brew was laid out on a table under an electric clock mounted on the wall. Henson was pleasantly surprised at her appetite.

"Don't you dare look at me like that," she said, a light sheen of grease on her shapely lips. "I haven't dirtied a plate all day."

"Ain't nothing wrong with satisfying your hunger."

Her tongue licked at her bottom lip. "Is that so?' Her gaze lingered on him.

From the other room just beyond the archway to the kitchen, a raised voice said, "Look, what them Bolsheviks did over there can't be repeated over here, Langston. They all Europeans and whatnot. And actually, there's plenty of oriental types over there too, but surprise, surprise, they don't seem to be the ones in power now, do they?"

"Nobody's saying it's perfect, Florence," Langston Hughes said to Florence Emery. From Harlem originally, the cabaret singer had moved to Paris and was a fixture at Eugene Bullard's Le Grand Duc nightclub.

She continued, "Look at the trials and tribulations that go down trying to bring together whites and blacks on the labor front. More than half the damn time it's the whites inside the unions who are the worse ones. They like to keep their precious little boilermakers and brick layer clubs white and all, right. 'Course they don't mind you New Negroes take some lumps for them on the picket line."

"Don't get me wrong," Hughes said, I'm not saying they've created a workers' utopia, but there are key lessons we can learn from them in our march toward equality here at home. All of us can't move to Paree you know."

"I sure as hell hope not," she said, head back, laughing, her hands on her hips.

In another apartment, the trumpet player was joined by a saxophonist and a clarinetist. After a false start, they jammed a rendition of "Black Bottom Stomp," then riffed into "San," and from that, a round of improvising solos. By then a guitar player had joined in, and the beat became more melodic as several couples began slow dancing. The couples included women with women, and nobody raised an eyebrow.

"Not bad for a man who's been out in nowhere living with the seals and the mudlarks," Stevenson said, the side of her face on his chest as they danced.

"I do try."

"Yes, you do." She looked up at him and they kissed.

The man and woman didn't rush away to satiate their growing passion but stayed at the party long enough to let it further blossom. Long enough that Willie "The Lion" Smith showed up after playing a gig at a local club. An upright piano was wheeled out of one of the apartments and he banged out several rousing numbers in his masterful stride stylings. A long cigar dangled from his mouth, and Florence Emery was cajoled into singing a couple of numbers with him.

The cheer and the music filed the building and spilled out onto the streets as Henson and Stevenson finally left the party. It was past one in the morning.

"I'll see you to your door," Henson said.

"That would be just lovely," she answered, warm from liquor and lust.

Her studio apartment was in a building with a butcher's shop on the ground floor that had a speakeasy behind a wall that could swing open. But the two didn't stop in for another drink. Soon, they were at the door to her fifth-floor walk-up, Henson's hand under her skirt, her leg around his waist. The two managed to get inside and tumbled into her bed. She had hold of him by a hand and stroked him as she nibbled on his neck and ear.

CHAPTER ELEVEN

While Henson and Stevenson kept house, Vin O'Hara tossed three kings onto the table. "I believe that beats your two pair."

"Shit," groused another more adept at safecracking than cards. He sat back and lit a cigarette while O'Hara gathered up several loose dollar bills that constituted the poker pot.

"Always a pleasure doing business with you gents," O'Hara said, rising and stretching. "But I gotta go see a man about a horse."

"You gonna ride that nag all night?" another player leered.

O'Hara showed even teeth. "Modesty forbids." He polished off his whiskey, folded his winnings into his pocket and after putting his coat on and placing his straw hat on his head, touched the brim. "See ya."

Somebody grunted, and O'Hara was out the door and walking along the quiet hallway, the hour was just past midnight. He took the stairs two flights down and out onto the sidewalk, looked around and walked up the street to his car—the company vehicle, as it were. It was a Ford Model A and was among several that belonged to Dutch Schultz that his men used in making their rounds. This included collecting his monies from various illegal endeavors or making a call to break a guy's arm or stick a recalcitrant so-and-sos head in the wheel well and put a foot on his neck to make him see matters the Dutchman's way.

Inside the car, O'Hara had set the spark lever up when he'd parked. He keyed the ignition on, and engaged the gas by pushing its lever to the right of the stick shift toward the dashboard. He gave a couple of squirts of fuel into the carburetor barrels, working the choke and cranked the engine. The car came to life and putting the spark lever down, he pushed the accelerator and gave the car gas. He let the brake off, put on the lights, and pulled away from the curb. Very little traffic was out this time of the morning in Hell's Kitchen or elsewhere.

He headed east, enjoying the neon glare of edifices like the Roadway, the Knickerbocker and the Winter Garden. The shows were over, but there were workers out on ladders, using their elongated poles changing the marquees. He turned, winding his way north, reaching Harlem in less than ten minutes. He drove through the so-called jungle area on 133rd, past the likes of the Clam House and Smalls' Paradise. A few more turns and he was cruising in front of the Cotton Club on Lenox Avenue. Several white patrons lingered out in front. A large man in a double-breasted suit threw his head back and laughed jocularly. The segregated club was run by transplanted English gangster Owney Madden backed by Chicago mob money. He and his manager employed black staff, and even had Duke Ellington heading the house band, but negroes did not go there to be turned away. Though, apparently, now and then O'Hara understood, a light-skinned colored gal, maybe the friend of one of the chorus girls, might be let in if she knew how to behave among white folks.

He parked near an apartment building on 145th and after remembering to put the spark lever down, as he best be away again shortly after the sun was up, locked the car. Tacked to a light pole nearby was a handbill announcing the upcoming presentation at Liberty Hall by Daddy Paradise, entitled, "Equality and Prosperity, the Road to True Freedom." Word was, numerous notables would be in attendance, including A. Philip Randolph and the Reverend Adam Clayton Powell, Sr.—these Harlemites, along with the likes of Queenie St. Clair, and rumor had it, numbers king Casper Holstein.

This whispering about his name was far-fetched and had originated with Miriam McNair to boost the gatherings' allure. He often didn't venture far from his nest at the Turf Club. Tickets were selling briskly.

O'Hara stood atop the stoop, the vestibule unlocked. He continued up to the fourth floor. When he reached there he wasn't winded. He knocked lightly on the door of apartment 4B. It swung inward before he'd finished, the person on the other side having heard his approach.

The woman was the arresting-looking Petersen who had made the two-way radio call from the car. She was dressed conservatively, and her hair was brushed away from her intelligent face.

"Hey, now," she said, stepping back to let him in.

"Hey yourself," O'Hara said, taking off his hat and coming inside. He had met her before, and was again struck at her mixed features. One of those black women who must have Cherokee or something like that in her family, he'd concluded. The door closed.

Sitting around a square table were three others including Oscar Dulane who nodded at O'Hara.

"OD," O'Hara said.

Dutch Schultz's man was the only white person in the room. He seemed at ease as he took off his coat and laid it on the arm of a club chair near the curtained window. He joined the poker game in progress.

"Deal me in," he said, laying a five on the table. "I'm feeling lucky."

"Good to hear," Petersen said, sitting back down.

"Dealer antes," said the other woman in the room, Venus Melenaux. As usual, she was dressed in a man's suit—or rather a man's suit tailored for her. She was the banker, and changed out O'Hara's bill for singles and four quarters. The game recommenced with a hand of five card stud.

On a sideboard were sandwich fixings, warm bottles of beer and corn liquor. At one point after several hands O'Hara and Dulane stood there. Dulane poured more liquor in his glass and O'Hara cut off a couple of slices of bologna, and, with a piece of cheese, put that between twin pre-sliced bread, packaged loafs of such having recently been introduced in markets.

"We're just gonna step out for air and a smoke," O'Hara announced, holding his sandwich.

"Don't be long," Melenaux joked, "I want a chance to earn my two dollars back betting into your flush that should have been mine."

"Yes, ma'am," O'Hara said, smiling and bowing slightly. He started on his sandwich while descending the stairs.

Outside, the two didn't shoot the breeze. They talked about Schultz's activities regarding Harlem.

"I don't know exactly what's in that crazy bastard's mind, OD," O'Hara said, blowing smoke from his cigarette into the air. "But I do know Flegenheimer is focused on the upcoming Daddy Paradise talk at Liberty Hall. Told his man Two Laces to sniff around and see what he could learn."

"Okay," said Dulane, eyebrow cocked. "I'll make a few inquiries of my own. And let Matthew know if I find out anything hinky."

"But careful asking around, yeah?" He took a last puff and, after throwing the cigarette away, dug on the side of his gums for the remains of his sandwich. He then swallowed.

"Like walking on eggshells," OD said.

"Ain't that the truth." They both returned to the card game.

Henson and Stevenson lost track of time and any modesty, and somewhere in the dead of dark morning, got to sleep after their romantic labors.

"Oh my," Stevenson said when she awoke in the morning, her mouth cottony and a dull ache behind her right eye. She looked over. Henson wasn't in the bed. But she could see him busy in her kitchenette, taking items out of the icebox.

"How you feeling?" he asked, chopping up an onion. He looked at her and not at his hand as he expertly worked the blade to dice the onion as a chef would.

"Fine," she said, scooting out of bed and fetching her robe in the closet, aware he eyed her nude form. She exited and used the facilities down the hall.

She returned to find bacon frying, and the aroma of fresh coffee had her salivating. Or maybe she just wanted more of her guest, fantasizing other wicked things to do with him. Stevenson straightened up the bed, and after folding it back into the wall, went to the table where Henson was serving the food.

"Is there nothing you can't do?" She dipped her nose toward the coffee, breathing the smell in deep, seeking to clear the fuzziness in her head. On the table was one of his throwing stars. She picked it up, examining the weapon.

He grinned at her, tearing off a piece of bacon. "Careful with that."

Holding it between thumb and index finger, she turned the shuriken. "What if you electrified this thing?"

Henson raised an eyebrow. "Huh?"

"It'll make it much more effective."

As they talked, Henson was impressed that Destiny Stevenson wasn't just a pretty face and a knock-out body.

"Miriam called me yesterday to glow about Charles' upcoming speech," she mentioned. "About how proud I'll be of him."

Henson chuckled. "Guess she's figuring to be your stepmom, huh? She made a face.

"You're not much on his ways?"

"I guess I haven't really sorted out what I think. My mom was his bookkeeper. She always told me he was my father, and it wasn't like he was a complete stranger to us growing up. But I'm not his only out of wedlock child."

"Have you met any of your half-brothers or sisters?"

"Two of my sisters, yes. I also think there's a son out there somewhere. Now, one of the half-sisters I met is a big believer in Charles' mission. Has some kind of position with his organization. I'm sure she'll be out here for the event."

"You think what he does actually, you know, uplifts the race?"

"Or is he just a huckster?"

Henson shrugged as he poured more coffee for both of them. "Plenty say he provides hope, tells us not to fear the white man, do for self—and, as he admitted the other night, in addition to the ones he runs outright, invests his money in other peoples' businesses.

The official name for Daddy Paradise's organization was the Peaceful Grace Ministries. They operated restaurants, a freight line, moving companies, gas stations and even a string of roadside motels for the negro traveler in the segregated south.

"Ministering to the body and the soul. Now if I'm not mistaken, he himself has said he is not a Christian in the traditional sense. He mixes in Catholicism, Buddhism and Santeria among other spiritual teachings."

She cocked her head. "You looking to join the cause, Matthew?"

"Just trying to get a sense of the man."

"Doesn't the New Negro have to be responsible for more than just themselves?"

"Yeah," he nodded, lost in thought.

She rose, letting her robe fall open. She straddled his lap, putting her arms around his neck. "Maybe right now you best concentrate on getting a sense of the daughter. Or are you out of too worn out from last night, Mr. World Explorer?"

"The Arctic got ice, baby?"

She kissed him, working her hand under his shirt. Like before, she marveled at the scar tissue her fingers caressed. The overgrown skin crisscrossed his body, testament to years of hard living.

Their lovemaking on the chair had it creaking and wobbling, but it didn't break.

Fremont Davis stood across the street from Matthew Henson's residence in the brisk morning air. He was in a topcoat and gloves, smoking a thin black cigar. Passersby gave him the once-over but kept on. Probably some he assumed thought him a landlord out seeing about one of his properties. Such a notion brought a small smile to his face as he puffed away, his keen eyes fixed on the window he knew looked out from Henson's living room. He'd brought one of his hunting knives with him, contemplating simply walking up to the man's place, knocking and putting the blade to him when he opened the door, the sleep not yet out of his eyes.. Not a kill strike at first, for he needed that sumabitch alive to tell him where he'd hidden the Daughter. He'd skin him slowly to get him to talk. Henson might, he also considered, be quick enough to evade the knife thrust and counterattack. Well, he concluded, matters were in motion for him to realize his goal. He'd made certain of that. Davis tossed the cigar away and strolled back to his parked car.

When they were done, Henson and Stevenson said their goodbyes. Downstairs he walked along, hands in his pockets. A group of kids, none of them no more than twelve, ran past him laughing and goofing with each other. What Stevenson didn't know was that he did have to be responsible for more than himself. Since his breakfast with Henrik Ellsmere it had been on his mind he needed to make things right with his son Anaukaq, Ackie he'd called him. He hadn't seen him in what, almost six years? Their only communication were infrequent letters back and forth. Was living his life, being rootless and taking off for parts of the country or the world whenever he felt like it so important? Sure, he'd rationalized that his kind of life was dangerous and no place for a child. But how could he visit on the young man being fatherless like he was early on in his own life. He caught a glimpse of his haunted eyes in a storefront window.

Henson stopped at a drugstore and made a call to his lawyer. It was still early, and he called him at home. The lawyer answered on the second ring. They exchanged pleasantries then Kunsler filled him in on what he'd learned so far.

"I haven't been able to track down Ellsmere," Kunsler said, "but I'm pretty sure the G-Men have a tail on me."

"Same here," Henson said. "He doesn't seem to be with me this morning, but could be they've got a team on us. Four at least, I figure. You find out anything about those red hots in the animal masks?"

"Now, there I've had a bit more luck. I've got a friend in the morgue who let me in to see the body of the one you put the pig sticker in. His name was Clyde Jessup, a known muscle for hire out of Chicago."

"Anything on who he was working for?"

"No, and no one has claimed his body."

"Okay, keep at it, Ira, we'll shake something loose."

"Hey, I almost forgot. I got a call yesterday at the office on a more pleasant matter."

"What was it?" Henson said.

"From Paul Robeson's agent. They'd like to buy you lunch and talk about Robeson playing you in a movie."

He chuckled. "That right?"

"That's what he said. What do you think?"

"I'm flattered. But he ain't gonna have no white woman call me nigger while trying to get me in the sack an' hack at my privates with a butcher knife. Shit." He was referring to a scene in a Eugene O'Neill play *All God's Chillun Got Wings* that recently starred Robeson.

Kunsler guffawed. "Christ, I'll make sure to specify that can't happen if we draw up a contract. Don't you worry, old son." He laughed again.

"Fact, I wouldn't be too crazy about that O'Neill fella being anywhere near this if it got going. Nobody will remember my book, Ira. It's the moving pictures that will be what will stick in people's minds in the long haul."

"Didn't know you gave your legacy so much brain space."

"Ah, you know what I'm saying."

"Yes, I do. Robeson's in London doing *Showboat* but is expected to take a break in a month or so to come back here and spend time with his wife and new son. I'll see about setting up a time."

"Okay, talk soon," Henson said, severing the line.

As he went back outside, he reflected on two things; was the fact the hood was out of Chicago—Daddy Paradise's base of operations—a coincidence? And on what Ellsmere had said about being held in a big house in Poughkeepsie. About it being near a park and its religious-themed stained glass windows. Poughkeepsie wasn't that big, and if he could get someone to fly him over its fancy houses, he might be able to find the mansion Ellsmere was held in. And he just happened to know a pilot.

He made a stop at Mr. Greene's newsstand. The bullet holes from the machine gun had been patched up, the white plaster in stark contrast to the weathered green paint of the wooden structure.

"Not that I like getting shot at, Mr. Henson," Mr. Greene said, "but business has picked up since then. People love them a sensation, don't they?"

"Yes, sir, they do." He bought a copy of the *Herald Tribune* and went on toward his apartment, but not directly to his front door. Henson stood at the end of his block, scanning both sides of the street before him. He recognized several of the parked cars and trucks, and did not see the tan Chrysler he and his lady friend had passed when they left the RCA building last night. Of course, that didn't mean there wasn't a new man watching him.

Upstairs he plugged in his electric percolator to make more coffee. In the bathroom, he started the water in his claw-foot tub, keeping it tepid despite the morning coolness that lingered. He stripped down and relaxed, the bathroom window open to the breezes as he read through the *Tribune*. He smiled at the antics of Walt Wallet in *Gasoline Alley* and *Tillie the Toiler* in the funny pages. This and the business with Robeson reminded Henson of the time writer George Schuyler shopped around the idea of a comic strip based on his exploits. Some black papers—and a few left-leaning ones—were interested, but by then Schuyler was criticizing several of his black literati, the "niggerati" as they were jokingly at times referred to by his Harlemite contemporaries, and had burned one too many bridges. By the time Henson was done, the water was icy cold, but he found it invigorating.

Back in his living room, he sat in his robe in his one plush chair next to a long ago bricked-up fireplace. There were two photographs on the mantle. One was of Henson standing between two Inuit youngsters, his arms around each of them. The younger one was his son Anaukaq, aged eight, and the older lad, nicknamed Luke, had been in his twenties. They all wore furs and were smiling broadly. That was the last time Henson had been north to see his boy.

The other was of Henson seated among celebrities like Reverend Adam Clayton Powell, Sr., Booker T. Washington, and Assistant U.S. Attorney W.H. Lewis. The occasion had been a dinner at midtown's Tuxedo Club to honor his "representing the race well." White America virtually ignored his contribution to exploration, focusing mostly on Robert Peary. For, while he was alive, Peary made sure it was his name, and his alone, be it in interviews or speaking engagements, that was associated with reaching the North Pole. This, despite his foreword to Henson's book, reading, "He deserves every attention you can give him." Maybe, Henson had considered over time, the humorless Peary did have a wicked sense of the absurd after all.

Tacked to the wall above the photo was a kaviak, a type of Inuit harpoon made of wood, ivory, and in this case, a tip made of iron. There was no iron ore in Greenland. When they'd first come to the village of Moriussaq, a thousand miles above the Arctic Circle, they couldn't help but notice the use of iron in the villagers' tools and weapons. While there had been Danes, Italians and other nationalities in the village before Henson and Peary, the villagers had not divulged the story or location of their sacred stones. That is, until Ootah told Henson, because the Polar Eskimos considered him one of them.

Henson poured a cup of coffee, absently blowing across its dark surface. He wandered back to then, the harpoon triggering a fond memory of being on hunts with his Eskimo crew— men who became close in the unforgiving icy plains of northern Greenland. Those times had a powerful hold on him. Those times, and the son he'd left behind. He finished his coffee and, after washing up a few plates in the sink, tidied up his apartment. Checking the time, got dressed and headed out to keep his appointment with Nikola Tesla.

"Edna, how goes it?' he said to his neighbor coming out of her apartment across the hall in her work clothes, a blue serge skirt and coat.

Edna Mullins worked in the chief clerk's office at the U.S. Customs House downtown. A good, solid, government job she might retire from on a modest pension.

"Oh fine, just fine," she said.

They descended the stairs together chitchatting.

"Don't work too hard," Henson said to her when they reached the street.

"Never as hard as you, Matt," she said, heading in the opposite direction.

Outside the tan car wasn't there and Henson detected no tail on him as he walked along. Nonetheless, he took a circuitous route to his destination.

The Service Hotel still had its previous name—the Earlington—inscribed in stone in a semi-circle of lettering etched over the front entrance. The Service moniker had been acquired during World War I when the hotel, which had fallen out of the hands of its previous owner, had been taken over for the recuperation of physically and psychologically wounded doughboys returning from the fight. It held some 200 rooms, some of them rentals by the week, and others converted apartments.

"Yes, Doctor Tesla is expecting you," said a sharp-eyed woman behind the front desk when Henson entered the lobby and told her who he was. "He's in the Tower Room at the top."

Up Henson rode in a quiet elevator and was let out in a gloomy chamber with a door across the small span of black and white tile floor. He opened it, and a sizzling bolt of lightning boiled the air in front of him. Instinctively, he ducked, reaching for the throwing star strapped to his shin under his pant leg. He also had another star tucked inside his waistband.

"Sorry, I thought I'd checked all the connections," a man with a pug nose in a lab coat. A wary Henson rose, empty handed.

"Stanley, who don't you and Jean see to all the connections, please?"

"Yes, Doctor," replied the pug-nosed assistant.

"One minute my good man," the Doctor said to Henson. He and Stanley got busy at a fantastic-looking machine like something of off the cover of *Amazing Stories* magazine.

They were joined by a female assistant also dressed similarly to Stanley. She wore glasses, and her hair was pulled pack in a tight bun. The device was made of metal, about five feet long and two feet in diameter. It was cylindrical in shape with glass tubes and wires protruding at numerous intervals. The thing rested on a tripod and there was wiring leading to a large box he figured was a battery. There were several squat black metal boxes with gauges on them connected to this as well. Finally, the Doctor disengaged from his tinkering and walked over to the explorer.

"Harlem's own Mr. Henson."

"Doctor Tesla," he said, shaking the offered hand. "You looking to fry one of your neighbors?" Henson asked, only half joking.

"If one of them was Edison, yes," Tesla replied solemn-faced.

The scientist-inventor was about medium height, with a heavy black mustache and eyes deep-set in an angular face. His white hair was cut as if by a near-sighted barber. The Serbian accent was pronounced, but his English was crisp and distinct. He wore cuffed pants and a shirt that seemed too big on his lean frame. The sleeves were rolled up past his elbows and there was sinewy muscle in those seventy-two year-old arms.

"But no," he continued, "I need to make many further adjustments

112

to the Electro-Pulsar. It still has much more work and experimentation to go through to perfect the shocker beam. Essentially make it wield a coherent beam of electricity."

"Like a cannon, only it shoots lightning bolts?"

Tesla said, "Exactly. As our penchant for making war and untold death on our brethren is inevitable, what if each country possessed the means to destroy the other? Would that not be a stalemate to such hostilities?"

"You might have more faith in humankind than has been demonstrated, Doctor Tesla."

"Nikola, if I can call you Matt."

"Nikola it is."

"You may be right, but we shall see. But, come, let's have our tea and biscuits as we discuss the matter at hand."

Set in the center of the roof was an enclosed eight-sided structure that once must have been the penthouse suite Henson surmised. But as they walked around a corner of this, he could see through the windows it had been converted from living space to Tesla's lab. There were numerous gadgets in various stages of either being built or torn down. Wires, black and grey boxes with tubes and gauges, Tesla coils of various sizes, gears, switches, and an assortment of all sorts of electrical and mechanical apparatuses were also in there on tables and work benches. On top of this was a radio tower of advanced design.

The two sat at a round glass table. On it was a teapot and European clear glasses set in silver holders. There was also a plate piled with rectangular British tea biscuits, and a pot of jam with a butter knife laying nearby. They sat, and after suspending a cube of sugar over each glass by a toothpick, Tesla poured their tea over the sugar into the glasses.

"Cheers," Tesla said, raising his filled glass.

"Na Zdorovie," Henson said in Russian, clinking his glass against the other.

"Do you speak it?" Tesla asked, also in Russian.

Henson knew the scientist was reputed to speak eight languages. "Enough to get in trouble," he answered.

The mustache lifted. "Then we better stick to English."

Chuckling, he said, "Maybe we better. You have any idea where the government is holding Henrik?"

"That's why I called you, as you were the last one to have seen our friend. I wanted to confirm that indeed he was being held by the authorities."

Eyebrow raised, Henson said, "You just happen to be listening to the radio then? Are you a fan of the Clicquot Club band?"

"I'm not adverse to swing music, Matt. I can still cut a rug," he said enthusiastically. "But that was my young assistant Stanley. We'd been working late as was not unusual and after knocking off as they say, he turned on the radio just as you were being interviewed."

"You knew about me and Henrik getting arrested?" Henson asked.

"I did." Tesla bit into his tea biscuit, crumbs accumulating in his mustache. "I have learned from bitter experience in this country, Matt, that one must be prepared for various possible eventualities. That merit is not always recognized. Other factors can intervene." He wiped the crumbs away.

He looked evenly at his guest. "Now of course I don't need to tell you that. But it's in that regard that I had heard Henrik had surfaced here in town and, well, had certain associates on the lookout for him. That no matter what has happened to him, his understanding of physics is unsurpassed, and I could use his help on several projects."

Tesla paused, looking into the depths of his tea but not drinking more. He continued, "Still, by the time I heard about the incident and sent inquiries about him to the station house, you both were long gone. And as there was no record of him being there at all, my suspicions were raised."

"You think you can run him down? Find him, I mean?"

"I shall try. As you will too, is that not so?"

"It is."

114

"And what do you know of his latest work?"

Henson considered his next words. "Is it that energy is all around us, Nikola? Unseen, but there, nevertheless?"

"Oh yes, Mr. Henson. I've devoted my life to that. I have, to be boastful, discovered the principals for transmitting power without wires. True power I mean. Radio being merely a..." he waved his hand in the air between them, "an expression of the lowest form of that."

He took his speared cube of sugar and swirled it in his tea. "And is Henrik onto a breakthrough regarding heretofore undiscovered sources of energy?"

"Don't know, all that bookworm stuff is way over my head. But I do want to find out who those guys in the mask were. Maybe this will lead me to where he is."

"It is certainly the case that various lines of investigation that start out parallel sometimes cross."

"On that, what do you know about the Weldon Institute? This effort by a gee named Renwick at futurism? I understand you spoke at a shindig he had."

A bemused look settled on his face. "I speak at a lot of affairs, for a lot of crackpots."

"But you do know him?"

Tesla shrugged. "Hugo Renwick and I have had several discussions about how to better society through technology. I've consulted on a few of his endeavors. He knew about my earlier patent on a tilted wing craft that could hover like what an autogiro does. Once in the air, the craft assumes the normal functions of an airplane. He even had me out to his airfield in New Jersey, offering my ideas on his experimental craft." He picked up the butter knife, lifting it straight up then trailing it along horizontally. "Like so, you see?"

"Very interesting."

"Mind you, his engineers have made substantial progress. I'm not so vain that I won't admit I didn't understand that it's only with a turbine can you solve the problem of stabilizing the airship long enough for the forward motion propellers to take over."

"You recall where this airfield is? I understand a friend of mine is putting his plane through its paces."

"I am proud to tell you that even at this age, my memory is... prodigious," he said, tapping an index finger against his temple. "I was driven out there by chauffer, but I can draw you a most accurate map."

Henson bit into a biscuit. The promise of the hunt always sharpened his appetite.

"You are referring to the young woman, Miss Bessie, is that not so? The first negro woman to get her pilot's license, yes? Indeed because of the short-sightedness of this my adopted home, she had to go to France for flight school if I'm not mistaken."

Henson nodded admiringly. "Yeah, man, she's something." He also knew that Robert Abbott, the publisher of the *Chicago Defender*, a city where Bessie had done some flying, supported her financially in her pursuit of an aviator's license.

"I would think so," Tesla agreed.

They talked some more then Henson said his goodbye, each man agreeing to let the other one know should they find Ellsmere. Thereafter, Henson made a phone call to Lacy DeHavilin and took a streetcar over to the Supreme Messenger Service on 44th Street in Midtown. He walked into the combination garage and dispatch office. Various cars, light trucks and motorcycles were coming and going or being worked on

"I'm looking for Jerry Culver," he announced.

Three white men were inside. They all glared at Henson. One of them in a grease-stained khakis shirt said, "We ain't hiring no coloreds today, boy. Bad enough we already been forced to add a couple of you all," he snickered.

In addition to the throwing star he had strapped to an ankle, Henson had a hunting knife affixed to the other. He approached the man who'd crudely addressed him. The other two tensed. He knew better than to be making a habit of burying knives in white men—but still.

"I'm not here for a job. I'm here to borrow one of your motorcycles. Or shall I tell Miss DeHavilin just how goddamn rude you were?" His friend owned a fair amount of stock in the enterprise.

"You're Matthew Henson," said one of the others. He was in dungarees and sweat-stained shirt. I'll be," he muttered.

"That's right." Henson and the mechanic stared challengingly at one another.

"Come on, then," said the other man.

Reluctantly he broke eye contact and walked out with the one he presumed was Culver. He took him over to an Indian Scout with saddlebags.

"You do know how to handle one of these babies, don't you? That there has 750 ccs." He glanced from the bike to Henson. "Miss Lacy said give you the best."

"I haven't spent all my time on dogsleds," Henson answered. He took a leather helmet with goggles off a shelf, and after mounting the motorcycle, got it running. "Much obliged," he said and rode out of the messenger service. Sure enough, using the map that Tesla had drawn, he got to the airfield in the wetlands.

Roaring up, he saw the experimental airplane outside a hanger. Three people were standing near it and turned toward him as they heard the motorcycle approach. Then there was the report of a shot, and a head exploded in red mist.

CHAPTER TWELVE

Henson purposely slid the motorcycle out from under him as the next shot punctured his front tire. He rolled on the ground like someone afire and smothering the flames. Quickly, he was up in a crouch and running to where the other two had scrambled behind the plane.

"Run, Matt," Bessie Coleman yelled.

"Who you tellin'?" he shouted back.

Another shot from the rifle sunk into the asphalt just behind where he was running full bore. He dove, and crawled to make it to the side of the plane to join Coleman and the mechanic Shorty Duggan.

"Any idea on who the hell's shooting?" Henson said.

"Damned if we know," the older man said.

"And that poor bird?" Henson said, pointing at the dead man.

"That's the fella Hugo sent over to see about our security," Coleman said.

"Shit," Henson said.

"Yeah," she agreed.

Two more shots rang out, puncturing the aircraft.

"Bastard," Duggan swore. "He's gonna tear apart our beauty, then us."

Henson looked over at the fresh corpse, then looked into the hanger. "Got an idea."

"You tend to have dangerous ideas," Coleman said with a tight

118

smile.

Henson went past the two, heading toward the tail end of the craft. From there, it was a open space to the hangar. Too bad he didn't have one of his smoke bombs with him. He turned back to Coleman.

"Can you make this contraption smoke?"

"I see what you're getting at," she said.

"You'll burn out the wiring," Duggan cautioned.

"You like being a sitting duck?" Henson retorted.

Duggan groaned, but said no more.

Fortunately for them, the door to the plane was on their side and they hoisted Coleman inside, not bothering to lower the step ladder. She cranked the engines as a gunshot shattered part of the windshield.

"Bessie," both men cried out.

"I'm fine. Get to it," she called.

She started the engines, careful not to flood them with too much fuel least they stall out. Like with a car and the mixture being too rich to burn off completely, she caused black smoke to eddy from the engine ports. As the cloud billowed, the dead man was obscured. Henson dashed to his body, having seen the man had a gun in a shoulder holster. He liberated the weapon. The smokescreen drifted in such a way that it provided cover for a running Henson. Though rifle shots punctured the shifting pall, he reached the hangar intact.

Henson grabbed a gas can, swishing it to make sure there was fuel inside. With that and an oily rag, he paused, waiting for the drifting black-grey smoke to snake back toward the plane. He then hopped on the wing strut opposite Coleman's pilot seat.

"You ready?" he said.

"No choice, in another minute or so, the engines will be fried." She released the brakes and began taxiing the plane, the smoke from the over-burdened engines blowing across the windshield. The shooter tried, but couldn't get a bead on the engine—at least not yet. They knew where the shots were originating, the sun was glinting off the long gun's barrel at the edge of the airfield among a copse of white pines.

The Skathi's frame shuddered and one of the engines threaten to seize as a bullet punched into its metal shell. Still, the craft rolled forward even though one of the tires had been shot and was losing air fast.

"Now or never, Matt," Coleman yelled. "She's about to shut down."

"I hear you." Henson had climbed atop the wing. At first, the smoke hid him, but now as the plane heaved to a stop, the propellers stalled, and his cover was beginning to dissipate. He felt his pockets, swore, and on his stomach, bent down to the cockpit.

"You got any matches?" he asked Coleman.

"Flare gun," she said, reaching for it where it was clamped inside the pilot's side door. The smokescreen was almost all gone, drifting upward into the clear skies. She handed it to Henson.

On a knee, Henson threw the can of gas as the sharpshooter continued blasting rounds into the wing and body of the plane., flung himself prone on the wing again, and shot the flare at the soaring can of gas and the rag. Grey at his temples, his aim was still true, and the can ignited with a whoosh.

The resulting ball of fire fell, the patch of woods began burning, and the shooting stopped. Henson jumped to the ground and ran, firing his handgun through the smoke in that direction.

"Have you lost your cotton pickin' mind?" Coleman yelled from the plane. "Get back here."

"He's making a break for it," he called back over his shoulder. He leaped among the burning trees and shrubs where the shooter had been, the wood crackling and popping as fire consumed it from within. The woods were damp from recent rain but unattended the fire would surely spread.

Ahead of him, Henson heard the shooter panting. It was harder to shoot back with a rifle given you had to stop and aim. In the chase, his handgun was an advantage. Farther along to his right, he saw a form hurrying through the growth. He shot at it, but didn't stop him. Henson crashed through into a clearing in time to see the rifleman behind the wheel of a two-tone Buick coupe. Henson shot out the back window, but missed the tire as the car sped away. The vehicle's bumper clipped a downed log as it went. Henson made a note of the license plate. He thought the car might have been the one his lawyer had noted a few days ago. He also noticed there were drops of blood on the ground. When he returned to the airstrip, the volunteer fire department had a horse-drawn steam-powered pumper putting out the fire. Additionally, there were several men with brass fire extinguishers on their backs also attending to the fire. He ditched the gun and came out of the forest.

"How the hell did this start?" the captain of the crew yelled at Shorty Duggan and Bessie Coleman, square head swiveling on his bull neck from them to the smoldering aircraft and back.

"Mr. Renwick will answer all your questions, sir," Coleman said.

"Yeah? And who's that, missy?"

"Hugo Renwick is your department's biggest donor. Or will be," Duggan said.

There was more back and forth between this man and Duggan. Coleman started to walk off.

"Just where the hell do you think you're going, gal?" the captain called.

"Make a call on the short wave," she answered.

"Hey now," he started but Henson got in his way.

"Let her make the call, cap'n." He said it gently, but his eyes were agates.

Had his men not been busy with the fire, the captain would have challenged back. As it was, he merely glared sourly at this uppity colored.

The blaze was soon extinguished. but the firemen remained, discussing holding the three until they could fetch the police. A black Ford with red trim drove onto the airstrip and a man got out from behind the wheel. He wore owlish glasses and walked with a slight limp. The man talked at length with the captain who, at one point, took off his hat, rubbing his hand over his crew cut hair. The man in the glasses then stood silently by as the captain addressed his crew.

"Alright, we're out of here."

"But captain—"

"No buts," he said, jerking a thumb at the trio. "Looks like they got them a muckety-muck to vouch for them." He turned and pointed at them. "But you can bet dollars to donuts I'm going to keep a watch on what's going on around here. Bunch'a coons and a brokedown mick up to who knows what. Sheet."

He clambered back on the wagon, the other firemen back into a battered GMC truck, and off they went.

Standing side by side watching them go, their clothes seeped in the smell of charred embers, Henson turned to Coleman. "You got another plane you can use?'

She shook her head, sighing. Duggan belly-laughed.

By the time a new plane was secured, it was getting on to dark and Henson knew his scouting mission had to be performed in daylight. The tire of the Indian Scout had been repaired and, though the front fender was in bad shape, the rest of the bike was okay. Henson and Coleman set a time for their excursion, and he started back to the city. The man who'd been slain was an ex state trooper, so they, too, had an interest in finding his killer. Henson told Coleman and Duggan the license plate number of the shooter, and they in turn provided it to the authorities. The flyer would also have one of Renwick's people track down the plate's owner.

Tired and hungry by the time he got back to Harlem, Henson stopped at a grocery store and bought some food. He rode home and parked the motorcycle on the street in front of his apartment. Given the bike was a v-twin, he removed the main spark plug wire leading one from one side of the engine to the other so the machine couldn't be started and stolen. Gathering his purchases in his arms, he heard the approach of footfalls. He straightened to see two white men standing behind him. One was tall and wearing a fedora, the other short and compact with a snap-brim hat. He recognized fedora as the one who'd tailed he and Kunsler previously. The other had been in the sedan. Henson was also certain the taller agent had been the one pretending to be asleep that night in the tan Chrysler outside the RCA building.

"Are you Matthew Henson?" asked the tall one.

"I am."

"We'd like a word with you. Won't take a minute."

"Make it tomorrow, would you? I'm just about to fix some dinner and hit the sack."

"You love your country, don't you, Henson?" the bulldog in the snap brim said. "Or maybe you and that red mouthpiece of yours are two peas in a pod hugging Karl Marx's underwear?"

"You gents with the Justice Department? The Bureau? That Hoover fella send you to talk with lil' ol' me?"

"You ought to be on *Amos n' Andy* you're so damn funny," the bulldog said.

"How do you know I'm not?"

"Look you smart mouth shine, I—" began bulldog.

The tall one in the fedora slapped the back of his hand against the other's chest. "Go on and get your chow, Mr. Henson. We'll take this up at another time."

"Good to know."

The tall one lit a cigarette, staring at Henson though the curtain of smoke. He turned and walked away. Bulldog lingered a moment, but then followed his compatriot. Henson went on up. He wasn't sure what to make of this development. The government men were now coming at him directly. They were probably wise he knew about their tails and figured why not, put the squeeze on him directly. For sure those two must have something to do with Henrik Ellsmere's disappearance. But if he'd told them about the Daughter, why the kid gloves? Why not just bop him over the head and work him over? Not that he knew where it was, but only he knew that pertinent fact. Maybe they hoped to spook him and have him lead them to it.

Well, Henson concluded, yawning while he fried a pork chop and beans in a skillet, he'd go at this again tomorrow when he was refreshed. He ate at the table in his living room near a window open to the night. A full moon hung in the sky and Henson wondered what his son Anaukaq was up to in his days and nights in his family's village. Chewing absently, he understood he wasn't a boy any longer, Ackie would be eighteen or nineteen now—a man by many measures. Older now than when Henson left home at twelve to strike out on his own and find the sea welcoming. He finished his meal and dug out his bottle of bathtub hooch from a cabinet. Never a big drinker, he poured himself a draught from the half-full bottle and it away again. He sat back down at the table and drank, staring out past the moon and stars and imagining. As if the time difference didn't exist, that his son was staring up at the same night sky.

In the brownstone on Striver's Row, two others were also looking up at the moon. Daddy Paradise and Miriam McNair had spent the day visiting potential donors to his foundation—for tax purposes, the Universal Prosperity and Inclusion Association—working on his upcoming presentation at Liberty Hall, and making love. Now they were both clothed in colorful silk robes, sitting side-by-side in the converted sun room on the top floor of McNair's home. The room was her meditation chamber, and contained all manner of artifacts from voodoo gris-gris to Catholic statuettes she'd obtained on a trip to Mexico. Overhead was a skylight through which the moonlight shined.

"If the meteorite exists, this could be a momentous time in our sojourn in this land. We were bound in chains and brought to these shores three hundred years and so ago," Toliver said, gazing upward.

"Oh, Charles, it seems so fanciful about this stone from space and what these white men seem to think it can do. It's almost beyond belief."

"Yet here we sit in comfort in a structure where invisible current provides us light and music from boxes of wood and metal. Things that in the lifetime of our predecessors would seem like the conjurings of a wizard or blamed on the Devil."

She nodded in assent. "But an unheard of source of energy? And for all you know this… meteorite or whatever it is that crashed on Earth centuries ago, well, surely it can be depleted, used up like coal burning in a furnace, can't it?"

Gently, he took his hand away from the woman and tented his ringed fingers over a belly that had been spreading due to too many fine meals. "That may be, Miriam. But I have read arcane texts indicating there are hidden chambers in the pyramids of Egypt and of the Aztecs in Mexico through which the enlightened could receive cosmic rays from space. Granting them who knows what sort of power, for lack of a better word."

Her eyes got wide.

"It may also be that whoever takes possession of this so-called Daughter can set their own price. From what I've been told, a piece no bigger than your hand once unleashed a tremendous lightning bolt that shattered large formations."

"More powerful than dynamite," McNair observed.

"But an energy it's rumored that can't be exhausted." He spread his hands as if to encompass the enormity of his statement. "Now, this was not a direct eyewitness to this event," he added, "but a second-hand account from someone who was with Mahri-Pahluk at the time." He smiled at the Inuit nickname for the explorer.

"How fortuitous then that you've been able to draw Mr. Henson into your orbit."

He looked at her unblinkingly. "Do you not see that as providence?"

"Or doom," she said, stiffening in her seat. "It's from that inhabitable land of ice and snow. What if that blue whiteness is not

125

what you and the others think it is. What if it signals the end of us, a new ice age?"

"Then the first temple of ice will be here in Harlem." A misty glare took ahold of him. "Think of it more in the sense of how so much of an iceberg is below the surface. Much like how the whites see us, dear Miriam. We know there is so much more to us as a people." He waved a hand. "Our renaissance is a prime indicator."

"Yet I fear a backlash. Just look at what happened to those prosperous blacks in Tulsa not too long ago."

He turned toward her, his hand on her knee. "Don't you see, my sweet? All the more reason this object from the heavens, sent to us by the god force you and I know oversees our lives, is meant to be the way in which we might well make millions…monies we can well use for any number of enterprises for the advancement of the negro people."

His hand moved upward, massaging her inner thigh.

She moaned slightly but caught herself from being carried away by desire. "Then it might be harnessed for destructive purposes."

"Only if it falls into the wrong hands. Between us and Queenie, we won't let that happen. Yes, she is about fattening her pockets, but she is sincere about our improvement. Both can be accomplished."

"This is so damn dangerous."

He smiled, his hand moving further up without interference. "And exciting."

McNair sat back, Toliver's hand now between her legs. "Yes," she murmured.

The moon continued to beam down on them.

CHAPTER THIRTEEN

Bessie Coleman brought the bi-plane in low over the parkland in Poughkeepsie. The morning sun ascended in the horizon. "We might be waking up some of the swells," she said to Henson, who sat in the seat behind her. "They don't have to roll out of the sack to make it to the assembly line like us proletarians you know."

"Yeah, well, too much sleep is bad for you," he cracked.

"How about I swing over those big houses over there?" she said above the roar of the propeller and engine. The plane was a WWI-era British made Bristol and had seen better days. It had been borrowed from a friend of hers, a one-legged air jockey named Bull Hogan. Patches and sewn up sections predominated its canvas skin. But Coleman's confidence in the machine remaining aloft had buoyed Henson, and off they'd gone from an airfield about 100 miles away.

They had been reconnoitering the area for nearly half an hour. Henson had seen one house with stained-glass windows, but knew from Ellsmere the house was three stories and this one was only two.

"Hey, just beyond those trees," he said, pointing in the direction he meant.

"Okay." A three-story Gothic Revival with turrets and gables came into view. A row of rectangular religious-themed stained-glass windows framed the second story of the mansion.

"I think that's John the Baptist's head on a plate in the middle,"

Coleman observed.

"Yeah," he said, hauntingly recalling his stepmother Nelle reciting Bible verses as she beat the hell out of him and his sisters. He shook it off. "Anyplace to set down?"

"Well," she drawled, "there is that bridge. Looks sturdy enough and plenty long enough."

"Girl, you done gone simple? What about the traffic?"

"They'd clear out when they see me coming." She half-turned her head to grin at him.

"And when the police come, what then? Even if we're not near the plane, they'll confiscate this relic."

They were following the ribbon of the Hudson when they both saw their possible solution below atop a rise of land off the river.

"Looks like it used to be a paper mill," Coleman said.

"Whale rendering was big around here once upon a time, too," Henson said, not sure why he should recall that bit of history or how he knew it. Numerous windows in the abandoned plant had been busted out and the doors boarded over. There was a good sized paved lot that must have been used for trucks hauling away loads of paper.

"Is that going to be long enough?" Henson wondered aloud, referring to the lot.

"Son, I can put this thing down on the head of an anteater." Coleman banked the plane and took a pass over the plant, evidently calculating the lot's length. She circled back and, cutting the engine speed, brought the craft down quickly, Henson's stomach suddenly in his throat. But she got them on the ground and taxied to a stop with room to spare ahead of the main building.

They got out. Cars passed by on the highway, but a plane landing at an abandoned factory didn't garner that much attention. Maybe the motorists thought this was some financier come to inspect his new property. With their leather helmets and goggles on, from a distance, you couldn't tell they were black—that might have been seen as an anomaly. Dressed in plain clothes, Coleman in khakis like Henson, the two made their way back to the mansion. Passing others on the street, both were pleased they were unmolested.

"Guess they figure we're the help what with these big houses around," Henson said to her.

"And it don't hurt we've seen a few of us colored out and about," the aviatrix noted.

"There is that," he replied dryly.

The house in question sat on a leafy hillock at the end of what would be considered more of a lane than a street. This, too, coincided with what Henrik Ellsmere had told Henson.

"Let's check out the garage first."

"Right."

The way the house was constructed, partially into the hill itself, the three-car garage was on level ground with earth and greenery over that. Creeper vines hung over the tops of the segmented doors. Each garage door had its own window set in the middle. Henson and Coleman, both on tip-toe, looked into each one.

"No cars," Coleman said.

Henson remarked, "Did they clear out after the professor escaped? Hedging he might bring the law back?"

"Or this joint isn't populated most of the time, anyway."

Henson nodded, pointing toward the house. "One way to find out."

To the side of the garage was a winding set of concrete steps. They took these up through shrubbery on either side at intervals which brought them to a portico and the expanse of the porch.

"The gardening hasn't been done lately," Henson noted. The shrubbery appeared to need trimming.

"So far, so good," Coleman said. She looked down onto the path and the homes nearby. "Can you see into the house?"

"No, the curtains are closed." Henson had moved to one of the front windows then came back over to Coleman. "Around back?"

Coleman was already in motion and he followed her. Due to the design of the house and the foliage, they were mostly hidden from view as they went around to the right of the house toward the rear along a dirt path.

"This might be to the maid's quarters," Coleman guessed, stopping at a door. There was a concrete path that led to the far side of the house and presumably another part of the roadway

"Keep your eyes open, Bess." Henson stepped close to the door and, using his ice axe, as quietly as possible chopped at the wood around the single lock until the door gave. They stepped inside, and he closed the door behind them, even though it no longer was able to latch. It was gloomy in the house, and smelled musty from the lack of human presence.

"Come on," he said.

"Okay, boss," she said, mimicking Stepin Fetchit.

"You're hilarious," he deadpanned.

Inside, the furnishings were tasteful and expensive, what there was of them. As Coleman had suggested, it seemed the home wasn't used full-time, but was meant to be a getaway of some sort. The icebox was empty, though there were some canned goods in the larder.

"A summer home?" Coleman speculated as they looked around.

"Somebody with the silver," Henson agreed. "But none of the furniture has been covered. Are they coming back soon?"

Coleman lifted a shoulder. They continued prowling. The two found the area that had been Ellsmere's lab, but it was cleared out. Upstairs, there were bedrooms, bedding untouched. Back downstairs in what would be the study, there were animals mounted on the wall.

"What?" Coleman said, noticing Henson drawing in a breath sharply at the sight of the heads. "These dead deer and whatnot bother you? You mean to say them stories they tell about you skinnin' a polar bear with just a butter knife wearin' a loincloth ain't true?"

He'd moved more into the room, glaring up at the head of the buck.

Coleman noted this. "Yeah, so he's a hunter like you?"

"I hunted for food or hide to wear," he said, distantly. Then

130

brightening, "I get it now. What with his hatchet men running around in animal masks."

"Who you talking about, Matt?"

He answered her as he jerked open drawers of a colonial-style desk. Nothing.

"Shit," Coleman hissed.

Henson looked over at her. "What?"

"Pretty sure I heard voices outside."

The front door opened on a creak. In stepped two older women carrying linens and cleaning supplies. From where they were in the study, Henson and Coleman could see them through the slightly ajar study door.

"Guess they're here to clean and shut the place up," Coleman whispered.

"Then we can find out who hired them. I already got a powerful notion, just want to confirm it."

"You gonna rough up them old gals, are you, Matt?" She spread her hand imagining a newspaper headline. "Famed colored explorer arrested after assaulting two old white women."

"What kind of idea you got?"

Coleman smiled. After getting a window open in the study and going outside, Coleman came back around to the front of the house and knocked on the door. It was opened by a heavyset, lined older face.

"Yes," said the woman.

"Excuse me, ma'am, but I understand Mr. Davis is hiring on help to keep this here fine house going while he's away?"

The other woman took in Coleman in men's pants and leather jacket. "You wear that getup all the time?"

"Huh?" Coleman said. "Oh no, ma'am, just got through with a job packing apples off a boat is all. I gots a maid's proper uniform and what not."

"Well, I don't know what Mr. Davis intends to do with this house

131

long term. Me and Ophelia were hired to dust and close it up for now." Her companion could faintly be heard humming as she began her tasks in another part of the house. Henson and Coleman had spotted various cleaning supplies, mop and so forth in there already. "You might check with the Albright Employment agency here in town. They're the ones who hired us, care of him."

"I 'preciate that," Coleman said and walked away. She met Henson back at the plane.

"You were right," she told him. "A Mr. Davis owns the place. Who is he?"

A grim-faced Henson explained, "Fremont Davis. Among other things, he owns a shipping line and fancies himself a big game hunter. Big wig in the Challenger's Club and was on the board of the National Museum who backed our seventh trip to Greenland."

"The one where you finally reached the North Pole?"

"No, that was the eighth. The seventh was to fetch the Tent."

"Get a tent?"

Henson was at the propeller and at her signal, turned the prop and the engine caught on the third try. He came toward the cockpit. "A name for a meteorite like you ain't never seen." He climbed in as she began turning the plane around to take off. "It was thirty-four tons and took us the better part of a year to dig it out and move it to the ship. The hardest time of all my years in the land of ice and snow."

"That's saying something," she yelled back as the plane gathered speed.

"You can say that again, sister." Henson sat back, not seeing the landscape drop away but the hunched backs of men sweating in sub-zero weather. "You can say that again."

CHAPTER FOURTEEN

"Heave, heave," yelled Jason Leeward as an assortment of white and Eskimo men in furs.

The men shoved the big rock off its hydraulic jacks—each designed to lift thirty tons—as others on the opposite side pulled the chains and ropes attached to the black craggy surface. They rolled the rock over again onto the wooden tracks on the ground, a kind of makeshift railway. At the end of the tracks, they'd be dug out, and placed farther along, then the process would be repeated. A process of heave, dig, roll, dig and do it all over again and again. This work had gone on for more than twelve months over less than 100 miles. They ate, slept and shat moving the rock which had been nicknamed "Ahnighito" by Peary—his daughter's middle name. Donkeys had been brought on this trip to help move the Tent. The bitter cold had killed the animals, and they'd been fed to the dogs. It was as if the more than fifty members of the crew and laborers had found themselves in Purgatory, and the punishment was only for humans and machines to undertake this seemingly Sisyphean task. Possibly an eternity later they may have been judged to have completed their duty. Several fingers and toes had been sacrificed along the way from frostbite or a slipped jack.

But damn if they had finally hadn't reached end of their journey. In sight was the bay, and the ship, the Hope.

"Take a break," Matthew Henson said in English and Inuktitut. A chorus of relieved groans went up.

"Hey, who put you in charge, darkie?" Leeward said. He was a lean, long-faced individual from some damn place in Kentucky.

"I told you about using such language," a bearded Peary said to Leeward.

"I've about had it with you and your pet monkey, Captain."

"Why don't you shut the hell up Leeward, and save your hot air for loading the Tent onboard." Henson said.

"It's Mr. Leeward to you, boy."

"I'll call you what I feel like."

Ootah, who spoke a degree of English, had positioned himself close to Leeward. By nature, he was a hard-faced man, but he now displayed a bland expression. His knife was in his hand under his furs.

Leeward was aware of this. "You won't always have your chink manservant nearby, Henson."

"I'm happy for just you and me to settle the score. Any goddamn time you want, Johnny Reb."

"Let it go," Peary said.

The two antagonists glared at one another until Leeward broke contact.

By mid-afternoon as it was reckoned, the largest of the three meteorites was winched onto the ship. This time of year, the midnight sun hung low on the horizon. The men and the environs were, at any given time, washed in various arrays of color. There wouldn't be darkness for another month.

Some of the laborers had feared the Tent was so heavy it would sink the vessel. Two years ago, when he'd first sighted it, Peary had estimated it weighed at least twenty-five tons. But once it had been unearthed, a better sense of its true heft had been determined at over thirty-four tons.

Henson sat on the starboard side of the boat, making notes in his diary. Kudlooktoo came over. He'd taken a shine to the youngster, and the young man was fond of him as well.

"Hey now, Luke. How's the professor?" Like many Inuit, the orphaned teenager had acquired an Americanized nickname.

"The same since he was brought back," he replied in English. "He eats and sleeps, and when he's not doing that, sits on his bunk talking to himself."

This had been Henrik Ellsmere's second excursion with the crew. The storms, the harsh conditions, the life so close to the edge, it got to even the most experienced. Ellsmere snapping had been unexpected, as there had been no warning signs. Or at least none anyone paid any attention to. But one day out on the tundra as the men moved The Tent along, the professor, who usually stayed in the encampment, had come out to see the progress. Making small talk with Peary, Henson saw the man abruptly stop, his mouth agape, like someone snow-blind and disoriented. He peered up into the sky, a man who suddenly couldn't recall how he got here.

"Professor?" Henson had asked.

"Yes, yes, I must get to my class," he muttered, looking right through the other man.

And that was that. He was helped back to his cabin on the ship, and Luke given the task to checking in on him.

"I'll go see him," Henson promised.

"Uncle Matt..." the kid began, having learned English from Henson, "There's a *fourth* rock from the sky, you know."

Henson put his pencil in the diary and closed it, setting it aside. "You mean a piece of one of the three?" There'd been fragments from the metcorites taken back for several years, and not just by the Americans.

"No," the young man said, his hair short as Henson had first cut it back then. "The holy man said in his sermon last Sunday. He talked about the brightest light from the stars since the birth of Jesus."

"Father Christofferson?" Every now and then a missionary type, usually a Dane, would show up and attach themselves to a group to convert the heathens and bring stray Christians back to the Lord. Henson read the Bible, but didn't put much truck with these sorts.

"Him, yes," Luke said.

"You know the father likes his...strong coffee," he said in Inuktitut.

Luke chuckled. "He was sober," he replied in English.

"And how would he know of this?"

"Don't know. But I had been thinking on this since then, and now with the big one on the ship, knew I should tell you before you go away again."

He clasped the young man on the shoulder. "Thank you, Luke. I'll check it out."

The teenager smiled, having pleased the other man.

Henson left The Hope and walked to the encampment of tents and igloos where the laborers resided. A yellow haze permeated the area. He got to Christofferson's ice brick houseas many non Eskimos had adopted using such structures., bent at the opening and called inside.

"Padre, it's Matt Henson. You have a minute?"

"Of course, Mr. Henson," he replied in his accented English. "Do come in."

Henson entered. Christofferson was sitting crosslegged, several loose sheets of paper stacked together on a small board on his lap. His hair was frost white and his Santa Claus beard reached mid-chest. It was close in here, and the smell of unwashed human body order and raw walrus was overwhelming. The priest was particularly fond of snaking on walrus heart. Henson sat.

"Luke tells me you claim there's four meteorites."

The fifty-three year-old clergyman looked at him a moment, then clarity shone behind his blue eyes. "Ah yes, right. I was making a point about God's wonders."

"But where did you hear about there being a fourth?' Henson understood there was probably only one meteorite originally that had broken up, and its pieces had fallen to Earth. Still, a fourth piece would have value. Plus, he would love to see that bastard Leeward's face if he could be the one to discover it.

"From a fine woman, a convert who is much devout," Christofferson said proudly. Like Henson, he spoke several Inuit dialects including Nunavut and Greenlandic.

Henson wondered if that was his way of saying he'd taken her as a mistress. He wouldn't be the first outsider, Bible-thumper notwithstanding. "She say where it fell?"

As an answer, the taller man uncrossed his legs and, crawling out of the igloo, stood up and pointed. Henson followed him. "She knew this story from her childhood. But in her version, it was not the trickster Torngarsuk who threw the Woman, and her Dog and Tent from the sky, but the beneficence of Seqinek. That this was a tear from her daughter who wished only the best for the first people." The word "Inuit" derived from Inuish, their word for people, as for thousands of years, the Eskimos thought they were the only ones to inhabit the Earth. The ones who had prolonged contact with Americans, Italians and what have you, also referred to themselves as Greenlanders

"The sun goddess you mean?" Henson said to make sure, referring to the Eskimo deity of Seqinek.

"Yes," the priest confirmed, pointing at a peak aglow with warm white against a terrain of stark white in the near distance. "At Robeson Point."

Henson considered the information.

As the Hope wouldn't be setting sail for another two days, Henson arranged for he and Ootah to set off, saying they would like to bring some seal meat along on the voyage. Once out of sight, they circled around to Mount Robeson. Henson had pointedly asked him not to tell his brother Egingwah. The latter was more attached to Peary, and they didn't want him gossiping if their two-man expedition didn't pan out. Mount Robeson was less than a half day's journey by sledge.

The two dismounted and tethered their dog when they reached their destination. To their good fortune, the ruddy-tinged sky was still clear, and for this part of the world, the weather tolerable.

"Did you think it would be lying around for us to see?" Ootah asked. He enjoyed ribbing his friend when he could. He'd also told him he'd never heard this story about the sun goddess. They poked around the base of the mountain for a while. Even looking up its side, there were no gouges or where a meteorite could have made impact.

Henson recalled that when he and Peary met with the museum's board, a man named Fremont Davis made mention of an astronomer friend at a university. The scientist, Davis had noted, was of the opinion these meteorites would have struck the earth hundreds of thousands of years ago, and any traces would likely be long gone—and yet there were the other three.

Motivated to one-up that cornpone cracker, Henson said, "Let's keep at it." But after another hour, ascending some yards up the mountain, no vestiges of iron ore or otherwise was discovered.

"I'm hungry," Ootah said when they reached level ground again.

"I hear you," Henson said. Hands on his hips, he walked about, looking at the ground. They were several yards from where their sledges were.

"Hey, wait," Henson said, trudging over to a spot where he saw a dark streak on the ground. He bent down, touching it with his gloved hand. "Not iron. Must be from another dogsled." He stood up, and as he began to turn away, the ground gave out under him.

"Matthew," Ootah yelled, running over. A trench had opened in the frozen ground and, though he was concerned about his companion, the seasoned hunter knew better than to rush to the edge and fall in as well.

Standing as close as he dared to the opening and leaning forward, he could see Henson on his back. But he hadn't fallen straight down into the exposed subterranean cavern. Rather, he had landed on a pack of hard ice that covered a formation of sloping rock that led to the cavern floor.

"Matthew, can you move?" his friend called out.

Henson moaned, eyes fluttering open. "I think so," he said weakly.

138

"I'm coming." Ootah began navigating the descent, the light fading from lavender to purple to black in the interior. It wasn't that wide, and his friend had been lucky he'd landed where he did. Below on the floor of the revealed chamber several stalagmites of ice poked upward, some taller than a man. They hadn't brought a torch, but, having long since gotten used to the half-light of summer, he could make out parts of the interior. He reached Henson who now was sitting up.

"How do you feel?' he asked in his native language.

"I think I just had the wind knocked out of me," he said. "Don't seem to have anything broken."

"Good." Getting a grip on him, Ootah helped him to his feet and the two went down to the cavern itself. There were number of stalagmites, and centuries of ice build-up had created outcroppings that protruded all around them, along the walls and overhead. It was hard to determine how large the space was, and how deep it might go.

"Water must seep in all the way from the bay from cracks and cervices," Henson observed.

"True," Ootah agreed, also looking around. He pulled back the hood of his fur parka and combed his long hair away from his eyes.

"Hey, over there" Henson said, pointing into a gloomy patch beneath an overhang of rock and ice. They walked over to find the remains of a dogsled and pieces of skeleton.

Ootah bent down and sorted through some of the bones with his gloved fingers. Momentarily he announced, "Dog and human bones." He glanced up at Henson. "Not sure, but I'd say two people, but one sledge."

Henson pursed his lips. "Maybe one of them was a woman, lighter in weight." Peary had brought his wife and young daughter along on at least one of their expeditions. Though he was pretty sure he hadn't introduced the missus to his mistress Ahlikahsingwah. Hell, Peary had even hired the woman's husband, and that man was proficient with a rifle.

He refocused.

"What happened to trap them in here? They both couldn't have broken a leg. One would have been able to help the other out."

His friend offered a blank expression.

The diffused light was tricky among the shadows, but Henson got closer to the tread marks from the sledge. He began following the trail which ended at a wall of ice.

"That's not from a ski," Ootah said standing next to him.

They both got out their ice axes and began chopping away, working up a sweat. Through the translucent layers, there seemed to be an object, greyish black and roughly shaped. The two explorers got more excited as they went, and after a half hour of chopping away, a portion of the object was exposed.

"She was right," Ootah exclaimed.

"Yeah," Henson breathed.

Embedded in the ice was a hunk of rock that looked like the Tent and its two mates. It was the smallest of the four, maybe the size of a two-person couch Henson figured. But there was something different about this specimen. Renewed, they kept hacking away and got more of the artifact exposed. It was black and craggy with depressions and outcroppings like the other three. Only its surface wasn't matte, but had a sheen to it.

"What is this?" Ootah said, touching a blue vein in the rock. The meteorite was shot through with those veins. They'd uncovered enough that a dome of the ore protruded from the ice.

"I don't know." Henson raised his axe high, hesitating for a second then struck the meteor's surface forcefully. After several more chops at it, he broke off a triangular fragment. He picked it up, the piece filling his palm. The blue evident by contrast. "Maybe Ellsmere's not so far gone he can't test it. Or, when we get back to New York, I can get it examined."

"You're not going to tell the others? Not even the captain?"

Henson scoffed. Peary had not dissuaded the Eskimos from calling him by a rank he'd yet to achieve. "Not yet I'm not."

Ootah regarded the other man evenly.

"What have you two jigs been up to, huh?" said a voice behind them.

As one they turned to see Leeward descending the slope. He had a revolver in his gloved hand. "I knew seal hunting was bullshit. I figured you two had found gold, but this…" he said, reaching the floor. "This could be bigger." He came closer, eyes glittering as he took in the meteorite. "It's different than The Tent," he said, excitement rising in his voice.

"You were gonna hog all the credit, weren't you, Henson? Tired of being in Peary's shadow? Well, huh, I can't blame you for that." He laughed and snorted. "Shit, I'm going to be famous."

"You?" Henson growled, starting toward him.

"Easy, now, boy," Leeward said, waving the pistol at him. "Take it easy. I'll make sure you and slant-eyes here get a mention in the footnotes." He laughed again. It sounded hollow and mocking in the underground chamber.

"Now, you two do what God made you for. Get to digging."

Henson and Ootah went back to work, gun on them. In another hour and a half, they had more of the rock exposed. Henson stood back. Both men's chests rose and fell, sweat coating their faces.

"Another break already?" Leeward joked. "Well, I wouldn't want to wear out my two mules."

Henson said, "You think your story will be believed, Leeward?"

"Why not, Henson? I'm the white man here."

"He's got you on that one," Ootah said straight-faced.

Henson pressed. "How will you explain you learned about the meteorite? How did you know to find it? And how are you going to stop me and Ootah from telling the truth?"

"Don't you worry your lil' burr head about that, son. Maybe you two will have an accident out here in the wild. I came here out of the goodness of my heart searching for you two, but you must have fallen into a crevasse." Leeward had been sitting on a rock, legs crossed like he was relaxing at the theater. He stood up, menace drawing his face tight.

"Break's over, get the fuck back to work and get me my meal ticket."

As Henson had challenged Leeward, he'd moved away from the rock and Ootah. But the revolver was aimed at his stomach, and he knew better than to try anything. He turned back to continue working. The meteor, more than half of it sticking out of its icy prison, had been loosened by gravity and its weight. It fell the few feet to the floor with a thud. As it struck, there were sparks, and a jagged finger of cosmic energy shot from it with a boom as a bolt of blue-white light.

Instinctively, the three ducked.

Ootah went prone. Leeward cursed. Henson was in motion.

He grabbed up a handful of loosened rock and ice at his feet and flung it at Leeward. The man had to raise his arms in front of his face to protect himself. As he did, Henson covered the distance between them with a bound and a leap. He bowled him over.

"Get off me, nigger," Leeward howled.

Henson tried to punch him in the face but Leeward moved faster than he'd anticipated. He got a knee between them and shoved Henson away. Both were still down but Leeward scrambled up, gun in hand, about to shoot Henson. An ice axe whistled through the air and sunk in Leeward's shoulder. Blood spurted from the wound and the hot numbness in his arm caused him to drop the weapon as he yelped.

"You goddamn chink," he yelled at Ootah.

Henson swung like he'd seen Jack Johnson do in a fight. His fist hit Leeward flush in the face, staggering him.

"I ain't done yet, snowball." Enraged, Leeward plucked the axe free from his shoulder and hefted it. Powered by desperation and greed, he charged at Henson, ignoring his wound, axe poised to do severe damage.

Henson back-peddled and, heel hitting a rock, fell over on his backside. Ootah came at Leeward but he slashed at him, driving him back. Teeth bared, Leeward lunged at Henson, who yelled shrilly.

Having nothing for defense, Henson latched onto the rock he'd tripped over. He drove its rough-hewn tip into Leeward's chest as he dropped on him. To his and Ootah's absolute amazement, in a flash of blue-white light, he exploded into flame as if he'd been roasted by a direct beam of sunlight. Not even enough time for him to scream. A rain of dark ash powdered Henson's clothes and face. He rose, and they both stared down at the charred remains of what had been John Leeward.

"Holy shit," Henson stammered.

"What was that?' Ootah said, awed.

Henson opened his hand. It was the piece of the meteorite he'd chopped loose for a sample. There was a smudge of blue on the tip of his index finger. He was afraid to rub his fingers together least the stuff ignite and burn him up, too.

"It *is* from Seqinek." Ootah said fervently.

Henson wasn't about to argue.

"Where's Leeward?" One of the crew, a mechanic named Peters, asked when Henson and Ootah returned to the three-masted Hope several hours after the incident.

"Leeward?" Henson said innocently, with a glance at Ootah. "We didn't see him."

His friend remained tight lipped.

Peary appeared, frowning at Henson. "You taking up smoking after all these years, Matt?"

"No..."

"Got some ash in your mustache." He walked off. His listing gait due to losing all his toes to frostbite.

A search party was hastily organized. The man's dogsled and team were found, but not at Mount Robeson—not that they would have found the meteorite or the burned corpse there. Leeward's dogsled was found near a snowy bank of headlands a few miles away from the cavern. There were tracks from the dogs and sled, but by mushing their teams back the way they'd come, the two had dragged snow shoes to better cover their own tracks. They had briefly considered killing the dogs and destroying the sled, but unless you were going to stew up the dogs as the last resort for food—as both men had had to do in the past—trained Malamutes and Huskies were more valuable than precious metals out here. And Henson didn't believe in killing innocent creatures.

From the faked location, Henson and Ootah knew the searchers would go out in increasing circles to find a trace of Leeward. The Hope's voyage was delayed, but despite all their searching, Leeward wasn't found. What had he gone off to investigate, they wondered? Had he stepped on what seemed to be solid land and fallen to his death in a crevasse? They were known to open like the maw of a snow beast, then go shut again without a trace, filling in on themselves from the impact of a body hitting from enough height.

"If and when the cavern is found, well," Henson reasoned to a worried Ootah, "who was to say who'd been there?"

"It's too bad. He had his faults, but to die in the cold, alone, frozen to death. He didn't deserve that." Peary said later to Henson as the explorers stood on the Hope's top deck, the chained down Tent behind them. It sat straddling the hold, suspended over steel rails. It was determined it would be easier to unload back in the States above deck rather than from within the ship.

"He's in the hands of the Lord now, sir," Henson said.

"As we all will be one day to answer for our deeds."

"Yes, that is so."

Peary regarded him evenly then walked away.

Henson and Bessie Coleman sat quietly and comfortably in lounge chairs in the back room of May-May's, closed up after the dinner rush.

At his behest, Lacy DeHavilin had invested in the diner and this room was his unofficial office. It was dark in New York City and the evening was chill.

"I know you and the cold are friends, but the rest of us ain't penguins," Coleman said. She bent to poke at the smoky logs in the wood burning stove. Embers sparked, and a tepid flame started up. She added a fresh log, closed the stove's door, and returned to her seat near him.

"You and Ootah covered up this Leeward's death? Even though it was self-defense?"

"That's right," he drew out. "I wasn't about to take my chances with the whims of the crew, all of them white. Hell this wasn't our first try at the Pole and each time I was the only negro. Sure, some were okay in their dealings with me, but I also knew several saw me as no more than Peary's uppity valet. Out there where the law was tooth and claw, who knows what they'd believe? Now, mind you, the other way around, well hell, Leeward would have said 'That nigger went crazy, his simple mind snapping from the pressure of having to keep up with us white men.' And Ootah, well, you ever hear his name, or the names of the other three Eskimos who were with us when we planted Old Glory at the top of the Earth, mentioned?"

"You've mentioned them in your talks."

He was impressed she knew that. "The white newspapers don't come to my talks."

"There is that," she agreed.

They each sipped their libations. He also didn't tell her how Peary had planned to leave him behind at their base camp and make the last surge to the Pole with only two other Eskimos. How he'd learned this overhearing two Inuit boys talking the night before. But Peary's estimations had been off. Henson could also reckon latitude and longitude. He could estimate a sledge's progress within feet, let alone miles. He'd been certain that their camp was already at the Pole. As Peary couldn't reconcile the colored Henson could be so adept,

Henson wasn't going to waste time arguing.

He had written about this publicly several years ago in the *Boston American*. But thereafter, didn't mention it—he couldn't without stewing in rancor and regret.

Finally, he said, "Peary got his pension from Congress, Bess. They've denied mine, more than once. Despite the facts, and me saving the commander's life. Twice." He said this reservedly, no more emotion behind the words than ordering a steak in a restaurant. He had long ago come to accept that fate was his to forge from life's adversities.

Coleman nodded knowingly.

He'd told her a version of the story of the cavern. He'd left out the meteorite they'd come to call the Daughter, short for the Daughter of Seqinek. She was told it was gold, and that he and Leeward and Ootah had battled, him killing the Kentuckian with a hunting knife.

"And this Davis fella, he wants that gold?" She said. "He kidnapped your Professor Ellsmere to get you to 'fess up?"

He'd also told her that Ootah and his brother Seegloo had hidden the gold. What *had* been hidden by the time he'd returned to Greenland was the meteorite with the strange power. A power he feared, then and now, would be used for evil. He also understood sooner or later he was going to have to tell her the truth. But first things first.

"Not sure. But I'm looking forward to meeting Mr. Renwick."

"Very good," she said, draining her glass. "See you tomorrow."

"Good deal." He walked her to the rear door and unlatched it. "You going to be okay? I am a gentleman, and all."

"Negro, please," she grinned, patting his cheek. She stepped out into the night and he watched her go, then closed the door.

He turned from the door when the phone rang. Not too many people knew the number to this back room. He put a hip on the desk and plucked free the receiver, while picking up the body of the instrument in his other hand to talk into the mouth piece.

"Hello?"

"Matt, it's Slip. Figured I'd take a chance calling you here seeing as how you don't keep a blower at your place."

"What you got?" When he'd talked with Latimore that day in St. Nicholas Park, he'd engaged his services.

"That egg who came at us in the park with the knife is a fella who goes by the sobriquet of Two Laces, though I have no idea why. But he's been known to do muscle work for Casper Holstein and Dutch Schultz."

"Not at the same time I'm guessing, since them two ain't exactly buddies."

The well-off Holstein was seldom-seen, at least in daylight hours. He was originally a poor boy from the West Indies and a pioneer of the numbers racket. Poet Claude McKay, among others, posited he invented the pursuit while working as a porter in a store on Fifth Avenue. He studied the way other lotteries had operated, relaying on who knew how their winning numbers were derived. For as little as a nickel, an aspirant could bet what would be the ending three-digit number derived from the tabulation of the daily New York Clearinghouse total, arrived at as the result of trading among banks. The last two numbers from the millions column of the exchange's total plus the last number from the balance's total -- both published in the late afternoon newspapers. In that way, no one could dispute what the winning numbers were.

They dreamed about them, they used the numbers of streetcars that stopped in front of their church, or the day of month of their grandma's birthday minus the date of the Emancipation Proclamation. And plenty in and around Harlem bet the numbers—particularly those who insisted they didn't. Holstein was reputed to own three apartment buildings in Harlem, he for sure owned the Turf Club, and was said to have a fine home out on Long Island. He'd also funded the literary prizes awarded by *Opportunity Magazine.*

"Correct. Two Laces was originally part of Casper's outfit, but they had a falling out over the usual story, a frail."

"I'm guessing the Dutchman is using Two Laces to help him move in on the Harlem numbers game."

"That's right. Like everything else that hothead covets, once he sets his sights on it, he'll stop at nothing to quench his thirst. At some point you have to figure it's going to be all-out war between him and the likes of Queenie and Casper. Let colored folk control that kind of money? Sheet. What self-respecting white man would let that go on?"

They both chuckled dryly.

"Any idea who on the force or in Tammany Hall he has in his pocket?" Henson said. As he'd predicted, there had been no report of the dustup at the apartment building where'd he rescued Destiny Stevenson.

"No, but he's been known to have meets over at the Cayuga Democratic Club"

The Club was a white-run organization that courted black votes in Harlem where the Club's building was located. An enterprising young man named J. Raymond Jones had started the Carver Democratic Club as a way to build up black voter empowerment.

Henson rolled a few ideas around in his head. "This has been very helpful, Slip."

"You want me to keep nosing around?"

"No, this is good, thanks."

"Thanks for the fifty."

The line disconnected.

As Henson locked up, he considered it made sense from the point of view of Dutch Schultz to kidnap Destiny Stevenson, as her father was tied in financially to St. Clair's loan operation. Maybe to force Daddy Paradise to sever those ties. Yet, except for sending Two Laces to brace him, the Dutchman had shown a restrained hand. That was not like him—this was a man who would bury an icepick in your head, then turn around and order a shrimp cocktail.

Walking toward his home, Henson wondered who had Schultz's ear and if this was about money and/or power. The attack on the airfield didn't seem to be his handiwork. He wouldn't use out-of-town muscle.

Back in his apartment, laying on his back in bed, not truly asleep or awake, he relived an incident that happened during that last push to reach the North Pole. He and the others were crossing a rivulet of moving ice floes. He was pushing a sledge loaded with provisions, no dogs. Just then the floating hunk of ice he was on tipped upward due to the shift of weight, and he was plunged into the bone-freezing water. His hood was torn off, and he let go of the sledge least it drag him down for good. But he was wearing fur gloves, and couldn't get a good grip on the ice. It was tantalizingly close, but might as well have been yards away. He was a goner and his only thought then was he was close, so close, to his goal.

Cold numbed his extremities, and try as he might, he couldn't swim well enough to remain aloft. His legs refused to kick, and he was having a hard time keeping air in his lungs. Ready to meet the Grim Destroyer, it was then an ungloved hand grasped him by the nape of his neck and, struggling together, he was hauled onto the floe. It was Ootah, who had not only saved his life, but managed got the rest of the supplies across as well.

They nodded stoically at each other.

His kamiks—sealskin boots—were removed and replaced, the water beaten out of his bearskin pants, and then they hurried to catch up with the rest. That was just how it went out there, all in a day's work. Peary, too, it turned out had also fallen into the water and had been saved by the other Eskimos.

Henson came fully awake. He hadn't recalled that near-death occurrence in a long time. Was it an omen of things to come?

CHAPTER FIFTEEN

"It does seem after solidifying matters in Chicago, Los Angeles is the city to expand in, Queenie." Charles Toliver and Queenie St. Clair walked along Amsterdam Avenue a little after breakfast. Each wore stylish clothes and hats. One of her crew trailed not too far behind doing bodyguarding duties.

Toliver continued. "Negroes in Los Angeles have been enterprising. They've started an insurance company, a film outfit, not to mention the two newspapers, *The Eagle* and *The Sentinel*.

"A legit bank, huh?" she said.

"Homefolks from Texas, Louisiana and Oklahoma are finding their way there. Escaping onerous racism for the more sunbaked variety," he said, grinning. "Jim Crow might be applied with a more subtle hand…."

"But it's applied nonetheless," she finished.

"Yes, ma'am," he affirmed. "But it's wide open out there."

On they went, discussing their plans. Thereafter, she returned to her office at the Palmetto Ambulance and Funeral Services. Venus Melenaux was waiting for her with a typewritten note she handed across. The numbers boss read it quickly.

"They're demanding fifty thousand dollars for the return of Casper." Queenie St. Clair said, sitting behind her desk, tossing the message onto it.

"That's the price," Venus Melenaux confirmed, sitting across from her. "We gotta let those bastards know it's gonna take us a few days to raise a ransom that steep. In the meantime, we need some proof Casper is okay. To our advantage, Dutch's men think we're part of his gang anyway."

"When the drop is made, they'll gun down whoever we send down and take the money," St. Clair determined.

"That's my figurin'," Melaneaux said.

St. Clair had followed up on the lead Tommy Riordan had provided. She calculated if she could be the one to free him, a grateful Holstein would be a useful asset down the line. Particularly if she could pull it off with Toliver and a few other bankers actually establishing a bank lending to negro businesses and would-be home owners out west.

"Okay, eventually a meet will be set, but we come loaded for bear."

Meleneaux's smiled and sipped her coffee. "Better clean off Papa's shotgun."

That same morning, Matthew Henson arrived ten minutes ahead of schedule at Hugo Renwick's estate out on Sands Point in Long Island. He'd been driven there by a chauffered Pierce-Arrow Runabout. Several of his neighbors saw him being picked up in the fancy car earlier. That wasn't as impressive as seeing the white driver holding the rear door open for him.

"Go on now, Matt," one said proudly.

"Have a martini for me," another said.

"Way to go, Mr. Matt," Henry the newsie had cheered, a raft of papers under his arm. He flipped the kid a fifty-cent piece, winking. "I want to see that report card, you hear?"

"Yes, sir," the thirteen year-old called back.

He'd been helping the orphan with his math and history homework when he could. He made a mental note to make sure he followed up with the youngster soon on that. Sitting in the rear of the fancy car,

151

Henson waved sheepishly at his neighbors as he rode away. The day was bright and clear, and he had to fight dozing as the car ran smoothly along the roadway. Eventually, they arrived at their destination. Henson tried to not gape at the immensity of the brick and wood structure set amid lush foliage as the car came to a stop at the front steps leading up from a circular, gravel topped driveway

Lavish was an understatement for the mansion and grounds. It was part Tudor and part medieval castle, 12,000 square feet that fronted the Atlantic. There was a tennis court, a six-car garage, a guest house bigger than most single-family homes, a boat house, and on and on. Henson wasn't so much envious as astounded. He shook his head and made up his mind to appear matter-of-fact in the face of all this excess.

"Hello, Mr. Henson, come this way," a pretty blonde-haired maid said, after opening the front door.

"Sure."

Henson was escorted out to the pool. There, lounging in chairs under an umbrella were Bessie Coleman, Shorty Duggan and another man he took to be Hugo Renwick. They had a half full glass pitcher and tall slim glasses beside them on a glass table.

"Look what the cat dragged in," Coleman said.

"Hey," he said to her and the mechanic.

"Mr. Henson, I've heard nothing but good things about you from Bessie." Renwick stood, the men shook hands.

"Thanks for having me, Mr. Renwick."

"Hugo, if I can call you Matt."

"Why not? This is some spread."

"It *is* a bit much," Renwick admitted, sitting back down again as Henson also took a seat. "But in my defense, it is also where the Institute is housed." He waved toward the house. "If things go as planned, this will be a citadel of the new world we're working to usher in." He paused. "That's why we're happy to have the talents of Miss Coleman."

"Us colored gals are doing big things," Coleman said.

152

"Have some lemonade and sit a spell." Renwick poured him a glass as Henson sat.

"What do you know about our work, Matt?"

He told Renwick about his meeting with Nikola Tesla. "But would what you're up to be a reason for violently attacking you?"

"Black and white working together as equals? That's a future some ain't too keen on," Duggan observed.

"A color blind world, huh?" Henson said dubiously. "How about a world where color only matters for identification? Where what you did and who you were was what counted?" Renwick countered.

"Amen." Henson held his glass up, tipping it toward the other three. He sampled his refreshment, enjoying the drink's tartness.

"Me and Shorty are still of the mind that shoot 'em up was about the Skhati," Coleman said. "It's a one of a kind aircraft any one of these greedy plutocrats would want to call their own."

"Would one of those plutocrats be Fremont Davis?" Henson asked.

Renwick leaned forward. "Curious that you brought him up. Isn't he the one who blocked you being accepted into the Challenger's Club?"

"I was young and foolish then," he retorted. When Henson had returned from the North Pole he'd been feted. It wasn't the same as what Peary received, but among black Americans in New York and elsewhere, and a smattering of white left and liberal press like *The Nation* and *The New York Times*, he did receive praise and recognition. Enough so that he had believed the all-white Challenger's Club of big game hunters and explorers would open its doors wide to him.

"My then-wife encouraged me to apply," Henson admitted.

"Eva," Coleman said.

"Yeah."

"Why do you say it's curious, Hugo?" Coleman said.

"I don't know about the attack on the airfield, but I have it on good authority that Davis and Dutch Schultz are working together for the time being."

Henson asked, "Why and how do you know this?"

"I don't go around with my head in the clouds all the time like my reputation suggests, Matt. I do attend to earthly matters as I have to protect my various interests."

"Meaning?" Henson said, irritated by his evasiveness. Or maybe he was just showing off to impress Coleman.

"About two or so years ago, he and I sat on the board of a petroleum enterprise. Davis, as you know, has most of his money tied up in an overseas freight business."

"That's how he became a big game hunter," Henson finished. "Using his freighters to take trips to Africa and Asia."

"Exactly. At that time there was a strike going on at the Brooklyn docks, tying up his and other owners' ships from loading or unloading. One of the straw boss longshoremen eager to please was an acquaintance of Mr. Flegenheimer, already on the rise. Seems the two had grown up together in the tenements. He made a call, and subsequently heads were broken. The strike was settled. I learned this after the fact, and that it was Davis okayed this action, not the others –though they, of course, benefitted too."

"And they're working together to do…what?" Coleman said. "The Dutchman supplying the muscle to make what happen?"

Renwick fixed Henson with a look. "There are various rumors as to what Davis is after. Some say it's about a secret cache of Alaskan gold. Others say it was to do with a hunk of precious ore unlike anything heretofore found on Earth." Renwick hunched a shoulder. "That fueled the idea in a handful of quarters that you and Peary brought more back from the Arctic than those three meteorites. That the fallout between you two was over who would control this…whatever it is."

Henson was clueless as to such rumors; it wasn't hard for him to remain blank-faced. But, eager to see what Renwick would say, he responded, "As you said, that's just gossip. Hell, I've encountered people who say we brought back one of them green men of Mars that

Tarzan fella wrote about in his yarns."

"I have heard talk of that nature as well," Renwick said. "That whatever it is, it is in fact of an extraterrestrial character."

"If that means out of this world, it sure sounds like it," Coleman noted.

Duggan said nothing, keeping his own counsel.

Henson had the feeling the industrialist knew about the Daughter, or at least had heard explicitly about it, and probably Davis had too. But how? He hadn't told Eva then, and they had divorced the following year.

He said, "Back here on Earth, I want to look into this parlay between Davis and Schultz."

"What's your angle, Matt?" Coleman asked.

"I've got a couple of clients to protect."

"Who?" Coleman said.

"Daddy Paradise and his daughter."

Coleman and Duggan cocked their heads.

"I'm betting she's out of the lollipop stage," Duggan opined.

"Funny," he intoned. It had occurred to him that the grab of Destiny Stevenson wasn't about Daddy Paradise and Queenie St. Clair and the numbers' profit. Not for Davis, anyway, but that would be a reason he could keep Schultz involved. And he was the wild card.

"Well," Renwick began, "let me have the kitchen rustle us up some food."

"Is he on the level?" Henson asked the others after Renwick left.

"You mean can he be trusted?" Coleman replied.

"I guess that's what I mean. Or part of what I mean. Will he stand by what he professes or is he full of hokum? Go the distance like Garvey no matter who comes after him?"

"Or do you mean like your buddy Daddy Paradise?" the aviatrix quipped.

Henson chuckled. "You gotta get your hands dirty if you want equality, Bessie. Ain't nobody gonna give it to you freely. We all can't be angels."

"I don't know if that's cynical or wise," Duggan noted.

"He's for real, Matt," Coleman said. "He knows he's a child of privilege and rather than gallivant around like a lot of dilettantes interested in the Negro Question or giving money to starving children in India, he knows he has to be about changing things for the long haul. We wouldn't be here if we thought different," she finished.

"Among his concerns, he's been big on supporting anti-lynching laws," Coleman added. "Not just talk, but providing money and fielding investigators like what the NAACP carried out."

"Okay, you sold me. He's on the level."

Henson tented his fingers and sat back in his seat, considering several options. Overhead a hawk came into view, circling, then going into a dive at an unseen prey beyond the hedges. Possibly he was imaging it, but the explorer had an impression of a stifled cry of a trapped animal floating to them on the wind. He sipped more lemonade. After a lunch that included more discussion about the aims of the Weldon Institute, Henson said his goodbyes and was returned to town by car.

On the drive back, he tried to think how news of the Daughter's existence might have become known. Moving the rock was a two-man job, at least. He had suggested back then to Ootah that he not use his brother to help, and his friend had assured him he that he didn't. He'd last seen Ootah in person when he'd been brought to New York about four years ago at the behest of the Clicquot Club Beverage Company as a reunion of sorts.

"Mahri-Pahluk," Ootah had shouted as Henson rushed over to him at the Brooklyn docks that day.

"Whoop halloo," Henson had shouted excitedly as both men hugged.

The two had lunch in Chinatown, as Ootah had a fondness for chow mein. They caught up on a lot of things, like Henson's son. He knew from infrequent letters transcribed by other explorers or

Christian missionaries—there was no written language among his son's people—that Anaukaq had a good life. His stepfather had long ago accepted the boy as his own, as had been related to him from the mother, Akatingwah, in a transcribed letter.

"He's getting to be quite the young man, Matthew," his friend told him while putting a mass of chow mein into his mouth. He'd first wound the noodles on a fork. "Yes, I know to use this in public among the kahdonah." He said, noting his friend's stare. The word meant white-skinned. Most of the customers in the place were.

"You need to see him. Letters aren't enough." His friend's English had improved markedly since the two had last been together.

"I know. I guess, well, there is the money, but that's an excuse."

"Yes, it is. You know how to get there."

Ootah had not stayed in Moriussaq all this time. He had been visited with a wanderlust after first seeing New York when the North Pole expedition had returned. For a while, he'd lived in Svalbard, an archipelago a few hundred miles south of the Pole. Via signing on ships and even a missionary tour, he'd been to Denmark, Russia and even lived for a stint in London where he'd obtained a tailored suit on Savile Row, which he now wore at their meal.

"Bespoke is what the English call it," his friend had told him, running his thumb up and down the underside of one of the suit's wide lapels. For the last few months, he'd also told Henson, he'd been back in their village. "Anaukaq's coming along as a harpooner," he added.

Henson beamed. His own family environment had not been nurturing after his folks died when he and his sisters were young. His stepmother, Nelle, was a cruel, unfulfilled woman who beat him and the girls. Finally getting up some size, he'd said his goodbye to her with a sock to her eye and a warning that he'd be back if she hurt his sisters. He certainly needed to do better by his boy. What exactly was holding him back? Did he need to be a success before returning? And what was success as measured by what he did now for a living? A part-time travelogue show on the radio, hawking soda pop and swinging on ropes through gangsters' windows. By hook or by crook, he could get back there if he really wanted to. After all, the Grim Destroyer didn't care who he claimed, and given his current career—if that's what it was—he could go at any time.

"I promise to make amends, brother."

Ootah stopped chewing, swallowed his food and, clasping his hands together, bowed slightly at the man across the table from him. "By Peeshahhah who guides our way through storm and dark of day."

"By Peeshahhah who guides our way through storm and dark of day," Henson repeated, also clasping his hands together and bowing slightly. They evoked the name of the Great Hunter. There could be no dishonor.

And yet here he was, no closer to retuning to northern Greenland than he had been those four years ago. They'd also talked about the Daughter during Ootah's several days in the city, which included the two being interviewed in *The New York Amsterdam News* and on the Clicquot Club radio show, plus a special broadcast from Abyssiniann Baptist Church. Ootah had said no more than that the Daughter had been secreted away, and that he and only one other knew where it was. Henson hadn't asked him who the other one was, as he'd assumed it'd either been Seegloo or Ooqueah, the other two Inuit who'd reached the North Pole. He didn't want to know. Imagining word of the discovery might be found out one day, he wanted ignorance about its whereabouts in case he should be tortured to reveal any details.

Of course, that didn't mean Egingwah hadn't spied on his bother to find out what he was up to. That made Henson sound as paranoid as Peary had become, but there you had it. Word of what Ootah had moved could have made it back to the commander here in the States. Hell, for all he knew Egingwah, or whoever, could have returned to America.

It was also possible that Davis, upon hearing of the possibility of the Daughter, could have mounted an expedition on the hush-hush and gone up there. That was certainly the type of thing he'd do, wanting to test himself and satisfy his curiosity. And who knew, maybe the good Reverend Christofferson got to talking to his mistress one evening and blabbed about the tear sent from the sun goddess. That he'd asked about it could have been the source of the rumors. Back in town, he asked Renwick's driver to let him off before reaching his home. From a payphone in a drugstore, he called Destiny Stevenson at her music shop.

"Hey, stranger," she said sweetly over the line.

"Didn't mean to disappear. I'm not that kind of fella."

"I know you're not."

"You busy tonight? Want to drop by my broadcast at Smalls and we can get something to eat after?"

"Sounds great," she said.

He gave her the details and rang off. He then walked back to his apartment, using the alone time to decide several matters, including what to tell the Weldon Institute. At his place, he reviewed the notes for his weekly broadcast and made his way to Seventh Avenue near 135th Street and Smalls' Paradise, "Harlem's Hot Spot" as it said on its menus. The cabaret was about two blocks from Striver's Row. The nightclub had an elongated marquee over the main entrance with the name of the place—minus an apostrophe—in relief letters and pulsing lights. The building it was in resided next door to the Mayfield Beauty Shoppe offering extra Marcelling. As the club was in the basement, Henson technically did his broadcasts for WGJZ in a supply room-turned-studio off the club floor. When the evening show was on, waiters would dance the Charleston while deftly holding trays and stomping the rug between the tables. The club could handle some 1,500 customers and was known to pack in hundreds more if, say, Cab Calloway's band was playing.

"How's it rollin', Matt?" the doorman said.

"If I had your hand."

"Yeah, man," the stockier one said, pushing the swing door open to the still closed club.

He was an ex-heavyweight who'd had a so-so career in the ring.

Henson walked through the club where the staff was busy setting out utensils and cloth napkins on the tables. Several musicians were on stage, blowing or plucking their instruments going over their arrangements. A horn player nodded at Henson. The broadcast room was behind and to the right of the stage. It was near the office, and he saw the owner, Edwin Smalls, seated at his desk doing paperwork. Always sharply dressed, his suit jacket was on a hanger behind him and golden cufflinks sparkled on his wrists.

"The Snow Leopard," he said, looking up briefly.

"Brother Smalls."

Past him, the studio had a padded swing door with a porthole window. On the outside was a hand-painted sign reading: "On Air", and over that, a red light had been installed. Beneath was a speaker, its heavy wire leading into the compact broadcast space. There were several folding chairs set up for listeners. No one was there, yet.

Inside, the engineer, Wally Carlyle was waiting for Henson. He was a youngish white man with a crew cut, natty bowtie and pressed blue shirt.

"Hello, Matt," he said.

"How's it going, Wally?"

"The same ol' jive, man," The engineer, a jazz fan, said. A control console had been built in the room. There were several other instruments in the small room, as well. Carlyle flipped several toggle switches on the main console, tapping his finger on the extended microphone to check the sound level. He noted the flux of needles on his gages and turned one two knobs with the precision of a surgeon. Henson locked the door and flicked on the "On Air" light.

He then sat on a stool at the end of the console, the engineer positioned the microphone on its swing arm over him. Both of them looked at the wall clock to check the time. Henson shifted in his seat, adjusting the microphone. He placed his papers on the console and cleared his throat. The engineer sat down, too and, eyes back to the clock, counted down with his fingers pointed at Henson. He got to his index finger and jabbed it toward the other man while he flipped two switches, bringing them live on the airwaves.

"And now, faithful listeners," came the mellifluous voice of stage actor Warren William over the recording lathe, "once again it is time for the weekly installment of Strange Journeys. From the Aztecs to the Yoruba, from the Ting Dynasty to the War of the Roses, you'll hear tales of tropical jungles in unforgiving climes, fantastic treks through the sun-drenched deserts of lost kingdoms and expeditions into the lands of ice and snow." A dramatic pause, then William concluded, "I give you now your host, the hunter, trapper, linguist, and storied man of tomorrow…today, Matthew Alexander Henson."

Carlyle winked at Henson as he stopped the recording device. It was a bit much, Henson knew, but Lacy DeHavilin had insisted on engaging William's services and had written the over-the-top introduction herself. Wickedly, she'd included a line about his privates being the size of a mule's but thankfully only he had read that passage. Though, dammit, he had the unerring feeling the unexpurgated version would show up one day, probably in her ribald memoir. Focusing, he began, reading a passage from his book.

"The route to Cape Columbia is through a region of somber magnificence. Huge beetling cliffs overlook the pathway, dark savage headlands, around which we had to travel, project out into the ice-covered waters of the ocean, and vast stretches of wind-swept plains meet the eye in alternate changes." Henson finished the reading and segued from setting the scene into a story about Roald Amundsen and the flight of the Norge, a dirigible designed by General Umberto Nobile, to reach the North Pole two years ago.

"The airship and her sixteen-man crew not only reached the Pole, but went on to Alaska as planned," Henson said into the microphone. "Overall, their flight covered more than 6,000 miles, a lot of that unexplored territory. Can you imagine?" he breathed, "what that must have been like? The excitement and exhilaration of seeing that uncharted vast area? I can tell you from personal experience, my friends, there's no thrill quite like it, you and the wilderness of snow and wonder."

The engineer dipped his head in appreciation of the picture Henson had painted.

He continued, "Unfortunately, my dear audience, once success was achieved, Amundsen and Nobile had a falling out, as each believed he should get the lion's share of the credit for the Arctic flight." He looked off into the distance, a crooked smile composing his features. "But really, the lesson to be learned in these sort of endeavors is that it's a team effort that's key. Only in working together can the hardships Mother Nature and mankind throw at us be overcome."

The engineer nodded.

"Next week, I'll conclude with the excursion the two were involved in earlier this year." He lowered his voice as he ended the sentence, an ominous foreshadowing of events. For both men had perished after recently having returned to the unyielding top of the world. Nobile had gone missing in the airship Italia, and Amundsen had joined the search for his estranged friend. His plane crashed and he'd died. Nobile was never found.

The half-hour broadcast also included Henson answering letters from his listeners. He rustled papers louder than normal for a sound effect at the start of this segment. "I have a letter from a Miss Thelma Rudolph who asks if I'll ever again return to the North Pole. She also asks why we don't have a fund drive among our churches to sponsor an expedition of a select sampling of our negro leaders and I lead them there." Henson set the letter aside, an open envelope paperclipped to it.

"Well, Miss Rudolph, that sounds like a fine undertaking, one that plucks the strings of my heart. But right now, what with rent parties a necessity and groceries going up in Harlem, seems it be best to concentrate money-making efforts closer to home. While we do own some properties but plenty of these buildings are in outside hands.

The Urban League recently reported that forty-eight percent of us colored renters pay nearly twice as much our white counterparts in other areas of New York. A four-room apartment north of Central Park goes for $55 versus the same going for $32 elsewhere. Many of us have boarders on different shifts sharing mattresses as a way to meet these exorbitant prices.

"Now don't get me wrong, I ain't calling for revolution, but I am saying like with those flyboys and their blimp, we need to put our heads together and pool our money and efforts for the betterment of all." The stool creaked as he shifted his weight. "Well the ol' clock on the wall and the steely eye from engineer Wally says it's that time again. I must take my leave."

Wally the engineer queued up the recorded music of the Clicquot Club Band. Over this, Henson talked as he brought the music sound level down some.

"And remember, there's only one discovery of refreshment for me my fellow travelers, Clicquot Club Pale Dry Ginger Ale. Yes, pale… dry…ginger…ale. Made from only the purest of ingredients including naturally sweet cane sugar. It is a refresher like no other." Henson flung his arms wide. Carlyle queued up a rapid-fire tom-tom beat like raindrops splattering on a tin roof to close out the program.

"Good stuff, Matt," the younger man said.

"Thanks, Wally."

"Say, I hear the muckety-mucks at Zenith are talking syndication. Looking to get your show picked up on a few more stations. They've been getting inquiries from Pittsburgh and Baltimore, and even in a place called West Memphis."

"Well, all reet."

"Ha."

Zenith Radio Corporation supplied all the radio equipment for the studio in the night club and had paid for the installation of the electrical machinery. The connection had been made years ago as Peary had used Zenith radios on his expeditions and had even appeared in a print ad extolling their virtue at one point. Yet, unlike other white controlled entities, the higher-ups in the company didn't pretend that Henson did not exist. There was a fondness for him among them it seemed. The two men said their goodbyes after they stepped back into the larger area.

"You sounded good," Destiny Stevenson said, rising from her folding chair.

"Why thank you, ma'am." He bowed slightly, taking her hand and kissing it as if a wayward count on holiday.

"Oh, you charmer."

They locked gazes, then he said, "I promised you dinner, as I recall."

"You did, here?"

"It gets a might rambunctious out there at the tables. I was thinking more intimate surroundings."

"You were, were you?"

In another part of town, the moon shone on a one-story garage where two others met in secrecy. They were in the office of Granady Truck Repair & Parts in the Bronx. The firm actually used the trucks to ferry illegal beer and stronger spirits across the five boroughs.

"Here it is," Detective Kevin Hoffman said. He handed a file folder to Dutch Schultz. The plainclothesman looked more dour than usual.

Shultz handed the file unopened to his driver and bodyguard, Vin O'Hara. The gangster turned to go.

"Aren't you forgetting something?" Hoffman said.

"Oh yeah," Schultz grinned, nodding toward O'Hara. He had a lit cigar between his kid-gloved fingers.

The driver reached into his coat pocket with his free hand and withdrew a stuffed envelope. He flipped it to the detective. As this happened, O'Hara managed to open the folder slightly and see the photograph clipped on top of the typewritten pages in there. He maintained his poker face.

"Don't spend that all in one place, Judas." Schultz laughed as the two hoodlums left.

Hoffman stood still for several moments then pocketed the envelope and departed as well.

At an eatery called the Sugar Hill Café on 144th Street near Amsterdam, Henson and Stevenson had a meal of smothered steak, collard greens and steamed carrots. More than once, Stevenson slipped her foot out of her low-heeled shoe and tapped her toes on his shoe. They had coffee after dinner.

"What else are you going to show a girl tonight, Mr. Henson?"

"You big city wimmen are kind of bold, aren't you?"

"We must be bold if we're to seize our future," she said.

He frowned. "Your father says that, doesn't he?"

"He does, indeed. And we have front row seats for the to-do."

He sipped contemplatively. "I talked to your father, and I'll be going over the security with OD day after tomorrow. Among the crew he's rounded up a few former bodyguards for Garvey. The kind of gents who didn't blink when they went up against them Kluxers."

"You expecting trouble?"

"No, but I don't want to get caught with my pants down."

"Oh, no, we wouldn't want that," she teased. "What about the police?"

"What about them?" he huffed. "They aren't providing any personnel, not even Cole Rodgers." He had more of his coffee. "You're not too full are you, Des?"

"I'm feeling pretty spry…pops."

"Good, wouldn't want you getting too sleepy yet."

"What sort of night do you have planned, Mr. Arctic Adventurer?" She leaned forward, whispering, "We gonna do some exploring back at your place?"

Grinning Henson said, "Before we get to that, we got us some burglarizing to do."

"Huh?"

CHAPTER SIXTEEN

"Five in the corner pocket," Fremont Davis announced. He leaned onto the pool table and his stick struck the cue ball dead center. The cue ball rolled over the green cloth. At first, it looked as if he was going to hit his opponent's ball, but it angled just enough away that it didn't and then banged against the five solid just so. The ball rolled languidly, and dropped into the called pocket.

Hugo Renwick drew on his cigar and let out a stream of smoke. He stood holding his pool cue. The two men were in the red velvet-wallpapered game room of the Challenger's Club.

"Nice shot," he said.

"One must keep a steady nerve." Davis stalked around the table, figuring out his next shot.

The club stood on the Upper East Side with Central Park in the background, in a four-story townhouse. Its façade was in the style of German vernacular architecture that harkened back to the days when Manhattan was a Dutch colony. It was made of brick and wood and there had been some recent renovations befitting the Beaux Arts style that had enthralled the modern-day customers of numerous architectural firms. It had tiered sloping roofs, and stood as a somber edifice to the desire for humans to uncover the mystery and wonder of the planet they lived on.

"Is that why you invited me, Davis? To remind me of your

resolve?"

The big game hunter stroked a finger and thumb down his goatee. "What if it's to join forces rather than work at cross purposes?" He tapped the tip of his cue stick on the table's rail. "The nine in the side pocket." He began lining up his shot. "The aims of your institute and mine are not diametrically opposed, you know."

"They are in how to achieve them."

Davis thumped the cue ball and it struck its intended target a glancing blow. The ball struck the pocket point and caromed away. Davis took a sip from his whiskey and, picking up his lit cigar next to it, he filled his mouth with smoke then pursing his lips, exhaled the fumes.

"No sense revisit our old arguments, Hugo. But you will grant me that human nature given new technologies tend to use them against each other to try and gain the upper hand."

"That include your views of the darker races, Davis?" He pointed his cue at the bookcase. "Is that a first edition of Mitchell's *An Essay upon the Causes of the Different Colours of People in Different Climates.* I see, too, Kant's *On the Different Races of Man.* Preposterous supposed scientific conclusions about the negro's primitive nervous systems, their superstitions and so on. I imagine there's a whole shelf devoted to phrenology around her somewhere. Possibly in your office upstairs."

Davis laughed and had another sip of whisky. "Hugo, you of all people believe in vigorous intellectual debate. Indeed, up in my office are books by Fredrick Douglass and W.E.B. DuBois. Books I've read cover to cover. I ultimately have the negro's best interest in mind, along with that of all humanity."

"Like your partnership with Dutch Schultz."

"I can't ride as tall a horse as you can, hobnobbing with that flying woman and so forth. Progress is messy work."

"Meaning I might have to get out of your way?"

"I had nothing to do with that attack on your airfield."

"But you know who did. Some other member of your little cabal,

I'm guessing."

"Not everyone is as tolerant as I am. You're employing a woman aviator—a black woman at that—and her Loyal Order of Hibernia mechanic." He tsk-tsked.

"One of my competitors figured to cash in on the Schultz angle. Blame him as cover for their deed." Renwick had been doing some digging.

"As I said, Hugo, it's messy work."

Renwick shot, dropping one of his striped balls in a pocket.

"Sit tight, and honk twice if you notice anybody going in." Henson and Stevenson sat in a seven year-old Chevy 490 he'd borrowed from May Maynard. One of its cylinders needed a ring job. It was night, and they were parked outside the Challenger's Club. Davis and Renwick's pool game some hours over. Henson's plan didn't include having to make a quick getaway, at least he hoped not. From where the car was, they had an eye on the front of the place. More than one window was lit in its upper stories.

"There's people in there, Matt."

"I don't plan to be doing any visiting."

"You know what I mean." She kissed him. Both hands holding his face to hers. Her fingers were surprisingly cold.

"I'll be careful."

Recalling her rescue, she asked, "You figuring to climb up the side and go through a window?"

He held up a ring of several skeleton keys. "Nothing that strenuous—until later."

They kissed again briefly. "You're just full of surprises."

"Ain't I?"

When Henson's admission to the all-white club had been rejected, he'd fumed and become depressed for a time. After all he'd been through, all that he'd endured, he'd proven his competence by white standards, yet still racist whim and caprice had won out. In the letter sent to him, the message read in part: "While we acknowledge your contributions to the momentous event that is the planting of our flag at the North Pole, you were nonetheless under the command of Captain Peary. And as such, akin to the Eskimos who were his bearers, you did not initiate the fundraising and strategies of these expeditions to northern Greenland. Therefore, at this time, we must humbly decline your desire to join our august body. Should matters change in the foreseeable future, please don't hesitate to contact us anew." It was signed by Fremont Davis.

"Should matters change," Henson had sneered. "When the goddamn cow jumps over the moon," he'd railed, drunk. He'd gone on a three-day bender and it was his then-wife Eva Henson, née Flint, who'd snapped him out of his tailspin. It had started with her slapping his face as he lay on the carpet in their apartment rank in his underwear.

"Matt, you drink yourself to death, and they win. Become a hermit and lock yourself away from the world, and they win. Or you can get your head out of your behind, write the story as you know it, and go on from there with your chin up."

Good thing he'd listened to her, as well as her invaluable work in editing and suggestions on how best to translate his diary entries and recollections into the original draft of the manuscript. It then went through more revisions in the hands of the publisher, Fredrick A. Stokes, sanitizing several sections, including the mention of the birth of his son, a relationship he'd had before marrying Eva. Stokes was worried if readers knew Henson had relations with an Inuit woman, they might wonder if the married Peary had been faithful. Stokes knew both men had had mixed-race offspring, but decided it was better for the Peary legacy not to bring this up. Henson had disagreed, but Eva had convinced him this first book would put him back out there, and less controversy the better. Later he could return to Greenland and reunite with his kin, and in a follow-up book, more of a memoir of his entire life, he could tell the full story. Grudgingly, he'd gone along with that notion. He was pleased with the yarn-spinner Stokes had brought in, a six-three gent bronzed from his boating in the Caribbean and an all-around outdoorsman. This fella punched up the action passages in the final manuscript.

Pausing at the delivery door in the rear of the building, he considered whether his wanderings had led to his divorce. Now, Destiny Stevenson sat on lookout, another good woman, it was turning out. Maybe this time he'd get it right. Henson used one of his skeleton keys to unlock the door. As his ex-wife had predicted after his account was published and there was renewed interest in his past, he could finally see his future.

Easing into the darkened kitchen, Henson was careful not to disturb any of the pots and pans in overhead racks. It was said the kitchen had been redesigned by the famous French chef and restaurateur Georges Escoffier. While Henson wasn't friends with the likes of the Club's head chef, he was friends with a handful of waiters and busboys, all of them black except for a few Filipinos. One of those waiters had been in May-May's that day discussing Negro League versus the white baseball players. Several years before, this man had made a set of keys for Henson on the sly after Henson had gotten the man's sister out of a tough spot with a boyfriend handy with a knife.

Leaving the kitchen, he moved along a passageway lined with portraits of the likes of Allan Quatermain, Phileas Fogg, Gertrude Bell, and several other notable adventurers. He reached a turn and went left, having reconnoitered sections of the club over time. It wasn't as if he'd planned to blow the place up, but had made it his business to know the ins and outs of the establishment. Maybe in the back of his mind he wanted to start a club for the forgotten and overlooked explorers, by definition non-whites, and to needle the stuff shirts of the Challengers Club, steal their layout.

To reach the stairs leading upward, he had to pass by the main drawing room. At this hour of the evening, although the kitchen was closed, and the front door bolted, there was a skeleton staff, as the club had an around-the-clock policy for certain members. And though he was no longer the president of the board, Henson knew Davis had an office on the third floor given his family claimed roots in starting the organization.

He had to be exposed to get to the stairs, and he waited, crouching at the end of the passageway. Henson was primed, like being out in the jungle or the tundra, alert for animal sounds—four or two-legged. He heard snoring and grinned. He crept along, the pocket doors to the drawing room were open about the width of his hand. He saw one of the old timers asleep in a plush chair, the bulldog edition of the newspaper wrinkled under his hand. At his elbow was an empty glass that probably once held a libation stronger than the ginger ale Henson hawked. Large polished elephant tusks, one on each side, flanked the brick fireplace. In its maw, the charred remains of logs were streaked with blots of red, as if eaten from within by molten termites.

Henson went past and in the gloom started up the stairs gingerly. From above—paused on the landing at the bend of the stairs—he heard creaks of the wood beneath the runner. He swore softly. If it was a member, he couldn't pretend to be a waiter. He wasn't dressed properly to pull that off. If it was one of the staff, he couldn't put them in the position of having to cover for him, placing their job—and maybe their liberty—in jeopardy. He climbed over the railing, but didn't drop down, that would have made too much noise. Rather, he hung there, hands gripping the outer string of the staircase. He hoped whoever was descending wasn't looking that close at the sides of the steps.

From where he was, Henson couldn't see feet or legs, but heard the approach. The footfalls faded away again as the person reached the ground floor and walked away. He clambered back over the hand-tooled mahogany railing and continued upward without further incident. He reached the third floor and the locked door to Davis' office. He tried using his skeleton keys, but was thwarted. Davis had changed his lock since he'd had this set made. At the end of the hallway there was a window overlooking the side street. He went out onto the ledge.

With his sealskin gloves on, Henson clung to the rough brick face, edging around the building on the narrow ledge. Fortunately for him, Davis commanded a corner office. He wasn't as noticeable up here as he might be directly out front. Also, there was partial cover from the overgrown branches and leaves of a looming maple tree.

Sure enough, the window wasn't latched, and he let himself into the room. It was spacious and decorated with various archeological and big game items. These included a stuffed and mounted lion head, a Nuxalk totem pole he identified, to an Egyptian New Kingdom sarcophagus. Various amulets, masks, statuettes and a variety of Japanese swords also adorned the office. Off to his right, an inner door was ajar. Soft light and low voices came from in there. Henson stiffened as the shadows got larger. He got unstuck and hid, not in the sarcophagus as no doubt the lid was nailed shut, but behind a 19th century rectangular standing Chinese hat chest. Engraved on its doors were four five-clawed dragons chasing a flaming pearl. It was set near a far corner, and he moved it out an inch or so from where it stood.

A cord was pulled on a green-shaded lamp. Illuminated in its warm light was Davis and a woman who had Asiatic features. But she was copper-skinned and her hair was frizzy. Davis was leaning into her, and her hip hitched onto the front of the desk. He had a hand around her waist and she held a martini glass. She sipped from it and gave him a quick kiss.

"Now, you behave," she said, taking him in over the rim of her glass.

"How do you expect me to with one so beauteous as you?"

Henson had to stop himself from chuckling.

"I am not so easily flattered," the woman said.

"Miss Petersen, you wound me."

"Not so's you'd notice. Not like our lion friend there." She pointed to the mounted head with her martini glass.

"Ha, he never saw it coming."

"That's what they all say."

172

They kissed again and left the room by the main door, holding hands. Henson stepped out from behind the piece of furniture. He reconsidered the racial makeup of the woman and concluded she was part Eskimo. The other part was white, and he'd guessed it must be Danish given her name, but not necessarily. He'd encountered biracial Inuit before, but he couldn't recall meeting one in New York. Her accent suggested she'd been raised among English speakers. She had to be the one Ellsmere had mentioned.

He went to the desk and was glad to find that wasn't locked either. Henson scanned through the papers in the middle drawer and found a stack of photographs with him as the subject. These he removed and looked at more closely, holding them under the light of the lamp. The photos had been taken recently, given the models of cars in the shots. More than one was taken from above, showing him leaving or entering his apartment building. He had seen these sorts of shots before, where the photographer used a telescopic lens. There had been a few with them at various intervals of their expeditions, and he remembered one of the photographers showing him that sort of lens. It looked something like a telescope. That fellow, assigned by *National Geographic Magazine*, used the lens to take pictures of polar bears from yards away. It was *National Geographic* who'd sponsored their last expedition, the one to finally reach the North Pole.

Davis was having him followed. But did he believe the Daughter was in the city? He looked through the rest of the photos and gritted his teeth. There was one of him on the grounds of Columbia University. He didn't think it was the day he'd been out there with Ellsmere's notes. He'd been on alert then, checking his surroundings and was certain no one had been watching him when he'd gone there to hide the papers in the basement. This shot was taken before then. Henson realized he'd have to be much more careful. Henson returned to photographs to the middle drawer, in the order he found them. Finding nothing else of interest, he closed the drawer and looked through the papers on the desktop.

On top of a sheaf of typewritten pages—minutes from a recent board meeting—he found a torn piece of newspaper with an address and name written on it in Brooklyn. He could tell from what he could read of the newsprint, this was a recent notation. A horn sounded twice outside, and he looked toward the window then back at the sheet in his hand. Leaving the papers in the desk, he committed the address to memory and had to pull his hand back from instinctively tugging the cord on the desk lamp. His senses heightened like in the wild, he was aware of footfalls approaching from the hallway. This time Henson didn't rush to his hiding place. He stood still at the door and listened, having determined it wasn't Davis and the woman returning.

"I'll start at the library," one voice said. Henson could tell it belonged to a woman of a certain age. And that she was black.

"Okay, I'll start on them offices on the third and work my way down." The two voices were heavy with years of thankless labor.

Off the cleaning women trundled, Henson heard a bucket knocking against a leg. He eased the door open and went along the hall and downstairs swiftly. Back through the kitchen and out the delivery door. At this time of night there was little traffic, and he walked across the street and got into the car with Stevenson.

"Thanks for the warning," he said.

"I saw them walking up, and figured if they were downstairs cleaning they'd see you."

"Good for me they were starting from the top down."

She got the engine going. "Are you always so lucky?"

He gave her a sideways glance as they pulled away. "Looks like I'll be testing that notion."

"How do you mean?"

"I think I know where they're holding my friend, Henrik. But I don't think me crashing through a window is going to get him out of where they have him."

She started out the windshield, glossy streams of reflected light bright against the glass. "What do you plan to do?"

He paused then, "Make some noise."

"Huh?"

He explained what he'd found. As they neared his place he asked her, "Circle the block, would you?"

"Okay."

As she did so, he spotted the tan Chrysler parked toward the far end of the block. He didn't see anyone in the car. "Park up here, okay?"

"What's up?"

"Seems a couple of eager beavers might have dropped by unannounced. And you know how I'm a stickler for etiquette."

She looked at him askance and parked.

"I'll be right back."

"Oh no you don't, Mr. Henson. I'm not getting cut out of all the action."

"This could be dangerous."

"I know," she said, squeezing his knee.

"Then follow my lead, got it?"

She saluted. "Aye, aye, captain."

Walking up to his apartment building, he put a finger to his lips and pointed up at his window overlooking the street. The shade was down, and the lights were off. But a beam from a flashlight briefly shone in the gap of the end of the shade and the windowsill.

"Who's up there?" she whispered.

He told her about the Mutt & Jeff team who braced him.

"You can't go stormin' up there and beat on them, Matt. They're government men and could shoot you without breaking a sweat, even in the heart of Harlem."

He wondered whether they were only searching his place, or lying in wait to waylay him and carry him off to work him over. "Let's see if I can flush them out. Come on."

They entered through the front door, but instead of going upstairs, he guided her along the passageway to a door tucked away in the dark under the stairs. He took out his skeleton keys, and unlocked it.

"How many keys you got?" she said in his ear.

Growling, he said, "I guess all that time in the Arctic taught me the Grim Destroyer can come at you from any direction. All around town I keep stuff socked away that might come in handy one way or the other. Never know when you're going to be in need."

On the floor, in the compact supply closet, Henson had another of his shoeboxes with a few smoke bombs in it. He got this and a cleaning rag out. They had to step back into the street as he didn't dare turn on the hallway light. But under the glow of a streetlamp he modified one of his bombs, explaining to Stevenson what he was doing—he swapped out the igniter and, using a torn strip of the cleaning rag, made a fuse he stuffed into the smoke bomb.

. They returned to his building and up the stairs they went. Tiptoeing to his door, he put his ear to the panel, and could hear the two going through his place. Maybe, he figured, they weren't too worried about him suddenly coming home and finding them, given they were G-men and, really, what could he do about them burglarizing his place?

"Light it," he said to Stevenson, holding the canister.

She struck a wooden match and got the makeshift fuse burning. He set the device down against the door and the two crept back to the stairwell, Henson counting to himself. Heading back down, he signaled Stevenson.

"Oh my God," she wailed.

"Fire, fire," Henson yelled.

They pounded down the stairs, wanting to be heard. They then rushed back outside. By now smoke was filling the hallway.

Upstairs at his door, the bulldog government man snatched it open, a sap in his other hand. "What the hell?" he snarled, the smoke bomb falling inward. The taller one came out of the bedroom in his fedora.

Somebody put on the lone overhead light in the hallway, and several sleepy-eyed tenants came out of doorways in their underwear, pajamas or hastily putting on robes. Light spilled from behind their forms. The two white men stood out like giraffes in a dog pound.

"Shit," The bulldog one said, picking up the now depleted smoke bomb. "That goddamn sneaky darkie."

"Who you callin' a darkie, cracker? And what devilment are you two up to in Matt's apartment?" Edna Mullins demanded, her hair tied up in a scarf. She pointed at the object in the shorter one's hand. "And you set that thing off pretending there was a fire? What you two pales up too, huh?" she repeated.

The bulldog one was inclined to argue. His colleague intervened. "Let's get out of here before you cause a riot."

The two stared away, Mullens and several others glaring at them as they went.

CHAPTER SEVENTEEN

"Okay, try this," Destiny Stevenson said, handing a throwing star she'd modified to Henson. Inset in the center was a copper disk the size of a quarter. "Use that plank of wood I set up," she added.

Henson hefted the weight in his hand and spun the shuriken at the plank. He bit his bottom lip as he did so. "I didn't compensate correctly." Nonetheless, the star struck the wood and electricity crackled after the center piece split open.

Henson said, "Wow."

"The problem is the casing is…temperamental, let's say. I'm worried if you walk around with that thing up your sleeve, it might break and shock you."

"I'll see what I can do."

"Right out of whaddya call it?" an impressed Bessie Coleman said.

"Science fiction," Stevenson said.

"Yeah," Coleman said, snapping her fingers. "I read one of those stories once, all about metal men and half naked blondes screaming a lot." She eyed Henson. "Got a stack of those on your nightstand do you, Matt?"

"He better not," Stevenson cracked. She began adjusting her copper disks.

"If we could get back to business." He did have a copy of *Weird*

178

Tales somewhere in his apartment, but no sense bringing that up.

They were in Stevenson's workshop, a converted back room of her music shop. The three stood before a workbench where she had modified some of Henson's other gear, and there were a few prototypes of her own making as well.

"What's this?" Coleman said, pointing at two capsule-shaped canisters joined in the middle by a short tube. All over it was silver, and the canisters were about the length of a comb.

Stevenson smiled, picking the device up. 'It's meant to disorient your foe. I figured that might come in handy, considering." She explained what the gizmo did.

Henson and Coleman exchanged a knowing nod.

They went over more of the equipment while Stevenson finished her tinkering. Afterward Henson tucked the devices away in two padded leather gym bags.

"Seven o'clock, don't be late," Henson said to Stevenson and Coleman.

"Wouldn't think of it," the flyer said.

Stevenson locked up her store, and the three left the building by the back stairs. He gunned the motorcycle to life and waved at the two women who got into a Ford.

Given he knew at least the two government men were bird-dogging him, Henson had taken precautions arriving here, doubling back at times, taking narrow passageways and so on.

Later, as the sun set, the three began converging on their target, the Granady Truck Repair & Parts company in the Bronx. The place was on Kingsbridge Road a few blocks from where it ended at Fordham. This was the address on the note he'd found in Davis' desk. Once he'd confirmed from Slip Latimore the business was a front controlled by Dutch Schultz, he was pretty certain this was where Ellsmere was being held. Near the garage he met the newsboy, Henry. This was far outside the young man's regular route, but he'd paid him to recruit a few of his fellow newsies from around here to keep an eye on the garage. They told Henry what they'd seen, and now he told Henson.

"There's the usual mechanics closing up in there," Henry Davenport him. "My pals figure no more than three of 'em in there this time of the afternoon, Mr. Matt."

He handed the young man a five. "Anything else I should know?"

The kid smiled at the money before tucking it away. "Yeah, there's two other mugs of the gat variety who hang around. Sometimes different guys, but always two of 'em."

"Now you're talkin'." He handed over another dollar and the kid went on, the bulldog edition of his papers under an arm. The frontpage story was about several underworld types associated with the Dutch Schultz gang shot dead in a grocery store in the Bronx. A hidden room was discovered, empty, but it was surmised recently occupied. Bullet patterns indicated handguns and a shotgun were used.

Henson, his gunny sack over his shoulder like a delivery man, and walked past an Italian delicatessen. Inside, through the open doorway, he saw an older woman conversing in Italian with the counterman who was wrapping up a length of hard salami. Rounding a corner, there was an empty milk wagon at the curb. A horse was not hitched to it, but there was a barn across the way and the smell of the animals was strong. Further along in a luggage shops' alcove, he met up with his compatriots. The shop owner frowned at the site of three negroes congregating in front of his window, not sure of what to make of two women wearing pants and leather coats. They walked back toward the parked milk wagon least they rouse the man further.

He told them what he'd learned. "I figure, we wait till the mechanics leave, then proceed with the plan."

"Sounds right," Bessie agreed.

Stevenson was at the corner, looking down the street at the garage. She had a dual clasp messenger bag in hand and strapped it around her torso as she walked back to the others. Looking around conspiratorially, she reached into the bag and handed Henson the modified throwing stars.

"I think these are more stable, less likely to go off prematurely."

"A perfectionist, huh?"

She flashed a wry look at him.

Coleman said, "A couple of the mechanics are just leaving."

"Okay, I'm going to get in position," Henson said.

Going back onto the main thoroughfare, twilight fell, the grey light much like the in between of the Arctic. A transitory state in which anything could happen. Now, three men stood outside, with one in a newsboy cap laughed at a clever remark from one of the others. Henson crossed the street before reaching them. Black folks weren't unknown in the Bronx, but they weren't plentiful, and he didn't want to draw unnecessary attention.

As if to taunt him, a street lamp came on as he passed underneath. Its bright white light illuminated his form sharply. But the men across the street weren't paying him any attention. One of them padlocked a chain securing the front bay doors, and the three departed, two of them walking off in the same direction, and the third the opposite. Henson lingered along the sidewalk, and when the mechanics were no longer in sight, double-backed to the facility. As he'd rode toward the garage, he'd reconnoitered the area. He walked through an overgrown lot of grass and weeds on the same block as the garage. Straight ahead, he came to the end of the lot at the wall of a two-story building. He knew from his scouting, there was a space behind the most immediate building bordering the lot to his right and a wooden fence. He went through the gap in the fence toward the garage. It was a narrow passage and he had to hold his bag in front of him. There was junk to get past and he climbed over. He was now at the rear of the garage where the gap. There was light from a window in the rear.

Carrying over the rusted hulk of a discarded metal cabinet, he stood on the thing and chanced looking in the window. He spied Henrik Ellsmere standing at a table, making a sandwich. Not having paper or pen to make a note, Henson decided it was best to not tap on the glass and communicate with the scientist. The room Ellsmere was in seemed to be a combination of work area and sleeping quarters. There was a closed door in the back and beyond that, he guessed, would be the men guarding him. He checked his watch; time to get a move on.

He got his grapple and line out of the gunny sack, and on the second throw, latched the hook onto the edge of the roof. Up he went, sealskin gloves on. There was no skylight, but there was a flush hatch for access. He pried the lock off, got the hatch open and, using a flashlight, worked the beam to see a set of built-in metal rungs in the wall below. Part of the floor was visible from where he was as well. He heard voices drifting upward and killed the light. Feeling in the square hole, he got his hand on a rung and down he went. He was in a small hallway and ahead of him was an opening onto the shop floor. A card slapped a tabletop below him.

"Glad when this babysitting job is over."

"I couldn't agree more," said the other one. "How long is Dutch gonna keep this bird on ice? When's the thing he's supposed to be working on getting here?"

"Who knows? We drew the short straw." A card was slapped down again. "Gin."

"Dammit," the other one said.

Henson looked at his watch, eyeing the sweep of the second hand. In less than twenty seconds came a knock at the front door. It echoed throughout the garage. Several work lights were on, throwing circular pools of illumination from their bulbs.

"Who the hell is that?"

"We due for a delivery of hooch?"

"Naw, not tonight." Chair legs scrapped across concrete as one of them went to the door. There was a slot there and he drew it back to see who was outside.

"Yeah?" he said to the face of the colored gal standing there.

"I'm your fairy godmother," Destiny Stevenson smiled sweetly.

"Huh, you drunk or you been smoking some loco weed? Maybe

you oughta come in and share it with me and my pal," he leered.

Her palm held upward, she blew a silvery powder into his face.

"What the fuck?" he declared, backing up, coughing and reaching for the gun in his shoulder holster. The hood got it free, but his muscles had become rubbery and his eyes rolled back in his head. He collapsed, unconscious, onto the oily concrete.

"Pauly?" The other hood got up in a rush, knocking his chair over. As he ran to the aid of his fellow gunman, Henson stepped out and clubbed him once, twice, on the back of his head with a sap. He went down hard. There was an entry door inset in the garage's bay doors and Henson opened this to let the two women inside. They went past a Kenworth truck being worked on and reached the room where Ellsmere was.

"Matthew," the white-haired physicist exclaimed, rising from where he'd been having his snack. "And ladies," he said, bowing slightly. "I heard the shouting, but didn't dare peek out." He touched a bruise on his jaw. "I'd been reprimanded for trying to sneak away previously." There was other evidence of his mistreatment.

Henson picked up an empty unmarked bottle and smelled the opening. "Let's blow," he said, tossing the empty onto the bed.

"Uh-oh," Coleman said, hearing the chain rattle on the front doors.

"You two hide," Henson suggested. There was no back door, and while he and the two others might have gotten away via the roof and his rope, he didn't think Ellsmere would make it.

The bay doors were swung open and a driver got back in his truck and brought the vehicle inside. He came to a halt and turned off the engine. He opened the driver's door and foot on the running board, leaned partially out of the truck and called out. "Alfonse? Pauly? Where the hell are you?"

"They're taking their naps," Henson said, appearing at the side of the truck.

"Where'd you come from, shine?" He was reaching into the cab, but Henson grabbed him by his leather coat and yanked him out of the truck. Just as he was about to sap the man, a flap of canvas put him on alert. He dove away as a hood with a shotgun clambered out the covered bed of the truck, blasting at him. Buckshot pelted the flank of a delivery truck that Henson dove under.

"I got you black boy, ain't no hiding from the likes of me." He stalked over, bending down to shoot under the truck.

"Hey now," Coleman said, stepping into view.

Quickly, the shotgunner spun around to fire, but Stevenson shot him first, dead center with the revolver she'd obtained from the unconscious Pauly. He went over onto his back, unseeing eyes locked on the ceiling.

"Destiny…" Henson began, having gotten back on his feet. He tried to put a hand on her shoulder but she drew back. "You saved my hide."

She glared at him, tears in her eyes. She bit her bottom lip, pounding her fists against his chest. "Goddman you, Matthew Henson. Goddamn you and your Grim Destroyer." She fixed on him. "Yeah, you want to do right by your people, but really, you make us sacrifice to your god of death. It's all about the challenge to you—you against the odds. Was your soul frozen out there in all that ice and snow, Matt?"

"Destiny, honey," he began. But he knew the mixed emotions she was feeling. He'd felt the same way when he first had to kill another human being.

"The Grim Destroyer of yours is a god of death you think you can outfox. But none of us beat death, Matt. None of us."

She went on some more then she let him hold her close, sobbing onto his shoulder.

"We better get out of here," Coleman said in a rasp.

"Try not to think about it too much," Henson advised, knowing the opposite would occur.

Stevenson didn't look at him.

The four left. "I better drive," Coleman said.

Stevenson had a hollow look on her face as Henson helped her into the Ford. He left his motorcycle up the block after removing the spark plug wire and got in the rear of the car with the professor.

"Are you taking me to the frog and his jade rock, Matthew?" Ellsmere said. The older man turned to look at his friend a grave set to his face. "The Frog Prince has the answers you know. How to unlock the secrets of Seqinek's gift to us."

Henson said softly, "Is that what you told them, Henrik?"

Ellsmere stiffened as if struck. "My dear, boy, I want you to know I held out despite physical violence and threats of more." There were bruises on his neck the other man had noticed. "The frog told me it's only you who will wield its power. Your destiny," he said, not being ironic.

"Okay, Prof, sure you right."

Henson wondered what were Dutch Schultz, and by extension Davis, able to get out of Ellsmere this go-round about the Daughter. His captors had given him laudanum to better lubricate his tongue, but that also loosened the moorings he was having on sanity, he feared. He didn't think taking him to a sanitarium was a good idea. He needed to be cared for but not so anyone could get to him in the condition he was in. He knew where he had to take him. Coleman stopped so he could make to make a phone call, and then they made one other stop.

"I'll see y'all later," he said to Coleman as he and Ellsmere stood on the sidewalk. Destiny Stevenson stared straight ahead. The aviatrix nodded and drove off.

Henson took Ellsmere upstairs to Nikola Tesla's apartment at the Service Hotel along with the scientist's notes, retrieved from the basement at Columbia University.

"I'll see to it that he gets the help he needs," the electrical wizard said, his hand on his colleague's shoulder, the notes in the other. "I, too, have had bouts of…uncertainty."

Ellsmere nodded, muttering.

Henson had heard like Slip Latimore, Tesla could spend hours feeding the pigeons in the park, no doubt lost in arcane calculations he was working out in his head. "I can't tell you how much I appreciate this. And as much as possible, keep him under wraps, okay?" He'd told him briefly about how they'd rescued Ellsmere. "I'm not sure for how long, but I've got the feeling this is coming to a head for good or for ill soon."

"I concur on your assessment, Matthew. Forces are at play. You should know your Mr. Davis is part of…a council, I suppose it could be called. A grouping of plutocrats and a selected assortment of members of the government who, it is fair to say, stand closer to the tenets of a dictatorship that they do to democracy."

"That doesn't surprise me. A nest of vipers, is it?" Now it made sense how it was the government could spirit Ellsmere away from lock up, but wind up back in the hands of Davis working in cahoots with this bunch.

"More like that of the Medusa of myth, it seems to me," Tesla said. "With Davis looking to be the main head from which these snakes writhe. A Medusa Council, if you will."

"You mean, if he could possess the Daughter," Henson said.

Tesla regarded his visitor. "Is it here in New York?"

"Let's just say I can get a hold of a piece of it if I have to."

"I understand. But you must keep it safe."

"On that you can put all your money, Nikola." To Ellsmere he said, "See you soon, Henrik."

"Yes, I'd like that," his friend said, absorbed in examining a gadget that looked like a coffee pot with tubes and wires sticking out of it.

Henson went back down to the street; a chill wind having kicked up. As people turned up their collars, buttoning up and bending their heads low, Henson walked along erect, invigorated by the cold wind. For this was when he was at his sharpest, when he was most aware that any mistake would send him into the embrace of the Grim Destroyer. How he best not be complacent, least that bastard come for him through the white haze and claim him.

Upstairs, the woman called Petersen appeared from a side room in the doctor's quarters. Ellsmere reacted.

Tesla touched the other man's arm. "Don't worry, Freja is on our side. She was my Mata Hari inside Davis' operation. It was she who left certain doors unlocked for you to escape from your velvet prison in Poughkeepsie."

"Well I'll be," Ellsmere muttered.

"Should I try and follow him see if he takes me to the Daughter?" Petersen said.

"No, I don't think that will be necessary, my dear. We need to know how close Davis is getting. That remains your concentration."

"Davis is playing for keeps, Naygoohock" she observed. She often referred to him using the Inukitut word for doctor. Tesla had correctly surmised a woman with Petersen's exotic looks—half Danish and half Inuit—would attract his attention.

He smiled thinly. "So are we."

Tesla escorted Ellsmere to a rear bedroom in his apartment suite, and he dozed off in a chair. The electrical wizard rejoined Petersen, who sat leafing through a magazine. They then stepped into the side room where she'd been eavesdropping on the conversation between Tesla and Henson. There, on two desks cater-corner to one another, were two consoles that looked at first glance like what a radio engineer might use. To a degree this was true, as the apparatuses were electrical in nature. The black metal constructs were festooned with several mesh screens, toggle switches, dials and gauges. Heavy cables led from each through holes bored in the plaster and lathe walls at the baseboard eventually connecting to the radio tower on the roof of the lab.

There were hand-printed labels over the toggles indicting a different office or an abode in which Tesla had planted listening devices. These were tea saucer-sized, created with help from his friend the electrical engineer and physicist Leon Theremin. Over time, he'd had them planted in the aforementioned locations to eavesdrop via his mastery of electricity. To not have his legs cut out from under him like in his decades-long battle with Thomas Edison, who he felt cheated him out of not only accolades but more importantly, his dealings as well. His listening disks, as he called them, were secreted in such places as the summer home of Henry Ford, an associate of Edison's, three in Edison's research lab in West Orange, New Jersey, and one most recently installed by Petersen in Davis' office at the Challenger's Club—Davis being a major stockholder in Edison's enterprises.

This was how he'd found out about the council, and thereby deployed Petersen to find out more. He'd also heard the conversation between Davis and Schutz the night Henson had rescued Daddy Paradise's daughter. Possibly he should have been more forthcoming in his first meeting with the explorer about this, but bitter past experience had taught him to play things close to the vest as they said here in America. Tesla had asked Petersen, the daughter of an old associate come to New York 'to expand her horizons' she'd said, to keep tabs on Lacy DeHavilin as her name, too, had come up once when Davis was on the phone talking about Henson. Subsequently, he'd employed his second story man, Jimmie Dale, to break in and plant a disk in the widow's home given she had wealth. But he soon determined given her political bent, she was the opposite of the kind of person they wanted on this Medusa Council.

Now, he and Petersen sat and tuned in various frequencies to see what was transpiring. Maybe he was paranoid, Tesla considered yet again as he turned a dial. But hadn't his obsession with perceived enemies yielded useful information of actual enemies? Wasn't it just as telling to be more than just revenge on who'd cheated him in the past, or the potential to damage him in the present, that the price of freedom was unrepentant surveillance?

Well, he allowed, sipping his tea, such a rationalization sounded good.

CHAPTER EIGHTEEN

After dropping Ellsmere off in Tesla's care, Henson was still brooding about what happened to Stevenson. Not only did he feel bad about her having to deal with killing someone for the first time, he had to also wonder if she was right. Had he become so inured to taking a human life? He'd been using his knife rather freely as of late, and hadn't paused to reflect on the import of removing someone from this world—persons who sought his demise, but still.

As he unlocked his apartment door and went inside, he stepped on something. He clicked on the light, and picked up a note that had been slipped under the door. At first, he figured it was from Destiny. He quickly read the message and swore under his breath. Henson closed the door and started for the closet to gather some of his equipment. But a knock on the door had him spinning on his heels and turning the knob.

A youngish white woman stood there.

"Yes, ma'am?" he said.

"You're Matthew Henson, aren't you?" There was a nervous quaver to her voice.

"I am. What can I do for you?"

"I need your help, please."

"Look, I'm in the middle of something kind'a urgent. Give me your name and a way to get in touch, and I'll get back to you, okay?"

Henson slipped the note into his pants pocket.

Her body shook, and she put a hand to her lipsticked mouth. "Oh, if…if you could just give me a minute of your time, I'd be ever so grate…" But she didn't finish. She got weak in the knees, and she pitched forward.

"Aw, sweet Lord." Henson caught the fainting woman and reflexively looked up and down the hall. Great, a passed out white woman at his door at this time of night. Lightly, he tapped her face with his open palm. "Ma'am? Ma'am, can you hear me?" No response. He sighed. He had no choice, he had to get her out of his arms. He set her on his couch. Then he figured he'd go across the hall and fetch Edna Mullins to help him, be a witness in case matters got out of hand.

He lifted her up and, as he got her inside his apartment, turned toward the couch. That's when he heard the onrush of feet and cranked his head around in time to see the bulldog G-Man raise his blackjack and bring it down on his skull. He had been grinning broadly when he sapped him Henson would note later.

He came to gradually, and wasn't surprised that he had a whopping headache. Henson groaned, shaking his head to clear the fog congealed in it. He was tied spread-eagle to the secured upright frame of a Murphy bed, sans mattress. The room was sparsely furnished, but then again, Henson knew this place wasn't used to entertain guests. His shirt was on but unbuttoned, the sleeves loose as well. On a small wooden table there was a coffee cup, an alarm clock, and a pair of black gloves. There was a water pitcher and bowl for washing your face on a nearby sideboard. Bulldog, his snap-brim hat off, sat at the table leafing through a newspaper. He closed it as Henson tested his bonds.

"I win the bet," he said.

"What bet?" Henson croaked.

"That you'd wake up before midnight. My partner said I whacked you too hard, and that maybe you needed medical attention. I said that burr head of yours was hard like a Mississippi mule's ass." He tossed the paper aside, letting it flutter to the floor. "Now I can get to work on your black hide."

"Fuck you," Henson growled.

Bulldog shook a finger at him. "Now you should know, hell's comin', boy, comin' for you." He slipped on the gloves. Stepping over to him, he hit Henson in the stomach causing him to vomit. "Ain't so tough now, are you? Shoulda been doing this to you sooner as far as I'm concerned. You gonna spill all your guts tonight, darkie."

Henson tasted the bile on his mouth and spat. "Like I said, fuck you."

Bulldog hit him in the jaw, snapping his head back, and making the springs in the fame squeak. He reared back to strike him again when a door to Henson's right opened. In stepped Fremont Davis, who coolly regarded the prisoner.

"That'll be enough for the moment. I'm sure I can reason with Mr. Henson." He paused, as if receiving a telepathic communication. "You are, after all, a responsible sort, aren't you, Matt?"

Before Henson could respond, the other half of the Mutt & Jeff team entered the room. He was carrying a paper bag and removed his fedora. He put the bag on the table and plucked a chair from a corner of the room. He turned it around so the straight back was toward Henson and straddled the seat as he sat. He folded his arms atop the edge of the chair's back, and regarded the explorer.

Henson was looking at Davis. "Taking off the kid gloves, Fremont?"

"You've forced my hand, old son." he said.

Henson considered this probably meant he wasn't going to get out of this alive. Even if he did, who would believe him that government men and a millionaire had kidnapped him to give him the third degree to find a meteor of cosmic power?

"What exactly can I do for you, Mr. Davis?" He knew the answer, but any delay from getting wailed on gave him a better chance of recovery.

"Where can we find the space rock? The special one?"

"I don't know. And why do you want it, now? I'm guessing you've known, or suspected, its existence for a while."

"You know, all right." Bulldog came forward again but Davis held up a hand. Jeff remained sitting, watching.

"Hear me out, Mr. Henson. Nobody's looking to cut you out of the recognition like what Peary did to you. You want to name the find after you, okay, I can make that happen. You want your picture in the paper standing next to the stone from space, fine, I can make that happen too." Davis knew negroes liked their baubles.

"You know me enough to know I could give a shit about that. If that's what I wanted, I could have had that years ago."

"Then what?" the goateed man said.

"You know damn well what. I want my cut, Davis."

"Really?"

Henson huffed. "Yes, really, white man. You think I'm a fool? You think I don't know what the Daughter is capable of? Sheet," he sneered.

Bulldog jabbed a finger at him. "You best watch your tongue. You ain't got the upper hand here."

"I don't?" Henson challenged. "You gonna beat me within an inch of my life to talk? I've suckled on polar bear tit and ate raw dog and smacked my lips for more…boy. I've marched through weather thirty below and took out my stiff dick to satisfy two Eskimo broads at the same time in a lean-to igloo while slurping down boiling penguin stew. Afterward, I had enough left over to chase down a walrus just so I could catch and skin 'em to wear his big teeth around my neck. You figure to make me all aquiver like that dame you hired to have me drop my guard? Go ahead."

"Bragging sonofabitch," Bulldog groused. "We'll see." At a nod from Davis, Bulldog went to work on him. "You and that Daddy Paradise think your shit don't stink," he grunted, driving a fist into

Henson's ribs. "Well I got news for you, sambo, you've been falling down on the job." Another blow to the body wracked the prisoner.

After more than a minute of steady pounding, he paused, panting from his exertions. Henson's head hung low, and blood dripped from his mouth and cuts on his face. Davis, who'd been standing off to the side watching, came back over. He gripped Henson's chin and lifted his head. He was surprised the beaten man wasn't glassy-eyed.

"You can take it, I'll give you that, Matt," the rich man opined.

"Huh," Henson said, a slight smile on his face. "If you kill me, you'll never find it," he managed to say.

"I'll make you talk," Bulldog vowed.

Davis wasn't so sure. And time was not a luxury. "Is it here in town?"

"You have to have me along. You palefaces go alone, especially them flashing your badges, you'll get gutted. See it's deep, deep in the jungle," he cackled.

"He's losing his mind," the shorter federal man said.

"No, I don't think so," Jeff said.

His partner glanced at him, his gloves smeared with blood.

"You can beat me all night and it won't make no nevermind," Henson said. "We can't get there until the day time anyway."

"You're lying," Davis said.

"Okay," Henson shot back. "How you know different?"

"Goddamn smart-aleck porch monkey," Bulldog hissed.

Henson looked at him balefully. "You already got a lot of explaining to do with me looking like this." Inwardly, Henson gathered his chi as had been taught him by the deformed monk Hiroki Kodama.

"Is it at Smalls Paradise where you do your broadcasts?' the taller G-Man asked, getting to his feet.

"You tell me, stretch. I bet you've already searched there, my home, and I'm sure May-May's too. Huh, you tell me?" Henson figured the photos Davis had of him had been taken by these government men. But did this working over mean Davis was working with this Medusa

Council, as Tesla had called it, to turn over the Daughter? But that meant the government would want it—or at least a piece of it. It didn't seem likely to Henson that Davis would angle to do that. He knew enough about him to know he'd want the power for himself. Maybe to sell to the highest bidder, but more than likely to make him even richer and more influential. Which meant he'd have to control the Daughter.

"What's the payday you promised these two?" Henson said.

Davis regarded him.

"This little meeting of the minds is off the books, ain't it? Like those mugs in the animal masks you imported from out of town to fetch Ellsmere back. Make it all hush-hush. Like you were playing ball, but all along working behind the back deals for yourself."

Bulldog exchanged a glance with the taller one. When they'd tortured the hood, he'd spilled that Davis was paying him. They went to Davis and demanded in on however the millionaire was going to cash in on this whatever it was he was after or they'd tell Hoover at the Bureau.

Davis motioned to the two, and they went into the side room, closing the door. Momentarily they returned. He adjusted his tie as he stood before Henson. "Let me understand. You'll take us to the meteor?'

"Yeah, 'cause you bastards might get smart and just leave me here to rot."

"We wouldn't want you to miss out on any fried chicken bonanzas," Bulldog cracked.

"Your mama likes my drumstick," Henson said, his banter misdirecting them as he continued to go within—calling up images of a snow-covered Mt. Hiel in Kyoto, of practicing martial arts bare-chested and ankle-deep in the white powder. He had to drain off any hesitations, channel his pain into resolve. His actions had to be fluid, effort without effort.

That got a rise out of Bulldog, but his partner stopped him. He was chuckling.

194

Davis continued. "If you take us to the meteor, why would you trust us to make good on a promise to cut you in—as you said, once we have it, we have it."

"Really?" Henson said. "Once you have it, so what? It don't come with a set of instructions. And I've retrieved Henrik from Dutch Schultz." As he suspected, that was news to the shipping magnate and the other two, given the looks on their faces. That confirmed for Henson that Davis, using Schultz, had been trying all along to get to the Daughter first.

"The prof has already doped out the rock's secrets. But you can only have him if I'm breathing."

Bulldog held his arms out wide. "Let me tenderize him some more."

"I gotta relieve myself," Henson announced.

"Go ahead," Bulldog said.

Henson rolled his head toward Davis. "I'm not talking about peeing. You want me messing in my pants? You want even more attention on me in the morning when we get there? Okay by me, it ain't like I'm the one who's gonna be embarrassed."

Davis turned to the tall one. He in turn took out a .45 from his shoulder holster under his coat. "Fine, you can have a bathroom break," Jeff said. "But you'll do it with this pacifier pressed against that thick head of yours."

To his partner he said, "Untie him."

"Shit," he complained, but did so. He wasn't careful slitting the ropes on Henson's wrist and ankles, nicking his flesh.

Freed, Henson stumbled forward, bending over slightly, hands gripping just above his knees. He sagged, and Bulldog stepped away quickly, refusing to hold him up. He'd counted on the agent not standing too close to see what he was up to.

"Come on," the tall one demanded. "Time's a'wasting."

"Just need to…get my…breath." As Henson straightened up, he flung the shuriken he'd tucked away in a watch pocket sewn

195

onto his pants' inner waistband. This was one of the electrified ones Stevenson had altered. He was faster than Jeff could pull the trigger. The throwing star sunk deep in of his neck. He twitched and shook as electrical current surged through him. He managed a shot, but the gun was already dropping from his hand.

As this happened, Henson grabbed the washbowl and threw it at Davis, who was clearing the revolver he had on him. The dishware broke on his face, and the man stumbled back, firing blindly at a moving target. Henson used a leg sweep to upend Davis, sending him to the floor. He then swung around and leapt, dropping Bulldog with a flying kick. Falling to the floor, he landed on his backside, but rolled onto this stomach. He scrambled like a man at an oasis after three days with no water. Bulldog had latched onto his lower legs, but Henson now had hold of the .45. The taller one had also lunged for him, but Henson had aimed the throwing star purposely. He was getting woozy from loss of blood.

Calmly, he clubbed Bulldog in the head with the gun and got to his feet. "Knock that gat away from you," Henson commanded Davis.

He hesitated, but knew from his fetal position on the floor, he couldn't bring his body around to shoot Henson before the explorer pumped slugs into him. Davis swept his hand, skidding the revolver across the floorboards.

"You better get his neck stitched close or he surely dies," Henson warned Bulldog.

The taller man held a hand to his neck, blood soaking his upper shirt. Pleadingly, he glared at his partner.

"You're gonna swing for this, Henson," Bulldog promised.

"We'll see."

Davis removed a shard of porcelain stuck in his cheek, momentarily examining the piece with a disinterested air. Otherwise he remained still.

"Don' worry, I'll take care of your boss," Henson said. "Skedaddle."

Having no choice, Bulldog got his arm under his partner to

support him and started toward the door. But as he did so, he shoved the wounded Jeff at Henson, which caused him to try and duck. He wasn't successful and the two went over.

"Goddamn slippery nigra," Bulldog hollered, jumping on Henson. The two grappled. Jeff groaned on the floor. Davis ran out the door to the hallway, then down to the street.

Henson leveraged a knee into Bulldog's chest and, moving his head sideways, took a glancing blow on his jaw from the government man. He swatted him again several times about the head with the business end of the gun. He sagged, and Henson got him off and was on his feet. Henson closed the door, keeping his gun on Bulldog who sat up on the floor. Blood clotted his hair.

"He's right, you'll hang for this, Henson." Jeff rolled onto his back.

"Yeah? You think the other members of this council will reward you for trying to sneak one past them? Trying to make a naked grab for a thing they feel entitled to 'cause they were born with silver spoons in their mouths?"

Bulldog glared at him. "You gonna bore us to death with a lecture?"

Henson knew that even though this was an underhanded operation, to linger here was not in his best interest. Bulldog or Jeff could concoct any kind of story that would bring G-men or cops down on him with a vengeance once he got Jeff to the hospital. He was desirous of sweating this chump to find out what Davis was up to, and he best be quick about it.

"How come Davis has a bee in his bonnet to get the rock *now*? Keep in mind, you sonofabitch, the longer you take to come across, the less chance your partner has of staying alive."

Jeff murmured. "We're not sure. But we know a few years ago, Davis was a backer of Tesla. The egghead is always going on about his ideas in articles and what not. Anyways, Davis got a hold of some kind of blueprint Tesla had tried to sell the War Department." He looked over at Bulldog who also spoke.

"From what we've pieced together, Davis had his own white coats working on this blueprint for some time. Apparently he's ready to test this thing."

Henson understood it had to be Tesla's damn electro ray device. With the Daughter who knew how many thousands of those could be powered?

"Get the fuck out of here," he growled.

The two left Henson standing in the middle of the room. For the first time in a long time, cold worked its way through his body.

CHAPTER NINETEEN

Officer Cole Rodgers stepped out of the Rexall drugstore carrying a grocery bag of several items, including a tub of Vaseline and hairpins. He was proud to be able to provide for his two ladies. He was in civilian clothes, and had treated himself to an egg crème at the soda fountain. On he walked, happy to have the day—or at least part of it—off. He had to report in for the swing shift later, but for now he had his apartment to himself. Cora and her sister had taken Irene shopping. She'd told him with a kiss that, as long as he left the windows open, he could smoke a cigar while he listened to music, or whatever he wanted to do to relax.

Crossing the street at an angle, he approached his building. He shifted the bag to his other hand and dug his keys out of his pocket. He got the door open and stepped inside the cool and inviting foyer. Heading toward the stairs, there was a stir in his peripheral vision and, turning, a man with a handkerchief tied over the lower half of his face was there, a .45 pointed at his head. He'd left his own upstairs atop his uniform.

"It's Kingdom Come time, cop," announced the man.

Rodgers instinctively closed his eyes, wishing he could see his wife and child one more time, if only to say his goodbyes. There was a loud retort as he prayed there was an afterlife. When he didn't feel a burning sensation or a breeze blowing through the hole in his face, he opened his eyes.

"Matt?"

"Hey, Cole," Matthew Henson said, a length of pipe in his hand. The masked man was lying at his feet. He reached down and took the handkerchief off.

"I know that mug. That's Two Laces."

"Yeah, Dutch Schultz sent him to kill you," Henson confirmed.

"Damn. Why me?"

The note had warned Henson. The message had been left by the man calling himself Vin O'Hara, and he'd stated that he was an infiltrator. The explorer had believed the message to be authentic. "Daddy Paradise's big speech. Get you out of the way just in case. You being a black cop on the Harlem beat and all. Even though your bosses already said you can't guard the event."

Rodgers said, "I intended to be there anyway."

Henson smiled at him.

"Say, what happened to your face?" Rodgers asked.

Henson chuckled dryly. "Long story. But right now, we have to save a whole bunch of people from getting slaughtered like Thanksgiving turkeys."

When Henson had learned about Davis' copying Tesla's machine, he'd confronted him.

"Yes," the aging inventor admitted heavily. "I've got it on good authority that after several years of failures, Davis was close to making a prototype of his own based on my idea. That's why I'd renewed efforts to perfect my Electro-Pulsar."

"How'd you find out what he was up to?" Henson had asked.

Tesla smiled lopsidedly. "Too many times over the years, Matt, I've made bad business decisions that have cost me financially and scientifically. Once it became clear that Davis was using me, I was determined to...reverse course, shall we say."

"In what way?" Henson said.

As Tesla began to answer, one of his assistants had rushed out of his rooftop lab and whispered in his ear. When he was done, Tesla had invited Henson to follow. In the lab was a wireless of an advanced design unlike anything Henson had seen before. Freja Petersen's voice came over the wavelength after Tesla spoke into his microphone. What she reported caused both men to gape.

Later, after his meeting with Tesla, Henson made a stop at the U.S. Customs House on the southern tip of the island. The building near Battery Park and the water's edge was considered a fine example of the Beaux Arts style. Henson was disguised as a delivery man, wearing a light jacket with the words "B. Jonas Freight" stenciled on the back. He also carted a wooden box on a dolly. Once inside, he wheeled his supposed delivery to a metal door and knocked. A face appeared in the shatterproof window on the other side of the door. The woman unlocked it.

"Thanks, Edna."

"Off course, Matt," his across the hall neighbor said, wearing her blue clerk's uniform. "You know how to let yourself out, yeah?"

"Absolutely."

Mullins nodded, and they began walking along a long windowless hallway, Hanson trailing with the dolly. They got to a juncture and they separated, giving her a half wave as he did. He passed another clerk carrying a clipboard going in the opposite direction, and nodded curtly at him. He got to a door and entered. There was yet another clerk there, sitting on a stool behind a counter. He was a beer-bellied middle-aged white man with the stare of years of earned boredom.

"Yeah?" he said, as if forming that one word was effort.

Henson took a folded piece of paper out of the breast pocket of his shirt. "Delivery," he said.

The other man didn't bother to extend his hand for the paper. It seemed after years on the job, he'd perfected to the atom the amount of energy he needed to expend to complete any particular function. He did look at the sheet as it lay on the counter before him. He then made a heavy sound in his chest like a bear rousing from hibernation. He pulled over a clipboard and made a notation on the top sheet.

"Take it on back," he said.

"Yes, sir."

Henson opened the low gate separating the well from the gallery in a courtroom. He wheeled in his box, and the bored man had to get off his stool to unlock another metal door, this one windowless. He was let into a two-story cavernous storage area of rows upon rows of metal shelves filled with wooden and cardboard boxes and other types of containers. Like in a library, at the end of each row there were numerical designations corresponding with a master list the clerk kept up front. The lazy clerk was supposed to personally take the deliveries in here. But Henson knew from Edna, he didn't follow the protocol. The disguised explorer wheeled the dolly in a ways, and then deposited it between two rows. Inside the box was a cheap reproduction of a Ming dynasty vase. At some point, a clerk would come upon this and simply figure it had been removed from a shelf and not restocked.

Henson walked deeper into the rows until he came to Row 51. He went down this aisle, the light gloomy and the air stuffy. A little past midway he stopped, having counted his steps like a kid in search of buried pirate's treasure. There, on the third shelf up from the bottom, he removed a small wooden crate. There was no identifying sticker on it, and a person had to look close to note one of its nail heads had been dotted with red paint. He used a screwdriver he had on him to pry the lid off.

He inhaled sharply, staring at the triangular piece of the Daughter he'd broken off and taken back with him to America. He slipped the fragment into his jacket pocket. He then tamped the lid back on using the handle of the screwdriver. He tried not to look excited when he stepped back out and passed the clerk. He needn't have bothered. The civil servant was busy sharpening pencils. As he removed each one from the sharpener, he blew loose graphite off the tips and diligently studied the results of his engineering.

CHAPTER TWENTY

People came by car, foot, bus, subway and even train from outlying areas to hear Daddy Paradise deliver his "Equality and Prosperity, the Road to True Freedom" speech at Liberty Hall. While the police were not officially safeguarding the negro firebrand, the commissioner had to do something once he got the call from Mayor Jimmy Walker's office. The charismatic democrat had received too many calls and visits from too many black pastors and other civic leaders—and a few whites as well—about the event, and the need to make sure there was no problems at the gathering. Then there was the stoic presence of mostly white officers around the perimeter who watched as many in their finery, including a number of whites, such as the escorted black arts patron Charlotte Osgood Mason, filed past to hear the celebrity spiritualist.

The ones Matthew Henson had recruited to provide security were either in position or roaming about the auditorium. Though everyone hadn't been patted down upon entering the hall, Dulane's crew, given their known associates and associations, kept hard eyes out for those they deemed worthy of such precautions. Due to a suggestion from Miriam McNair, there were several women on security duty as well. Individuals who objected either relented, or were turned away.

Running about forty minutes behind, eventually as the bulk of the people were seated, the program got underway. Miriam McNair, in a sequined gown, came out on stage in a sequined gown to a round of polite applause. The podium hadn't been set up yet but there was an upright microphone upon which harsh white light shone from the rafters. She spoke into this.

"Some of you know me, many of you don't. But be assured I won't be taking up too much of your time as the man of the hour will soon be out to give his address. My name is Miriam McNair, and I want to acknowledge several groups and individuals who worked tirelessly to pull this event off. First off," she continued, splaying her fingers against a gaudy broach she wore, "I have to, of course, mention the women of my loose-knit organization, the Bronze Orchids."

That got another round of applause, and McNair continued to name those who had a hand in organizing and doing outreach for the event. She finished, then did an introduction.

"I would like to bring out a young woman, the niece of one of my members. She is quite something and will lead us in song to truly set the mood for this most special evening. You will find her voice amazing." McNair said her name and turned to extend her arm, waiting for the teenage girl to step out on stage. She got to the microphone, and McNair gave her a brief hug then left. The young woman took a big gulp and began. She was part of the Abyssiniann Baptist Church choir and she began a rendition of "Lift Every Voice and Sing" the so-called Negro National anthem.

Dulane, in charge of security, prowled backstage. He and a few of the others had been provided communication wonders by Nikola Tesla. These radio-signaling apparatuses, rectangular, about eight inches long with stubby antennas protruding from there tops, allowed Dulane to communicate with other key personnel. Tesla guaranteed the range of the radios was nearly a mile. The crowd stood, swaying and singing along to the young lady's exuberant song. Or rather, most stumbled over the lyrics, mouthing words that rhymed with the correct ones but weren't accurate. When the song ended, there was vigorous clapping and shouts of joy.

"You ready?" McNair asked Daddy Paradise.

"As I'm going to be," he replied. He was dressed in a three-piece suit, eschewing pin stripes for a demurer look in charcoal grey, white shirt and dark blue tie. A heavy silver chain was attached to his pocket watch in the vest pocket. There was a fob on it of the cross-legged, smiling Buddha. When wearing the watch at dinner parties and the like, the fob invariably garnered attention and an opportunity from the spiritualist to pontificate upon the depth and breadth of his teachings.

As was his custom, he'd rehearsed his speech from the typed text. After doing that several times, he then made key notes on index cards, specific ideas and points he wanted to make sure he covered. Prepared in that way, he could generally speak extemporaneously yet be secure with his cards before him if needed. The two stood in the wings as the teenager came off stage.

"You are on your way to stardom, dear," McNair said to her as she walked past.

"Thank you," she said as her mother came over and hugged her tight.

Dulane and a large gentleman, some six feet five of muscle and gristle, were near the couple. He had the two-way radio to his ear, listening. He took it away and said to Toliver, "Everything's good, Brother Paradise."

"Thank you," he said.

"Good luck, Charles." McNair kissed him on the cheek.

In turn, he kissed her hand and walked out on stage where a podium had been set up for him. The audience rose to their feet again, clapping and waving. In the VIP rows, the gathered were a range of Harlem's labor, religious and community leaders as well as representatives of the underworld. Those in attendance included A. Philip Randolph, who was not particularly religious, but understood he couldn't ignore the pull this man had on the members, men and women of the union he headed, the Brotherhood of Sleeping Car Porters. Near him was Queenie St. Clair with Venus Melaneaux resplendent in a tux, tails and a top hat in hand. St. Clair made sure not to be smirking. But now, having rescued Casper Holstein, she really was the queen of the rackets as far as her contemporaries were concerned.

Also in attendance was also writer and poet Langston Hughes, and Zora Neale Hurston was covering the event for *American Mercury* magazine. An Episcopal priest and several reverends, including T.C. Stafford, were present. Others not in the VIP section were there representing *Opportunity* and *The Nation*, while Jessie Redmon Fauset, though no longer the literary editor of the NAACP's *The Crisis*, was nonetheless covering the speech on special assignment for the magazine. Several photographers were there as well.

Hands outstretched, Daddy Paradise said into the microphone, "Please take your seats, beloved. You and I have a momentous journey to begin tonight. One that, I hope, will start us on the way to peace and prosperity. For surely not from City Hall or the White House, will our salvation come. No, my friends, only we can deliver us for us. Only we can do for ourselves because only we can rely on ourselves." His voice had steadily risen, and he began to thump on the podium using his index finger, the sound picked up by the microphone.

"And don't misunderstand, I'm not talking about negro for the negro businesses, though there is certainly nothing wrong with that. But I am talking about something more, far more. Something that will lead us to true financial fulfillment. But that is merely a fraction of the whole equation. For it is not a handout from the government or a free lunch in a bar that I'm talking about tonight. Neither Hoover nor Smith can get this for you. For you see, we all have it, that's the beauty of it." He dabbed at his forehead with a folded up monogrammed handkerchief even though he wasn't perspiring yet. Toliver knew people liked to see their preachers working hard.

"That which we must tap into is within us. In the fabled East it's referred to as chi, the universal essence, the life force that unites body, mind and spirit. But I'm not here tonight to get us lost in a bunch of mumbo jumbo and metaphysics. Oh no, I'm here tonight so that we can shake off the shackles of self-doubt and worry, of 'I can't,' and 'the white man won't let me.' Damn that." He paused, scanning the audience, pacing back and forth behind the podium then returning to latch onto its sides like a drowning man onto a life preserver.

Grasping the microphone, Daddy Paradise leaned his mouth close to the instrument. "Dare I say, *God* damn that," he blared into the microphone. His white-hot challenge echoed throughout the auditorium.

The crowd erupted gleefully, more than one pastor cringing.

The sound of those hoots and claps made their way to three men at an apartment building under construction that overlooked the facility. Liberty Hall, which tonight was filled to capacity, was a sprawling one-story building with catwalks and warrens in its upper reaches. From the vantage point where the three killers sat watch, they looked down on the rooftop section where the main auditorium was. The unexpected presence of the police had caused the plotters to reassess their plans, but they were still going forward with the job. Because really, what choice did they have? These men worked for Dutch Schultz. They'd brought with them a prototype of yet another way for human beings to destroy one another. But this method was unlike any other heretofore seen. It was a version of Tesla's Electro-Pulsar. It was a death ray.

But different from Tesla's design, this version looked more like a bazooka with cables connected to it leading to a squarish generator the size of a living room radio. Smartly, the generator had a built-in handle and wheels like a dolly. Tonight, the experimental device was to be used to slaughter a number of Harlemites, particularly the rivals of Schultz—Queenie St. Clair and Daddy Paradise being the number one and number two targets. Schultz would also not bat an eye given the ray would cause the death of a goodly number of notables and would serve as a lesson that he would brook no opposition. He knew that it wasn't just Daddy Paradise who invested with Harlem's gangsters to provide capital to those denied capital. Schultz also calculated should either of his main targets survive in the resulting devastation, either one of them would be seen as a pariah, a jinx. He'd be finished as a would-be black messiah and therefore the natural order of things would be secure.

"We just gonna blow up the roof with this thing?" one of the hoods had asked earlier. They knew from a supplied floorplan approximately where the main auditorium was located.

"It would bring down part of the building but that's no guarantee we'd get Queenie," another said. A side of his face was marked from a childhood bout with chicken pox. They had considered letting fly with a blast or two as people milled in. But a number of Klieg and other types of carbon arc lights, including some of Edison manufacture, were on, and they feared being spotted by the law. Now the lights were off and the police less concentrated. There were, however, lights illuminating the hall's entrance and one of the men had a set of binoculars. The idea was the police would think a bomb went off inside the place giving the hoods time to clamber down from the construction site and disappear in the dark and the confusion.

"There's either gonna be a break or we wait till it's over," the third one said. This was Eddie, the machine gunner Henson had bested when he rescued Destiny Stevenson. Eddie, wearing another colorful tie, was determined to even the score. "Once we spot her lordship, we let her have it and we're dust."

"Okay," agreed the first one. He badly wanted to smoke but knew not to take the chance of lighting up and giving away his position. He and the others sat waiting, conversing now and then to pass the time. Some minutes later he began looking down at the entrance to the hall through the pair of binoculars they'd brought.

"You hear that?" he said, lowering the binoculars.

"Yeah," Eddie said, "is that a plane?"

Before the other one could reply, a spotlight suddenly blazed from overhead.

"Shit," cursed the pockmarked one.

Overhead, Bessie Coleman brought the Skhati into hover position. Henson was strapped upright on the wing operating the spotlight recently attached there. He highlighted the three on the apartment building. Unknown to the hoods or Henson and Coleman, the building was owned by Casper Holstein through one of his fronts. He had not shown for tonight's speech.

"Is that the cops?"

"Can't be, they ain't got nothing like an autogyro do they?"

"Then we shoot it down," Eddie said.

A gunshot rang out from Henson causing the three to duck. He'd surmised from previously reconnoitering the hall and its environs with Dulane this site might be where the gangsters would zero in on the hall. There was a feral glint behind his eyes as the wind tore at him on the wing. He supposed Destiny had spoken a truth about him in the garage. He couldn't help it, putting his fate on the line was exhilarating. The Grim Destroyer be damned. Tonight, he was laughing in his face… tonight he was dealing justice from the skies. He almost laughed out loud, but caught himself.

"Come on, blast them with the ray, then do the joint and let's get the hell out of here before this place is crawling with cops," one of the other hoods yelled.

"Dutch warned maybe we might get three or four blasts out of this thing. It ain't perfected," the other said.

"I know," Eddie said. He brought the weapon to his shoulder, aiming at the light. A stream of white light shot from the tube. But even as this happened, he knew he'd missed. Coleman had maneuvered the plane out of harm's way. But the ray didn't dissipate. It reached its apogee, then curved downward just as rapidly, striking a parked car, exploding the gas tank. Several other vehicles went up, and a storefront was blown out. A section of vehicle spun through the air and sheared off the top of a hydrant, sending up a stream of pressurized water.

Up in the plane, Henson put the light back on. He said, "I'm gonna fix these birds before they hurt somebody. Swing me over the top floor."

"All right," she said, "but even though that thing has limited range, I ain't looking to get fried."

"I hear you, sister."

Now the hoods were shooting back with their handguns. But Coleman zoomed the plane around and Henson shot back. A round sizzled the air less than inch from his temple as the aviatrix brought the plane back to hover momentarily over the partially completed fourth floor, the top.

"Whoop halloo," Henson yelled, dropped onto a section of wood framing.

"We're bust, let's get out of here," Pockmark said, already moving toward a ladder. Down below there was shouting and running around. The police were trying to assess what was going on and maintain order. Because of the explosion, patrons were already rushing out of Liberty Hall as internal security tried to prevent people trampling one another.

Pockmark was wheeling the generator, and Eddie carrying the ray tube. The third hood trailed. The spotlight snapped back on, and now the cops on the ground could see him. They began firing up at the building. But since this was only revolver fire, there was little chance of being hit. Still it was only a matter of minutes until the police converged on them they knew.

"We gotta leave the generator," the third one said. The plane could be heard receding.

"I'll still be able to get a shot off at the hall when we get to the ground," Eddie said. He'd been instructed the device should be able to store enough energy that even uncoupled, it would fire once.

Pockmark and the other hood yanked the wires free from the generator. They'd used ropes to get the thing up here.

The three moved quickly, descending the ladder to the exposed second floor and from there, they'd take another ladder. Only, now a policeman was climbing up and was shooting at them. They fired back, hitting the officer, who fell.

"Not so fast," Matthew Henson said. Coleman operated the spotlight with a cable attached to it running into her cockpit. There were voices from below, more police gathering and figuring out how best to storm the upper levels.

"The fuck," pockmarked said. He brought his gun up and Henson shot him dead with Two Laces' .45. Henson had a handkerchief wrapped around his lower face. The other two stood frozen. "Drop 'em and kick the gizmo and the gats over," he commanded.

"Go to hell, Henson," Eddie said. "You ain't fooling anybody with that Deadwood Dick get-up."

The third hood shot at Henson, and simultaneously Henson shot back. The hood's bullet missed and Henson's bullet got him in the leg.

"Bye, bye, Henson," Eddie said. He had him flat-footed and triggered the ray gun. But the weapon was an inferior copy of what Tesla was working on. No electric beam lanced at him. Rather, the device hummed loudly. It got hot in Eddie's hands and began smoking.

"Oh shit," Eddie said, mouth hanging open.

Henson was already in motion. Down below, people reacted to a ball of light suddenly lighting the dark up there on the building under construction. Jagged tendrils of electricity boiled the air, their twisted columns of energy surging in various directors. Some of the bolts hitting the hall, causing damage to the brick work but not the intended large-scale murders envisioned by Dutch Schultz. Two of the hoods were instantly incinerated. Eddie had thrown the weapon away from him but was caught in the resulting fireball. He was blown off the floor under construction and his electrocuted body landed on the ground to gasps.

"What was that?" several people said. The wood planking began to burn.

"Fire, fire!" several yelled.

Using his grapple and line, Henson hurriedly descended the far side of the building as the police arrived, flashlights and guns out. Henson's form was obscured by black smoke as flames consumed the framing, some of the beams so new they still smelled piney. The whole thing was burning now, and one of the cops, a track runner in high school, was dispatched to a call box to get the fire pumpers to the site. They had to make sure the conflagration didn't spread.

"Okay, everybody, we're getting this under control," one of the officers yelled in front of the hall.

On the ground, a sweating Henson got his grapple loose. He hid his gear in the cab of a pick-up truck and wiped off and left the .45 underneath it. He then jogged away in the semi-light of flickering fire.

There was barely contained milling of the crowd in front of Liberty Hall.

"What the hell's happening?"

"Is it the end of the world?"

"Where's my car? I gotta get out of here."

"Everybody, please" a policeman said, "let's remain calm. We've got the situation under control."

People's restlessness increased for several slow minutes as various police cars roared into view and disgorged their personnel. The Klieg lights were put back on, casting bright lights on anxious and fearful faces. Daddy Paradise appeared, surrounded by OD, his large associate and other members of the security detail.

"Please, brethren, let's allow the police to do their job," Paradise stressed. He stood atop one of the police cars addressing the crowd. "It doesn't appear anyone was hurt, and it seems a great catastrophe has been averted." As he spoke, two horse drawn water pumpers raced around a near corner and arrived at the burning structure.

"You see," Paradise said, "there's no reason to panic."

One of the cops tried to pull him down, and was stopped by a sergeant who'd come on scene. He was the one who'd arrested Henson after the shoot out from several days ago. He tossed aside a dead cigar stump and muttered, "Let him talk. We don't want a fire *and* a riot on our hands."

There was a lot of murmuring and jangled nerves, but at the urging of Daddy Paradise along with Langston Hughes and several of the pastors, an edgy calm settled on the crowd. It helped that water was being sprayed of the flames.

While many watched, unbeknownst to them, the police had begun a sweep of the neighborhood looking for Matthew Henson. He soon emerged from Liberty Hall. He'd changed clothes, having stashed them in the janitor's closet the day before.

"Arrest him," the sergeant shouted.

"On what charge?" Ira Kunsler said, having been in attendance, and appearing at his client's side.

"Suspicion of murder," replied the sergeant.

"Who?"

He pointed at the smoldering corpse being carried to an ambulance. Photographers' flashbulbs popped, momentarily illuminated parts of the corpse's form as he was stowed away. One of the sergeant's officers who'd tried to get up on the building had briefly seen the outline of a fourth man. A black man, he knew. And who else around here could have probably used a rope to climb the hell down from there so fast?

"I've been inside all night seeing to the safety of the event," Henson said.

"Bullshit," a cop said as he and two others had their hands on him, their nightsticks at the ready. A palpable jolt of indignation went through the crowd.

"They're trying to scapegoat, Matt," someone yelled.

The edgy calm was fast dissipating.

"What evidence do you have?" Kunsler said beside Henson as the law tried to get him into a prowl car. But the crowd wouldn't part.

"We know he was up on the building," the sergeant said.

"Yeah, who's your eyewitness? A night owl?"

"I have good cause."

"You have a witness to identify him?" Purposefully, Kunsler raised his voice. "You mean you're going to take the word of one of the hoodlums had tried to assassinate Daddy Paradise at face value?

Because there's a whole bunch of people who will attest to him being inside this whole time," he bluffed, though knew Henson could get a few on security to lie for him.

"I saw him throughout the night inside the hall," a new voice announced.

Head turned to gaze at an elderly woman in her best Sunday-go-to-meeting clothes complete with an ostentatious hat with a rainbow plumage. Mrs. Celow stared defiantly at the sergeant. She was the person who'd let Henson use her apartment to drop down on Eddie and the other thug holding Destiny Stevenson. She was a righteous woman, but she figured the Lord would forgive her for lying on behalf of Mr. Henson. He was Harlem's own.

The cops looked around nervously. A captain with a lantern jaw muscled his way over to Henson and Kunsler. There were at least twenty police cars occupying the street. "All right, mouthpiece. You make sure your client comes down to the precinct tomorrow to answer questions. Understand?" He'd already recognized the dead man as one of Dutch Schultz's underlings. There was also that Two Laces gee they had on ice as well. He was making noise he wanted a deal in exchange for ratting out the cop who put him onto Cole Rodgers. No matter how he tried to keep a lid on all this, it was going to come out and then this business was going to blow up big time.

As the gathered clapped, Henson left in the company of his lawyer, flashbulbs going off in their faces like grenades. The two men went past Venus Melenaux and Queenie St. Clair. The two women exchanged a shared indecipherable look.

"That was close," Kunsler said, driving away from Liberty Hall. Grey smoke could be seen through his rear window as the burning building was mostly extinguished. "Imagine if that goddamn ray gun actually worked? Something like that in the hands of that coo-coo bastard Schultz.

His friend regarded him grimly. "Think I ought to turn over a piece of the Daughter to Tesla?"

Kunsler drove along, silence building between them. "If another madman should posses that kind of power." He shook his head. "Isn't it better we have a way to check him?"

Henson nodded.

"What about Davis?" Kunsler asked.

"He ain't the type to go back into the woodwork."

"Yeah. But look, you saved the day, Matt. The black and white press are gonna latch onto the Dutch Schultz angle we feed them. Not to mention the mystery of the thing they had up there and the unknown aircraft."

The explorer smiled wanly as he sat quietly. That night he stayed at Kunsler's place as the press was camped out in front of his apartment building. He made a phone call.

"Hello, Destiny," Henson said when the receiver was picked up on the other end of the line.

"Hello, yourself," she said.

They talked for a long time. Then he went to sleep, gathering himself for the last push.

CHAPTER TWENTY-ONE

As Kunsler had predicted, the black and white newspapers were filled with news about the attempted massacre at Liberty Hall. Though it was the negro press that had the best frontpage pictures of the burning building and the famous Harlemites, their faces a chiaroscuro play of light and dark as they watched the building burn. One of the black presses evoked the Greenwood incident instigated by whites, the Tulsa Black Wall Street slaughter of 1921.

While the dead hood was identified as a known associate of Dutch Schultz, there was as yet no hard evidence linking the gangster to the crime. Through his lawyer, Schultz denied any involvement and expressed his outrage at such a heinous act by clearly deranged individuals. Kunsler was busy fielding calls for interviews for Henson from such outlets as *Time* and *Look* magazines, as well as a Greenwich Village illustrator named Elmer "E.C." Stoner, who it turned out was a negro and was interested in collaborating with the explorer to produce a comic strip based on his exploits. He'd sent over some sample sketches and the two were perusing these. And in further consultation with his client, it was determined that *The New York Amsterdam News* would get first crack at a Matthew Henson interview.

As to what had exploded up there on the partially completed building next door to the hall, it was put forward by the police the hoods must have had grenades with them and one was struck by a bullet. Various eyewitnesses countered that as they told of seeing a bright flash and discharges akin to lightning. This in turn was the source of vigorous speculations in cafes, beauty parlors and many a speakeasy over watered down gin—in and out of Harlem.

To the chagrin of many in Washington, D.C., including those on the so-called Medusa Council, Daddy Paradise's stature had increased. He might not be the black messiah, but as he had hired Henson and the latter, the black community knew, had prevented mass killings. The spiritualist at this moment in time was ascendant. As donations flowed in, Paradise announced he'd hired architect Vertner Tandy to design and oversee the building of an all-glass and metal pyramid-like structure. This edifice would utilize the fairly recent process of chrome plating for its details, and would house a spiritual sanctuary, offices, a trade school and local businesses. Further, Matthew Henson was being hailed as the Hero of Harlem in presses of all stripes in and out of New York. Denied his proper recognition after reaching the North Pole, he was now, all these years later, the toast of the town.

Reverend Stafford, the informer, was racked with envy. His government contact was no longer available to him, the phone number disconnected. He received no further communication from the Bureau though he tried several times reaching out to them.

Before those occurrences, still jailed in the Tombs in Lower Manhattan, Two Laces lay on his cot in his solitary cell smoking a cigarette, when one of the jailers appeared at his bars. "There's a mouthpiece here to see you, Two Laces." He had a key in the lock and was opening the cell door.

"About damn time," the crook said, sitting upright and grounding the cigarette out under his feet. He yawned and followed the jailer along the hallway of other jail cells to a room down another corridor. He stepped inside, his eyes having to adjust to an unexpected gloom.

"Hey, what goes?" he said, the door slamming shut behind him. "Where's the shyster?" he said. There was a table and two chairs in the room, but no one sitting down.

A hand came from behind, covering his mouth, as a muscled arm pulled him back. Two Laces had his hands on that arm and was trying to break free when the knife blade opened the front of his throat. He gagged on his own blood, holding hands to his severed throat as he impotently trying to prevent his life from gushing away. He fell to his knees, his sweat-stained shirt soaked crimson. A foot in his back sent him over onto his face, dead.

Detective Kevin Hoffman briefly regarded his handiwork. He replaced the knife in its scabbard beneath his pant leg. Then removing his gloves, he stepped out into the vacant hallway and exited the central lock-up. There were spots of blood on his shoes.

Dutch Schultz exited the Hotel Astor to his waiting Packard Phaeton. The sun was bright and the birds chirped overhead. He should be in a good mood, having just had a series of his sexual fetishes indulged by the two working girls he'd paid well for the efforts. But the debacle at Liberty Hall haunted him, and if anything, he only got madder and more determined that he was going to take over the Harlem rackets from those coons who were laughing up their sleeve at him. Nor could he believe that Luciano and the others on the commission were giving him shit about this. They kept telling him he didn't see the bigger picture and that it was in the interest of everyone to have the colored run the numbers to keep the peace and they'd still be able to take their cut. Fuck that. The kidnap he put on Holstein had been busted up by that broad St. Clair. With his man Bernstein headed for a stint in the big house, busted by that negro cop Rodgers who he'd put the hit out on. These turns of events were absolutely infuriating. And it continued to rile him that St. Clair had been saved by that burr head Matt Henson no less. The same cocksucker who saved Rodgers. He vowed that he too was going to get what was coming to him. Schultz needed to get drunk.

"Take me to my saloon," he said to his new man behind the wheel. Word had reached him that Vin O'Hara had been gunned down in

Newark over a gambling debt. Though so far, no body had been found. Too bad, he'd liked the kid.

As they pulled away from the curb a guy riding a bike passed by their car on the driver's side, nearly crashing into his pristine vehicle.

"Hey, asshole, if you put a scratch on my car, I'll lop off your ears," Schultz yelled.

"Queenie says hello," the bike rider said, tossing an object through the car's open window

"Jesus and Mary," the driver said, eyes wide on the bomb on the floorboards. Like a cartoon come to life, it was a rough-hewn cannon ball-like sphere with a lit fuse sticking out of it. A modification of what had been called coal torpedoes during the Civil War. As his boss screamed and the driver reached for the bomb, the thing went off. The explosion blew the roof off the Packard, sending the shorn metal and one of the driver's severed arms pinwheeling through the air. Schultz had managed to get partially out the rear door, and was sent flying through the air across the sidewalk. He collided with the brick face of a building, breaking numerous bones, his clothes partially burned away and the skin dangling like tinsel from his scorched back and legs. But he was still breathing.

The bomb thrower was Venus Melenaux dressed in knickers, rolled up sleeves, and a newsboy cap. She rode on, ditching the bike a few blocks away in an alley where she'd left a skirt to wear to disguise herself as a lady.

At the hospital that afternoon, as reporters were kept at bay by the police, his hoodlums stationed in the hallway, the Dutchman was consumed with fever and frustration. Morphine pulsed in his veins. He was in traction and wrapped in bandaging. A nurse put a finger to her lips for her co-workers to be quiet as they witnessed his mumblings interspersed with rants.

"Yeah, I did him good. Tied a rag soaked in clap sores around his eyes, leaked in and made him crazy in a Siberian tiger who rode him till he got home."

"The last train carried the loot all the way under the mountain of the moon where it'll never be found only I know the way." He would chuckle and thrash, rattle on and at various intervals remain silent for long stretches.

"The prince is sure to come to dinner if the feathered octopus says so. But the cosmic girls piloting the blimps will want orange payment."

As the setting sun projected light and shadow slanting though the Venetian blinds, he'd been quiet for nearly half an hour. From somewhere nearby a radio broadcast a swing orchestra. The sound muffled through the walls of Schultz's room. During a break, the announcer did a commercial for Clicquot Club Pale Dry Ginger Ale. Schultz licked his chapped lips and began mumbling.

"Yes, yes, of course," he gulped, "Henson is not to be touched until the time of the sun goddesses returns with her forever light of blue. Oh, great and awful Grim Destroyer, grant me this passage down the tunnel of the seven spears that I too may rescue the fruit cups."

As the wounded gangster babbled on, Matt Henson received an envelope by messenger at his residence. It had the look of something you'd get inviting you to a dinner party. Inside was a note on cardstock. He read this and set this and envelope aside. At his cupboard, he had a taste of his bathtub hooch and sat in his lounge chair in the living room, staring at the mantle but not seeing it. As Kodama had taught him in the monastery in Kyoto, he centered himself in himself to reach the exquisite state of unconcerned immersion. He moved his mind past the jumble of mood, feelings and doubts to clarity—vibration of the soul in harmony with his body. To achieve zen, to not focus on calculation which led to miscalculation, he sought to be absolutely alert. Necessary was the ability to arrive at the state where an inner reserve of energy could be summoned at the most critical juncture. For he had an evening engagement at the Brooklyn docks in Red Hook, and did not wish to make it a one-way trip.

"Did you know during the draft riots several negro gentlemen having been pursued for blocks and blocks by enraged whites had sought refuge at the Challenger's Club?" Fremont Davis, his arms folded, leaned against a pile of coffee beans in burlap sacks stacked high and long against the bulkhead. During the Civil War, Congress passed compulsory inscription. This in the wake of the Emancipation Proclamation being enacted. Added to that, the well-heeled could pay for a poor person to take their place in the draft. Wage-earning whites revolted against Lincoln's "nigger war."

"Were they turned away?" Henson finished, climbing down into the ship's hold from the main deck. While there was still cargo in here, from fifty-pound bags of apricots to coffee to machine parts in wooden crates, all of it had been shoved off to the sides allowing for a squared-off mostly bare center. It was cold outside, and a chill wind whistled around this metal cavity. Henson had come without a coat on, braced and invigorated by the frosty temperature. As far as he could tell, only he and Davis were on the ship, the SS Robeson.

Henson wore his workingman's clothes and boots. Davis was in dungarees and a worn loose cotton shirt, western-type boots on his feet. Probably his hunting clothes, Henson figured. There were lights strung up at regular intervals along the walls providing illumination—though the shadows lengthened the more you moved away from the center area.

Davis straightened up, chuckling. "In fact, my dear departed grandfather Solomon who was head of the board then, sent word that what was happening out on the streets of the city was a travesty and that no innocent man nor woman seeking shelter would be harmed on his watch." He motioned with his hand. "Those gentlemen and several others were secured in the club's basement. Fed, bedded and safeguarded during the duration of the disturbance."

"Very noble."

"Do you know why I turned down your application for membership, Matthew?" Davis kept his gaze on Henson.

"To get back at ol' granddad?"

He shook a finger at him. "Ha, no. I knew full well of your contributions to reach the North Pole. I knew full well you deserved to be the first black member of our august body."

"But…" Henson said, orbiting the one small table there was in here. On it was a silver serving tray with two hunting knives laid out ceremonially. Their blades had been vigorously polished.

"But it was business, plain and simple. Had I championed your application, it had been made clear to me from other, shall we say… more short-sighted members, that certain contracts I was in pursuit of would not be forthcoming. That meant ships shipping, jobs, food on the table and the clothes on the backs of the families of my workers. The needs of one can't outweigh the many."

"Really, it was a sacrifice on my part, only I didn't know it."

He shrugged. "Wanted to clear the air on that. I have the negro's best interest in mind, Matthew."

"That a fact?"

"You scoff, but what is it you think I intended to do with the Daughter?'

"Considering you gave the Dutchman the ray gun, kill a lot of black folks."

He shrugged. "Again, just business. You know I wouldn't have kept that hothead as an ally for too much longer. But I will admit, I was curious to see how the weapon would operate."

"Not too good, it turned out."

"My scientists theorize the meteor will be the proper stabilization element. For you see, that's what this power will be in my hands. I'll bring stability and order. Mark my words, there's unrest in Europe and sooner or later the skies will be filled again with the screams of dying men and women. Imagine what could be accomplished in the judicious use of several of the death rays?"

"You figure to be the dictator of the world? Or America at least."

"Setting the terms is how I see it. There's a place for a man like you in such a vision, Matthew."

"I'll pass."

He looked sincerely disappointed. "I imagine in that exclusive interview you're set to conduct with *The New York Amsterdam News*, you'll be naming names, raising certain allegations."

"Most assuredly. Yet, I'm sure you're not worried about that."

"No, but there's others who want you made an example of, make sure you're put back in your place."

"An example for any other uppity nigras," Henson cracked.

"Yes," Davis said wearily, "there is that. But I've already concluded I'll have to get you out of the way. By my hand, not some rifleman on a roof as some had suggested. This has to be between you and me. Hunter to hunter."

Henson imagined bulldog suggesting the sniper approach. "Now that you've figured out the meteorite isn't here in town, if I'm dead, how will you find it?"

"I'd wager your friend Ootah knows. And one way or the other, I'll track him down and wrest its location from him." He said this without rancor, like listing items for a trip to the grocery store.

Henson cursed.

"What? I own a freight line." He swept his hand about indicating the hold. "I'm well connected here on the docks. You think an Eskimo can show up here a few years ago and that doesn't garner attention? Especially one palling around with a black man. Now, mind you, there had already been rumblings about a gift from the heavens."

"The priest, Christofferson," Henson said, after a pause.

"Indeed. Did you know he published a book in Denmark about his time in the Arctic? You're mentioned in several places, quite favorably. He writes about the time he told you about the Seqinek fable."

"So?"

"So, when Ootah was shown around Copenhagen by the priest, he apparently let slip more than he intended. How you two had nearly lost your lives in an underground cavern. But he clammed up thereafter.

223

Still," he gestured, "that was an inadvertent corroboration."

"Why made you believe the story in the padre's book?"

"I believed it because Leeward kept a dairy. Peary turned everyone's diaries over to the Natural History Museum, except for yours. Being enamored of your expeditions, envious even, I poured over those documents. And I'd read your rather tame memoir twice. Too bad you weren't allowed to tell it straight. I mean, you mention Leeward, how sad it was that he 'accidently' lost his life. But his account makes it clear of what he thought of you. A fellow like that must have truly grated on your nerves."

"He did," Henson admitted. It also occurred to him Davis must have been searching for Ootah before now. But once the millionaire determined he didn't have the Daughter close, it was better to get him out of the way should his friend get wise and try and send word to him.

Davis was near the knives again. "Curious then he should disappear in the crevasse. Maybe you and Ootah bumped him off simply because he was a Son of the Confederacy who deserved it. Or maybe there was another reason. I knew deep down it wasn't a gold strike or a stratum of coal you were protecting. That sort of wealth doesn't seem to motivate you, Mr. Henson. And even if greed was your North Star, you would have returned to extract those riches. But the Daughter is so much more than mere earthly treasures."

"Here we are, then."

"Yes. No more artifice, no hidden machinations of would-be puppet masters. Just you and me, and our will to survive. As it should be." Like he was a salesman indicating watches in a counter case, Davis gestured toward the knives. "Please, be my guest."

Henson picked up one of the knives. The handle below the curved metal hilt was carved hickory and had heft to it. Davis picked up the other knife and backed up several feet from his opponent. The unstated rules were simple, fight until one of you couldn't any longer. No throwing the knife, but you could use your free hand. If you ran, then your cowardice and shame would be the stone around your neck forever. Besides, the only way out was up the rungs and the other man would sink the knife in your back before you made it out. Knives extended, the two circled each other. Davis feinted, and Henson blocked with his blade, the clinking of the steel echoing in the cavernous space. Again, they moved around each other warily, eyes alternating from glancing at the other's knife then to their face, then to the weapon again.

Henson charged at Davis with an underhand thrust. The millionaire side-stepped, and Henson punched him with a solid left. Davis' head reared back but he wasn't that stunned, and mostly avoided a slash from Henson's blade, though he did slit the other's sleeve and the forearm underneath. The two shifted more, their blades striking and sliding off each other. Moving closer to each other at one point, Davis successfully grabbed Henson's wrist, yanking the other man off-balance. The knife was raised in his other hand and he plunged it downward, intending to sink it into Henson's chest. Henson acted fast and drove the flat of his blade against the other knife.

Both men grunted and gritted their teeth as they now had their respective left hands on the other's lower forearm, the knives momentarily locked as they each pushed them to overpower the other. Henson turned his body, trying to whip Davis around. But he let go, and stumbled. Henson pressed the attack and Davis swiped at his chest, driving him backward. His shirt marked the path of the knife along with a diagonal line of blood underneath.

Once more, they allowed several feet between them as each man sought an opening to attack. Davis hunched forward, then, twisting to the side, made Henson miss with his thrust. Davis' knife pierced Henson's upper thigh, but he pulled free before more damage was done.

Davis leaned his upper body in again, tossing the knife back and forth between his hands to try and throw Henson off as to which direction he'd make his assault. In a burst and a blur, the knife in his left, Davis brought the blade up toward the other man's stomach.

Fortunately for Henson, his reflexes were faster, he and ducked aside, chopping his knife at the other's wrist and lower arm of his knife hand.

"Shit," Davis swore, a deep wound lacerating that part of his arm. He moved off, sweat dampening his brow. He went far enough away that he bumped against some of the crates. Their creaks a graveyard resonance in the momentary silence.

Henson didn't come forward, but kept the distance between them. He knew a wounded Davis was a dangerous man, one not to be underestimated. Plus, in that gloom he might not see the flash of the knife until it was too late. His leg was hurting but he was too excited and too scared to let that bother him now.

Davis moved into the light, the knife low, but pointing upward in his fist. Henson rushed him, and their blades hacked at the other as if they were using broadswords. The shipping magnate twisted in such a way that Henson next jab at him went past and Davis sliced at his shoulder, drawing blood again. The other man moved away instinctively, keeping his hunting knife poised to prevent Davis from charging him. He, too, collided with cargo, and dove away as Davis lunged. The end of his blade sunk into one of the crates. As he pulled it free, Henson pressed his brief opening and nicked Davis' side. Davis made a defensive slash and Henson had to sidestep out of range.

Both men were breathing through their mouths as they circled one another in the center of the hold. They leaned in, jabbing and slashing, neither gaining an advantage over the other. Each was bleeding, and both knew they couldn't let their guard down. Davis lunged and Henson defended. But rather than backpedal or duck aside, he came at the thrust, his forearm in swift motion under the knife hand, knocking it aside with his forearm. In a blink, Davis' midsection was exposed, and with a grunt, Henson, seeing the other movements slow down as if viewed through thick amber, his own mind empty of anything but being, drove his knife underhanded into the area just below the curve of Davis' rib cage.

Davis' eyes saucered and he staggered. This time, when he

collided with an assortment of crates, he remained still. He looked down at his fatal wound and then at Henson. The explorer's mouth was set in a line, the bloody knife in his hand.

"Davis...I," he began.

"Seems you have the better of me, Mr. Henson." Red spittle foamed on his lips.

Henson wasn't sure what he felt.

Davis, hand to his wound, walked a few steps toward his vanquisher. Blood was slick on the skin of his hand and soaked the front of his shirt. He put a hand to his throat and plucked loose a thin chain around it. "This is yours, now."

Henson frowned at the oblong medallion on the end of the chain.

"It's Diana, goddess of the hunt," he said, holding the keepsake before him, then it dropped from his slick hand. "As it should be," Davis muttered, weaving on his feet. He did a half-turn and began walking as if to leave the hold. But he only got a few feet then wilted to the floor, his ankle tucked behind the other like an exhausted dancer who'd come to the end of his strenuous workout. He lay on his back, his vacant eyes looking up out of the hold into the cold night air.

Henson wiped his fingerprints off every surface he could think of in the hold including the rungs. He finished. He'd just killed one of the wealthiest white men in the world and the police would be all over this ship looking for clues. He didn't think Davis though, who had no immediate family, could come after him from the grave. But there were the others who sat with him on that Medusa Council, Tesla had called it, as well as Davis' relationships with various shareholders in various enterprises. Some of them, if they figured it out who had killed him, may not see this as the fair fight it had been.

Well, fuck 'em, Henson concluded, as he picked up the medallion. If this was the deed that the white world would recognize him for, having mostly ignored his accomplishments as an explorer and later as a kind of daredevil for hire, well then, so be it. He would hold his head up high as they marched him to the gallows. He was his own man and damned if he had to exist in anyone's shadow.

Back up top, he looked about the hulk of the darkened freighter, its crane masts in blacker relief against the dark. Not too far away there was light and activity on another cargo ship, but it didn't seem there was any attention being paid to him. Nonetheless, he stayed in the shadows as much as he could as he left the ship and walked among the warehouses. His shirt was bloody, and while he was bold about his larger act, he knew only too well his current appearance was more than enough motive for a couple of white cops to stop him and maybe he might not make it back to the precinct this time. Common sense tempering his arrogance, he stole a shirt left out on a clothesline with other items behind a tenement. He felt bad about this, these were working folks who could ill afford the loss. He left three dollars secured by the clothespin and continued on.

When he finally made it back home and into his bed, after attending to his wounds, he lay there signing in his throat, katajjait it was called by the Inuit. Though mostly performed by women, he'd been taught these guttural rhythmic sounds by Akatingwah, his son's mother, and he'd sung them to the child when the boy was an infant to entertain him or calm him to sleep. Henson imagined he was near a dying campfire in the Arctic never dark. When he awoke at daylight, he didn't know how long he'd sung, but his throat was sore as was his body.

CHAPTER TWENTY-TWO

Nikola Tesla swung the Electro-Pulsar about and unleashed a coherent bolt of energy that bored a hole through a five-inch steel plate mounted upright on a table several yards away. Several electrical oscillators were connected by cable to the machine. The beam was modulated so that it didn't continue through the metal, though it could have easily if the calibration hadn't been so precise. He shut the device off, a whine diminishing inside its casing as it powered down. The others gathered near him were silent, amazed and fearful of what they'd just witnessed.

"The light of the gods in human hands," Henrik Ellsmere marveled, his face anxious. His equations were the key to tapping into the space stone and metering its flow.

Tesla had a faraway look on his face.

Bessie Coleman walked over to the steel plate and touched the metal. "Cold, it's a cold light that bore through," she said, looking from Shorty Duggan to Hugo Renwick who seemed on the verge of tears. The five of them stood in the hangar of the Weldon Institute's private airfield in the Jersey wetlands.

Coleman broke her silence. "I don't know what to say."

"I do," Destiny Stevenson said from the hanger's opening. She had a gun in her hand. "This thing will not prevent war, but instead bring wholesale slaughter to a world already beset and bestride with troubles. It must not be." She drew in a breath slowly. "And if any of you won't do anything to prevent this, I will expend any and all efforts to make sure this…death ray is never fully realized."

Tesla said, "Miss Stevenson, surely that is too pessimistic an outlook. Think of the good that could be achieved with a device such as this." He rested a hand on the Electro-Pulsar atop its tripod. "A person trapped under fallen rocks or timber, a wall collapses, and—"

"Then they'll be counted among the dead if conventional means can't save them," Stevenson said sharply. "Better that than the death toll this wickedness could and will unleash." She pointed at the instrument, "And all because of that tear of the sun goddess."

Inside the pulsar was a piece of the piece of the Daughter Henson had given Tesla. It was the power source.

"I think you're overdoing it, Destiny," Coleman began. "I realize you're still bothered by what happened in the garage, but you have to look past that, honey."

"Look past destruction on an untold scale?" she challenged.

"Dr. Tesla would see that wouldn't happen," Duggan chimed in.

"Yeah," Stevenson snorted, "ask Edison about that."

"That's not fair, Miss Stevenson," Renwick said. "Progress is always fraught with uncertainty. Through the institute, we can wield this responsibly."

"Bullshit," she said, stepping in more, the gun level before her.

"You plan to gun us all down in the name of mankind, lass?" Duggan said.

"I plan to make you fools come to your senses."

"Remember that gadget you showed us?' Coleman said.

"What?"

The aviatrix threw the twin joined canisters Stevenson had shown her and Henson several days earlier. Designed to disorient, it exploded at Stevenson's feet with a flash and a bang, causing the other woman to stumble backward. Duggan was on her and took the gun away.

"God damn you all," she said, blinking hard to clear her eyes.

"Wait," Tesla said. He walked over to his machine and opened a hatch in its side. The piece of the Daughter was secured there by two metal rods and wiring. He got the fragment loose and handed it to Stevenson. "Hold onto this, throw it in the river, hide it away do with it as you will. Perhaps you're right. These recent events do have me questioning my ideas. I pride myself on always knowing the answer I seek. Now I don't know."

"Seqinek shall guide her," Ellsmere muttered.

Lacy DeHavilin poured some punch into her glass. A dark-eyed woman in pearls walked up beside her. They were at a function.

"Hello, Marie," DeHavilin said to her.

"Hello, yourself. How was Cuba?" Marie LaSalle asked.

"Relaxing and fulfilling. Though I wish a certain someone had been there with me."

LaSalle smiled. "A certain someone who was in all the news because of his saving the day at Liberty Hall?"

DeHavilin winked at her as a man with a walrus mustache in a black suit took to the podium.

"Thank you for coming out today," he began. "I know in one way or the other our beloved Fremont Davis touched the lives for the better of those gathered here in this institution, the Challenger's Club."

As the speaker went on, LaSalle glanced at the mounted enlarged photograph of the late Fremont Davis, silently toasting Matthew Henson.

The ship, a Patoka-class oiler called the Mesquita sat listless in its berth. Destiny Stevenson stood on the dock near Matthew Henson, the two gazing into each other's eyes.

"Write if you get work, kid," Ira Kunsler joked.

Henson turned to his friend and the two men hugged, patting each other on the back. "I wouldn't have made it without you, Ira."

"You're gonna get me all weepy," he sniffed.

"Take care of yourself, Matthew." Cole Rodgers stuck out his hand.

Shaking it, Henson replied, "You too, Cole. I look forward to reading about you in the papers. Give 'em hell, brother."

They grinned at each other. Henson embraced Stevenson again. "Once I square things with Ackie, maybe we come back here or maybe you'll learn to like walrus-fur coats."

"Maybe." She gave him a crooked smile.

"Tell Victor good-bye for me," he added. He was referring to her father's half-white son who'd disguised himself as Vin O'Hara to get the goods on Dutch Schultz.

She nodded and kissed him.

Henson hefted his duffle bag on his shoulders and giving his friends a half wave, turned and walked up the gangplank onto the waiting ship and his return to the Arctic.

Acknowledgments

Reading Mr. Henson's memoir *A Negro Explorer at the North Pole* set me on the path. But it was Dr. S. Allen Counter, who wrote the introduction to that edition which lead me to his book further illuminating details about Henson and those expeditions, North Pole Legacy: Black, White and Eskimo sealing the deal for me. Counter's book informed the reader about Henson's, and Peary's, half Inuit children along with other tantalizing reveals I just had to incorporate in this effort of re-imagining an individual given short shrift in history -- but could be remade as a tall tale in the style befitting our heroes and heroines.

About the Author

Gary Phillips is the son of a mechanic and a librarian. He was weaned on too many comic books, Dashiell Hammett stories, reruns of the original Twilight Zone, and experiences ranging from community organizer to delivering dog cages. His 1950s set graphic novel the Be-Bop Barbarians riffs on race relations, jazz, police brutality and the Red Scare. His novel *Violent Spring* was the first such mystery set in the aftermath of the 1992 civil unrest, and he edited the Anthony award-winning anthology *The Obama Inheritance: Fifteen Stories of Conspiracy Noir*. He is story editor on FX's *Snowfall*, about crack and the CIA in 1980s South Central where he grew up.

Visit him at www.gdphillips.com

MATTHEW HENSON

AND THE TREASURE OF THE QUEEN OF SHEBA

BY GARY PHILLIPS

Ethiopia, 1928

Italian Infantry Sergeant Piero Labreza cleared the thicket carrying a World War I era Beretta submachine gun. Finger on the trigger, he scanned the terrain before advancing into the open, walking across the hardpacked ground toward a raised platform hewn from basalt on top of which stood a series of obelisks of varying heights, one of them as tall as a four story building. On these stelae were carvings of images and words which, even this peasant's son understood bore import. Behind the obelisks was a terraced pyramid which sat in a shallow depression in the earth.

"The captain was right," he uttered, awed at his surroundings.

Shifting his attention back to the task at hand, he proceeded in search of the stranger who'd taken out two of his patrol. Originally, the orders had come down to travel from their outpost in Eritrea and cross the border into this sector of Ethiopia. Given the precarious relationship between the two countries—fascist led Italy being a colonial occupier in the Horn of Africa—this was supposed to be a secret retrieval expedition. So, a stranger aware of their presence was not a good thing on several levels.

A figure darted out from behind an obelisk and ran toward the pyramid. Instinctively the soldier sergeant rattled off a several rounds from his weapon, but the man was gone. Yet, where? He hadn't seen him go up the steps to the pyramid's doors. Warily he went onward, realizing the captain would have him skinned him alive for disobeying orders of not killing the man. But what was he supposed to do? How the hell was he going to bring him back alive? At least, alive enough to answer questions.

The sergeant licked parched lips. The captain had ordered his platoon to split off to find and capture this man. All they knew was he was black, his nationality undetermined, though the consensus was—from brief glimpses of the big shouldered mustached man—he was not Ethiopian. Kenyan, maybe? But something about him suggested he wasn't that, either. Whatever. The plan was to bring him back to camp, torture the bastard, find out who he worked for, then kill him and leave the body out to be eaten by nature's four-legged predators.

"We mean you no harm! Surrender now, you know you're outnumbered."

"Really?" came the distant reply also in Italian, though not as fluid. "You don't want revenge for the death of your comrade? I certainly would."

Smart man, the sergeant reflected as he looked up at the pyramid. From what the captain had told them, this pyramid wasn't used for burials like in Egypt. And unlike churches in his homeland—ornate, with Rococo flourishes reflecting their Baroque roots—this red stone ziggurate was composed of several tiers, rising some four stories then leveled off to a flat area. Here and there were also window openings. Atop the flat area was a sort of miniature three-sided pyramid that maybe was a story and a half.

Taking a deep breath, he mustered confidence. What with his sub-machine gun, extra magazines and the two grenades, he'd bring this buck back and earn the admiration of his commanding officer. It was about time he was awarded a better rank, wasn't it? This place was called Alexum and had remained long hidden from outsiders' eyes according to his captain. Up the flight of steps to the wooden double doors he paused, listening. He then used the barrel of his rifle to open the already ajar door and, crouching low, stepped quickly into the dark interior.

Inside the vaulted chamber, he could discern shapes, some sunken, others in relief, carved into the floors and walls. Easing forward, he passed through a shaft of light streaming in from a high window. Then a whistling and before he even fully registered the sound, his hand was impaled by a knife.

"Dammit," he swore, lifting his gun hand to see it wasn't a knife, but some sort of five-pointed star, each triangular segment a sharp-edged blade. His hand throbbed. But there was no time to deal with that. Footfalls had him whirling around. Orders be damned, he let loose another burst of bullets. But, again, his target disappeared. He cautiously stepped forward, and was struck hard in the face by the bottom of a boot.

The assault bowled him over and the owner of that boot, Matthew Henson, one of the first men to reach the North Pole, landed upright after his flying kick. Henson smashed his fist into the bridge of the soldier's nose as he tried to aim his gun. This staggered him, blood staining the man's lower face. In a blur of Henson's hands, the firearm went clattering and briefly airborne, the soldier wound up on his back on the floor.

"Don't worry," Henson said in English, smiling down at him, "you won't be in pain long."

"The hell are you—" the sergeant began, but wasn't able to finish as again Henson's foot lashed out. This time it was two vicious blows to the downed soldier's head, knocking him out. Dressed in worn khakis and a blue sweat-stained cotton work shirt, sleeves rolled up past his elbow, Henson hefted the unconscious man over his shoulder in a fireman's carry and off he went.

The base camp of the once seven—now six—man patrol consisted of a few tents, their armaments, rations, water, and the vehicles they'd driven: an armored car outfitted with tank turret, and an Opel Blitz light truck. The other three sent out to locate Henson had returned more than forty minutes ago. They were now certain Sergeant Labreza must have been fallen at the hands of the mystery man.

"Could be he's hiding in that lost pyramid of yours," suggested the corporal.

Captain Enzo Moretti nodded slightly. When the patrol entered the country, Moretti had told his men their goal was to ascertain the Alexum's existence and once that was done, attempt to secure a specific artifact. The men believed they were doing this on behalf of their superiors or maybe even Il Duce himself. Moretti didn't disabuse them of that notion.

"Hey, you guys! Help me, huh?" a voice cried out.

"Labreza," the corporal said, taking out his holstered Beretta.

"Hold on," the captain advised, hand raised. "Our enemy is clever and might not be alone." He, too, had his sidearm out. "Cautiously, eh? Fan out."

In a clearing, they spotted the sergeant tied to a cross of

wood beams splayed on the ground. Deep gouges in the ground indicated he'd been trussed up elsewhere and dragged here. He didn't appear to be hurt beyond his obviously-broken nose. He was clad only in his underwear.

"I got slapped awake and here I was," he explained. "The sonofabitch broke my fingers on both hands." He wiggled his thumbs.

"Oh my, Labreza," one of the men joked, "did you and your dusky companion's lovemaking get out of hand?"

The men cracked up.

"Ha, ha, very funny," Labreza said. "And for your information, that sprite we're chasing is an American."

That shut them up.

Labreza told them what little he'd learned while they got him loose. Meanwhile, Henson was sneaking into camp from another angle. Using one of the grenades he'd taken off the noncom, he pulled the pin and was just about to stick it down the barrel of the turret on the armored car when the soldier's whose leg he'd broken hobbled out of his tent to relive himself.

"He's here, he's over here," he yelled. Fortunately for Henson, the man's pistol was back in his tent. He fell down trying to race back into the tent to retrieve it.

Inside the armored car, several artillery shells ignited when the grenade went off. There was a big boom and a hail of shredded pieces of metal and rubber. A table-sized piece of makeshift shrapnel pirouetting through the air severed one of the soldiers in half as he double-timed back to camp.

Henson was already gone.

Ears ringing, the captain glared at the dead man. Grimly he addressed his other men. "We must hunt him down and finish this. If we can take the American alive, fine. If we have to kill this…whatever he is, so be it."

Wordlessly, the remaining four mobile members of the patrol checked their weapons and set off on foot. The one with the broken leg said a prayer for them as he buried the other soldier. The sergeant, still in his skivvies, looked on helplessly.

"This way," Captain Moretti said after he'd consulted a hand-drawn map. He'd paid an Arab trader handsomely for it back at their military outpost in what the Italians called the First Born Colony. The trader claimed he'd drawn it from memory a year before when he'd last come though this area. He'd held onto it until finding a buyer who knew its worth.

By late afternoon the soldiers arrived at the Pyramid of Alexum—said to have been one of several palaces built for Makeda, better known as the Queen of Sheba.

"Magnificent." As if it were an attractive woman, the captain's fingers caressed the symbols on one of the obelisks. He marveled at the significance of this find, lost in visions of glory back in Italy.

"Captain?" the corporal said.

"Right. Look, men, I better tell you the truth. We're not here on orders."

"What?" one asked.

"But, we take care of this impertinent Negro, we will all be rich men, I wager."

The other three traded looks.

"Come, let us be bold." Captain Moretti marched off, his machine gun at the ready.

One of the men shrugged, and followed the captain. The remaining two did as well—if only to exact revenge for the deaths of their mates.

"Looks to be only this one way in," the corporal remarked,

hoisting his rifle and fingering his holstered sidearm. They stood in front of the still-open double doors of the pyramid.

"Don't forget, the sergeant had two grenades," Captain Moretti said. At the doors, he crouched down looking for a trip wire across the opening. Satisfied there wasn't one, he rose and went inside.

Looking around, Moretti pointed at one of the privates, "You and I take this floor, you two take the second. There may be hidden chambers, even traps, so be careful."

"You mean traps installed by the ones who built this?" The corporal said, sweeping his hand around.

"Yes," Moretti admitted.

"What were they guarding?"

The captain smiled. "We shall see."

There were stairs leading up, and the corporal and a private named Calabrese ascended them to find themselves on a kind of mezzanine. It appeared there was no way beyond. On one wall was inscribed a large disk that repeated some of the symbols and text found on the obelisks. With the sound of stone scraping against stone, the outer ring began to rotate. An inner ring also started spinning in the opposite direction.

"What should we do?" Calabrese gaped.

"Hold," the corporal said, his rifle held low but aimed at the disk. The rotating stopped. Some of the inscriptions had aligned, but neither man knew what that meant.

"Look," Calabrese said, pointing. A section of the far wall had opened. "Well, do we go in?"

"We don't have much choice." The corporal paused at the opening, looked inside, then stepped through. He turned back to signal the private. "Come on, it's okay."

The private started to follow the path the corporal had taken.

Halfway there, the floor dropped beneath his feet and he fell through, swearing then wailed once.

The stones slid back into place.

The corporal gulped and considered running back to the stairs but wondered if he'd make it without falling as well. And if he did, the others would surely brand him a coward.

"Damn." He turned back. There were more inscriptions along the walls. There was also a conference-like stone table built into the floor with modern portable chairs around it. The pyramid was in current use he concluded.

"Hey," he called out in English. "We just want the American. Give him to us and we'll be on our way." A bird landed on the window, chirping merrily. He glanced at it.

"No need to shout, I'm right here."

The corporal wheeled about, firing his rifle, even though he knew he would be too slow. Rounds from the sergeant's confiscated machine gun blistered a ragged diagonal across his torso. The corporal fell forward onto the stone table, a wide-eyed look on his face, then rolled off onto the floor. Henson was on the other side of the table, smoke rising from the barrel of the machine gun he held.

Downstairs, the two heard the commotion and rushed to the stairs.

"Corporal!" the captain called out. He called out again, then ascended, followed by the private. Upstairs, they saw the corpse of the corporal, staring dead-eyed at the ceiling. The captain closed the man's eyelids.

"You think Calabrese went after him?" The private said hopefully, indicating an opening in the wall beyond the table. An opening that hadn't been there moments before.

The captain didn't answer. Ducking his head inside the next

chamber, he walked on through. The private shook his head and once again trailed his commanding officer. The two were now in a passageway that somehow allowed sunlight in though neither could detect the source.

"Doesn't look like a way out of here," the nervous private whispered.

"We're coming to another hallway," the captain said, whispering as well. "Be ready."

At the corner they paused. Goaded by his desire to plunder the pyramid's perceived riches, he stepped into the new hallway, his machine gun leveled before him. The two went along until an unfamiliar sound greeted them.

"What is that?"

"Quiet," the captain ordered.

There was a humming beneath their feet. What sounded like gears meshing became evident and a vibration thrummed up through their boots into the legs.

"The hell?" The private panicked, trying to run back the way he'd come, only now the floor went sideways and loomed upward, causing him to fall into the captain. Both men crashed to the floor which continued to slope up, then tilted to one side then the other, keeping them off-balance.

"We have to crawl," Captain Moretti yelled, using his elbows to move forward, pistol pointed ahead. On he went in the gloom, the indirect light having ceased. Seconds later the floor stopped moving. As the two got to their feet, there was a new sound, stone scraping on stone. A hidden door slid open, harsh light causing them to squint. Moretti put a hand up until his eyes adjusted. In that revealed doorway a figure appeared, backlit and unmoving.

"Devil," Moretti hollered as he churned off rounds at the

figure. His bullets didn't affect the shadowed man who remained standing and unharmed. Again, he fired, but the panel in the wall slid back in place. Moretti ran to the spot but could detect no creases in the solid surface.

"Let's get out of here, leave this cursed place," the private said.

Moretti dropped his machine gun and grabbed the man, screaming in his face. "You fool. There's a treasure worth millions in this pyramid and I mean to have them."

"*Them?*"

"The three crowns of the Queen of Sheba. Each was said to have been imbued with wondrous properties. One was to have been forged from a rare element extracted from the center of the earth, the second made from an unknown gemstone mined from the Nile, and the third from a glowing rock from space itself."

"That's a fairy tale, Captain."

Moretti backhanded him. "It's true, and they and whatever else this pyramid holds will be *mine*. And mine alone you grape-stomping peasant."

"No, they won't," Henson said.

The captain and the private were again bathed in bright light, this time from the end of the hall. And again, Henson's figure dominated the doorway. Both men fired at him with the same impotent results.

"Mirrors, it has to be," the private declared. Yet no glass had shattered.

The captain was no longer interested in logic. He ran at Henson, emptying his gun until it clicked dry, screaming profanities at the top of his lungs. He went through the image which evaporated into ethereal wisps around him. He found himself in a large space, the walls here rough and unfinished.

He looked over his shoulder, but the opening was gone—that wall solid once more. He tossed aside his now-useless machine gun and unholstered his handgun, moving along. His boot stepped on something that yielded and, taking another step, he felt something slither over his boot. He looked down, snakes covered the floor.

But the floor had been barren seconds ago.

Given his background, he absently identified some as Kenyan carpet vipers and African puff adders. Both species were venomous. He started to laugh at the joke of it all as he pumped bullets into the beasts with his pistol until it, too, was emptied. A puff adder coiled around his leg and he snatched it off. But it struck like a bolt and sank its fangs into his forearm.

"Dear God, he is the Devil, he's commanded all the snakes in the world to come *here!*" More of the serpents twined about him, and withering down into the pile of the hissing creatures, numerous sets of fangs latched onto him, filling him with so much more venom. Captain Moretti soon gratefully succumbed to the eternal blackness.

Uncontested, the private was allowed to stumble out of the Queen's pyramid. An armed Matthew Henson was there to greet him. The private dropped his gun and held up his hands.

"When you get back to your base," Henson began in Italian, "that is, if you can find your way back, tell them your captain went mad with greed and killed the others when you found out he'd lied to you. Or make up whatever story you three want to, I don't care as long as none of you try and come back *here.*"

"I don't—" he began.

"If you think your superiors will believe the truth, go ahead. If you don't get court martialed or shot for desertion."

Finished, Henson left the bewildered soldier and picking

up the man's gun, was soon swallowed in the shadows of the pyramid. Thereafter he ascended stone steps at the back of the ancient edifice to the flat area and the smaller pyramid there. A sweep of wind and dust kicked up, though the air had been still moments before. The wind soon subsided, and standing before Henson were three figures in ceremonial garb.

They spoke to him in Amharic which he didn't understand, but their import was clear. One of them handed Henson a wooden chest the size of a desktop radio. He made to refuse the gift but the three insisted. He dipped his head in thanks, and departed.

Eventually, he got back to Addis Ababa and the hotel where he'd first received the message from his buddy, decorated WWI aviator, jazzman, and boxer Eugene Bullard. Somehow at his club in Paris, Bullard got word about the trader and the sale of his map to the captain. Knowing it would take him too long to get there himself, he cast about and found out Henson was in this part of the continent on another matter and had reached out.

"This arrived for you while you were away, Mr. Henson," the desk clerk said in his crisp English.

"Thank you." He took the telegram and, unfolding it, read the brief message.

Matthew Henson—needed immediately back in Harlem, USA—matter of life and death—money no object.

He cocked an eyebrow reading the name of the sender. Henson refolded the message and asked the clerk to charter a flight back to the States.